15

The Annotated
Pilgrim's Progress

THE ANNOTATED PILGRIM'S PROGRESS

with helpful notes, essays on the life and times of John Bunyan, and an index to persons and places and what they mean by Warren W. Wiersbe.

by John Bunyan

MOODY PRESS
CHICAGO

Notes, essays on the life and times of John Bunyan, and index to persons and places and what they mean.

Library of Congress Cataloging in Publication Data

Bunyan, John, 1628-1688.
  The annotated Pilgrim's progress.

  I. Wiersbe, Warren W. II. Title.
PR3330.A2W54   828′.407   80-427
ISBN 0-8024-0229-1

All quotations from John Bunyan's other works are taken from *The Complete Works of John Bunyan,* edited by George Offor, 3 vols. (1853; reprint ed., Grand Rapids: Baker, 1977).

Illustrations, with the exceptions of those on pp. 7, 24, 27, 32, 93, and 113 are from *1800 Woodcuts by Thomas Bewick and His School,* edited by Blanche Cirker, 1962, and are reproduced by Permission of Dover Publications, Inc.

Printed in the United States of America

THE
Pilgrim's Progreſs
FROM
THIS WORLD,
TO
That which is to come:

Delivered under the Similitude of a

DREAM

Wherein is Diſcovered,
The manner of his ſetting out,
His Dangerous Journey; And ſafe
Arrival at the Deſired Countrey.

I have uſed Similitudes, Hoſ. 12. 10.

By *John Bunyan.*

𝔏𝔦𝔠𝔢𝔫𝔰𝔢𝔡 𝔞𝔫𝔡 𝔈𝔫𝔱𝔯𝔢𝔡 𝔞𝔠𝔠𝔬𝔯𝔡𝔦𝔫𝔤 𝔱𝔬 𝔒𝔯𝔡𝔢𝔯.

LONDON,
Printed for *Nath. Ponder* at the *Peacock*
in the *Poultrey* near *Cornhil,* 1678.

Original title page

Contents

Introduction 11

The Pilgrim's Progress —
Text and Annotations 13

The Life and Times of John Bunyan 183

The Puritans 189

Important Dates Concerning
Bunyan and the Puritans 195

Index of Scripture 197

Index to Persons and Places
and What They Mean 205

Introduction

The purpose of this book is to allow John Bunyan to speak for himself. *The Pilgrim's Progress* has not changed since 1678, when it was written; it is still a classic and always will be a classic. But Bunyan's readers have changed, and many people who want to enjoy *The Pilgrim's Progress* and profit from it are baffled by some of the symbols and allusions. Bunyan's original readers were better taught in the Bible than the average reader today, and some of Bunyan's personal life that shows up in the text was better known to them than to us.

I suggest that you keep a copy of the King James Version of the Bible at hand while using this book. Where Bunyan quotes a verse or phrase, I merely give the reference. Where he makes an allusion to Scripture, I quote the original. Where the passage alluded to is too long for quotation, I give the references and sufficient material for you to understand what he is saying.

There are also references to Bunyan's personal Christian experience, as well as to political and religious circumstances of his day.

It is possible to read *The Pilgrim's Progress* and benefit from it while knowing nothing about Bunyan himself or the historical circumstances of his life. But knowing these extra facts will give greater meaning to what he has written.

If you have never read *The Pilgrim's Progress*, I suggest that you read it through and enjoy it. Use the marginal notes only where you actually need help in understanding the text. Then, after you have read it, go back and read it again, using the marginal notes and your Bible. Take your time, read carefully, and think about both the text and the Scriptures. You will discover new truths that will make *The Pilgrim's Progress* and your Bible new books to you.

If you are not "a pilgrim," I trust that using this book will help you become one. If you are already on that pilgrimage to Glory, I trust that this book will make the pathway brighter and more victorious.

The Author's Apology
For His Book

::

WHEN at the first I took my pen in hand
Thus for to write, I did not understand
That I at all should make a little book
In such a <u>mode</u>; nay, I had undertook
To make <u>another</u>; which, when almost done,
Before I was aware, I this begun.
  And thus it was: I, writing of the way
And race of saints, in this our gospel day,
Fell suddenly into an allegory
About their journey, and the way to glory,
In more than twenty things which I set down.
This done, I twenty more had in my crown;
And they again began to multiply,
Like sparks that from the coals of fire do fly.
Nay, then, thought I, if that you breed so fast,
I'll put you by yourselves, lest you at last
Should prove *ad infinitum*, and eat out
The book that I already am about.
  Well, so I did; but yet I did not think
To show to all the world my pen and ink
In such a mode; I only thought to make
I knew not what; nor did I undertake
Thereby to please my neighbour: no, not I;
I did it my own self to gratify.
  Neither did I but vacant seasons spend
In this my scribble; nor did I intend
But to <u>divert myself</u> in doing this
From worser thoughts which make me do
  amiss.
  Thus I set pen to paper with delight,
And quickly had my thoughts in black and
  white.

apology. Defense. Bunyan felt it necessary in this poetic preface to explain how his book was written and why it was published. He did not want anyone to think he was being careless either in writing it or in publishing it.

mode. An allegory. This is a form of literature in which persons, events, and objects have a deeper meaning than what is apparent in the story.

another. Probably *The Heavenly Footman*, which was published after Bunyan's death. Based on 1 Corinthians 9:24, this book has several ideas in it that parallel *The Pilgrim's Progress*. Some scholars think it was *The Strait Gate*, published in 1676.

to show. Not only did he not *intend to write* this book, but he also did not *intend to publish* it. Bunyan had published at least a dozen books by 1678, when *The Pilgrim's Progress* came out, including *Grace Abounding to the Chief of Sinners* (1666). He was not sure that his allegory, quite unlike his other works, would be accepted or do any good.

divert myself. Writing the book kept him occupied with spiritual thoughts while he was in jail.

13

For, having now my method by the end,
Still as I pulled, it came; and so I penned
It down: until it came at last to be,
For length and breadth, the bigness which you
    see.
    Well, when I had thus put mine ends to-
    gether,
I showed them others, that I might see whether
They would condemn them, or them justify:
And some said, Let them live; some, Let them
    die;
Some said, John, print it; others said, Not so;
Some said, It might do good; others said, No.
    Now was I in a strait, and did not see
Which was the best thing to be done by me:
At last I thought, Since you are thus divided,
I print it will, and so the case decided.
    For, thought I, some, I see, would have it
    done,
Though others in that channel do not run:
To prove, then, who advised for the best,
Thus I thought fit to put it to the test.
    I further thought, if now I did deny
Those that would have it, thus to gratify;
I did not know but hinder them I might
Of that which would to them be great delight.
    For those which were not for its coming
    forth,
I said to them, Offend you I am loath,
Yet, since your brethren pleased with it be,
Forbear to judge till you do further see.
    If that thou wilt not read, let it alone;
Some love the meat, some love to pick the bone.
Yea, that I might them better palliate,
I did too with them thus expostulate:
    May I not write in such a style as this?
In such a method, too, and yet not miss
My end, thy good? Why may it not be done?
Dark clouds bring waters, when the bright
    bring none.
Yea, dark or bright, if they their silver drops
Cause to descend, the earth, by yielding crops,

such a style. Now he defends his style of writing by presenting several arguments. (1) Dark clouds in nature bring rain and fruitfulness. (2) Fishermen and hunters use "bait" to catch their game, and so must he if he is to catch the reader's interest. (3) Nature often puts jewels in unlikely places, and there are jewels in his book. (4) Other writers have used the same approach, including Bible writers, who present types, symbols, and metaphors. (5) Life itself often brings the light out of the darkness.

14

Gives praise to both, and carpeth not at either,
But treasures up the fruit they yield together;
Yea, so commixes both, that in her fruit
None can distinguish this from that: they suit
Her well when hungry; but, if she be full,
She spews out both, and makes their blessings
    null.

You see the ways the fisherman doth take
To catch the fish; what engines doth he make!
Behold! how he engageth all his wits;
Also his snares, lines, angles, hooks, and nets;
Yet fish there be, that neither hook, nor line,
Nor snare, nor net, nor engine can make thine:
They must be groped for, and be tickled too,
Or they will not be catched, whate'er you do.

How doth the fowler seek to catch his game
By divers means! all which one cannot name:
His guns, his nets, his lime-twigs, light, and
    bell;
He creeps, he goes, he stands; yea, who can tell
Of all his postures? Yet there's none of these
Will make him master of what fowls he please.
Yea, he must pipe and whistle to catch *this;*
Yet, if he does so, *that* bird he will miss.

If that a pearl may in a toad's head dwell,
And may be found too in an oyster-shell;
If things that promise nothing do contain
What better is than gold; who will disdain,
That have an inkling of it, there to look
That they may find it? Now, my little book
(Though void of all these paintings that may
    make
It with this or the other man to take)
Is not without those things that do excel
What do in brave but empty notions dwell.

"Well, yet I am not fully satisfied,
That this your book will stand, when soundly
    tried."
Why, what's the matter? "It is dark." What
    though?
"But it is feigned." What of that? I trow
Some men, by feigned words, as dark as mine,

carpeth not at either. Does not critize either of them.

engines. Devices. An allegory is merely a device to "catch" his prey.

lime-twigs. Twigs that were smeared with "bird lime," a sticky substance that held the birds fast.

pearl. An ancient superstition that there was a jewel (the "toadstone") hidden on, or in, the toad's head; that is, beauty in the midst of ugliness. Shakespeare mentions this in **As You Like It:** "Which like a toad, ugly and venomous, wears yet a precious jewel in its head." He was wrong on both counts, for toads do not have jewels, nor are they poisonous.

dark. Difficult to understand. "To understand a proverb, and the interpretation; the words of the wise and their dark sayings" (Proverbs 1:6).

feigned. Made up, imaginary.

15

Make truth to spangle and its rays to shine.
"But they want solidness." Speak, man, thy
   mind.
"They drown the weak; metaphors make us
   blind."
  Solidity, indeed, becomes the pen
Of him that writeth things divine to men;
But must I needs want solidness, because
By metaphors I speak? Were not God's laws,
His gospel laws, in olden times held forth
By types, shadows, and metaphors? Yet loath
Will any sober man be to find fault
With them, lest he be found for to assault
The highest wisdom. No, he rather stoops,
And seeks to find out what by pins and loops,
By calves and sheep, by heifers and by rams,
By birds and herbs, and by the blood of lambs,
God speaketh to him; and happy is he
That finds the light and grace that in them be.
  Be not too forward, therefore, to conclude
That I want solidness, that I am rude;
All things solid in show not solid be;
All things in parables despise not we,
Lest things most hurtful lightly we receive,
And things that good are, of our souls bereave.
My dark and cloudy words, they do but hold
The truth, as cabinets enclose the gold.
  The prophets used much by metaphors
To set forth truth; yea, who so considers
Christ, his apostles too, shall plainly see,
That truths to this day in such mantles be.
  Am I afraid to say that holy writ,
Which for its style and phrase puts down all wit,
Is everywhere so full of all these things —
Dark figures, allegories. Yet there springs
From that same book that lustre, and those rays
Of light, that turn our darkest nights to days.
  Come, let my carper to his life now look,
And find there darker lines than in my book
He findeth any; yea, and let him know,
That in his best things there are worse lines too.
  May we but stand before impartial men,

16

To his poor one I dare adventure ten,
That they will take my meaning in these lines
Far better than his lies in silver shrines.
Come, truth, although in <u>swaddling clouts</u>, I
  find,
Informs the judgment, rectifies the mind;
Pleases the understanding, makes the will
Submit; the memory too it doth fill
With what doth our imaginations please;
Likewise it tends our troubles to appease.
  <u>Sound words</u>, I know, Timothy is to use,
And <u>old wives' fables</u> he is to refuse;
But yet grave Paul him nowhere did forbid
The use of parables; in which lay hid
That gold, those pearls, and precious stones that
  were
Worth digging for, and that with greatest care.
  Let me add one word more. O man of God,
Art thou offended? Dost thou wish I had
Put forth my matter in another dress?
Or that I had in things been more express?
<u>Three things</u> let me propound; then I submit
To those that are my betters, as is fit.
  1. I find not that I am denied the use
Of this my method, so I no abuse
Put on the words, things, readers; or be rude
In handling figure or similitude,
In application; but, all that I may,
Seek the advance of truth this or that way.
Denied, did I say? Nay, I have leave
(Example too, and that from them that have
God better pleased, by their words or ways,
Than any man that breatheth now-a-days)
Thus to express my mind, thus to declare
Things unto thee that excellentest are.
  2. I find that men (as high as trees) will write
Dialogue-wise; yet no man doth them slight
For writing so: indeed, if they abuse
Truth, cursed be they, and the craft they use
To that intent; but yet let truth be free
To make her sallies upon thee and me,
Which way it pleases God; for who knows how,

swaddling clouts. Swaddling clothes, such as babies were wrapped in. You do not reject the precious baby because the garments are humble.

Sound words. "Hold fast the form of sound words" (2 Timothy 1:13).

old wives' fables. "But refuse profane and old wives' fables" (1 Timothy 4:7). These were superstitions that only ignorant old women would accept.

Three things. (1) I am not forbidden by God to use this approach, so long as I am telling truth. (2) If God so guided me, then let us accept His leading and "let truth be free." (3) The Bible uses this approach, and I am seeking to tell Bible truth.

Better than he that taught us first to plough,
To guide our mind and pens for his design?
And he makes base things usher in divine.
3. I find that holy writ in many places
Hath semblance with this method, where the cases
Do call for one thing, to set forth another;
Use it I may, then, and yet nothing smother
Truth's golden beams: nay, but this method may
Make it cast forth its rays as light as day.

And now before I do put up my pen,
I'll show the profit of my book, and then
Commit both thee and it unto that Hand
That pulls the strong down, and makes weak ones stand.

This book it <u>chalketh</u> out before thine eyes
The man that seeks the everlasting <u>prize</u>;
It shows you whence he comes, whither he goes;
What he leaves undone, also what he does;
It also shows you how he runs and runs,
Till he unto the gate of glory comes.

It shows, too, who set out for life <u>amain</u>,
As if the lasting crown they would obtain;
Here also you may see the reason why
They lose their labour, and like fools do die.
This book will make a <u>traveller</u> of thee,
If by its counsel thou wilt ruled be;
It will direct thee to the Holy Land,
If thou wilt its directions understand:
Yea, it will make the slothful active be;
The blind also delightful things to see.

Art thou for something rare and profitable?
Wouldest thou see a truth within a fable?
Art thou forgetful? Wouldest thou remember
From New Year's day to the last of December?
Then read my fancies; they will stick like <u>burs</u>,
And may be, to the helpless, comforters.

This book is writ in such a dialect
As may the minds of listless men affect:
It seems a novelty, and yet contains
Nothing but sound and honest gospel strains.

chalketh. Marks out, outlines a course to follow.

prize. "I press toward the mark for the prize of the high calling of God in Christ Jesus" (Philippians 3:14).

amain. Suddenly, with great vigor. Several people in *The Pilgrim's Progress* made good beginnings, but did not reach heaven.

traveller. This book will convert you and make you a pilgrim on the way to the Holy City. Bunyan's aim was not to entertain, but to evangelize.

burs. Burrs. By using imaginative pictures in his book, he helps us remember what he has said. We can easily forget sermons and lectures, but stories stick with us, like burrs.

18

Wouldest thou divert thyself from melancholy?
Wouldest thou be pleasant, yet be far from folly?
Wouldest thou read riddles, and their explanation?
Or else be drowned in thy contemplation?
Dost thou love picking meat? Or wouldest thou see
A man i' the clouds, and hear him speak to thee?
Wouldest thou be in a dream, and yet not sleep?
Or wouldest thou in a moment laugh and weep?
Wouldest thou lose thyself and catch no harm,
And find thyself again without a charm?
Wouldest read thyself, and read thou knowest not what,
And yet know whether thou art blest or not,
By reading the same lines? Oh, then come hither,
And lay my book, thy <u>head, and heart</u> together.

John Bunyan.

head, and heart. Bunyan believed in a balanced Christian life, with the mind and the emotions involved. Truth ought to enlighten the mind, stir the emotions, and motivate the will. The Puritans did not believe in empty emotionalism; they wanted light as well as heat.

The Pilgrim's Progress

IN THE SIMILITUDE OF A DREAM

As I WALKED through the wilderness of this world, I lighted on a certain place where was a Den, and I laid me down in that place to sleep: and as I slept I dreamed a dream. I dreamed, and behold, I saw a man clothed with rags, standing in a certain place, with his face from his own house, a book in his hand, and a great burden upon his back. I looked, and saw him open the book and read therein; and as he read, he wept and trembled; and not being able longer to contain, he brake out with a lamentable cry, saying, "What shall I do?"

In this plight, therefore, he went home and refrained himself as long as he could, that his wife and children should not perceive his distress; but he could not be silent long, because that his trouble increased. Wherefore at length he brake his mind to his wife and children; and thus he began to talk to them: O my dear wife, said he, and you the children of my bowels, I, your dear friend, am in myself undone by reason of a burden that lieth hard upon me; moreover, I am for certain informed that this our city will be burned with fire from heaven; in which fearful overthrow, both myself, with thee my wife, and you my sweet babes, shall miserably come to ruin, except (the which yet I see not) some way of escape can be found, whereby we may be delivered. At this his relations were sore amazed; not for that they believed that what he had said to them was true,

wilderness. The book begins with a wilderness and ends with the crossing of a river. This parallels the history of the nation of Israel. The Israelites wandered as pilgrims in the wilderness for forty years, then crossed the Jordan River to enter the promised land. The Puritans looked upon the church as God's Israel and this world as a spiritual wilderness.

Den. The town lockup on the bridge in Bedford, where Bunyan was confined for six months in 1675. It was then that he completed *The Pilgrim's Progress.*

a man. This description of a lost sinner is taken from several Bible references: "all our righteousnesses are as filthy rags" (Isaiah 64:6); "for mine iniquities are gone over mine head: as an heavy burden they are too heavy for me" (Psalm 38:4); "but to this man will I look, even to him that is poor and of a contrite spirit, and trembleth at my word" (Isaiah 66:2). The fact that his face is turned away from his own house indicates his willingness to forsake all (Luke 14:33).

a great burden. His sense of sin. Later he tells Master Worldly Wiseman that he got the burden by reading the book (see page 34). By revealing our sinfulness, the Bible increases the burden. The Puritans called this conviction. As a travelling tinker, Bunyan carried a sixty-pound anvil on his back.

the book. The Bible. Bunyan's note here is Habakkuk 2:2 — "Write the vision, and make it plain upon tables, that he may run that readeth it." In his autobiography, *Grace Abounding,*

Bunyan writes, "I was then never out of the Bible . . . still crying out to God, that I might know the truth, and way to heaven and glory."

What shall I do? The cry of the convicted sinner: "Men and brethren, what shall we do?" (Acts 2:37). "What must I do to be saved?" (Acts 16:30). See also Habakkuk 1:2-3.

our city. Its name is "City of Destruction" (page 25), and it is borrowed from the wicked cities of Sodom and Gomorrah, which were destroyed by fire and a "fearful overthrow" (see Genesis 19:23-28). Bunyan wrote this in 1675. The great fire of London was in 1666.

carriages. Treatment.

condole. To grieve over.

Evangelist. The "evangel" is the good news that Christ died for the sins of the world, was buried, and arose again (1 Corinthians 15:1-4). An "evangelist" is one who tells this good news to others and seeks to bring them to faith in Christ. (See Acts 21:8 and Ephesians 4:11.) Bunyan is probably depicting John Gifford, his pastor, who helped to lead him into his experience of salvation.

condemned. "And as it is appointed unto men once to die, but after this the judgment" (Hebrews 9:27). Bunyan adds Job 10:21-22 and Ezekiel 22:14.

but because they thought that some frenzy distemper had got into his head; therefore, it drawing towards night, and they hoping that sleep might settle his brains, with all haste they got him to bed. But the night was as troublesome to him as the day; wherefore, instead of sleeping, he spent it in sighs and tears. So, when the morning was come, they would know how he did. He told them, Worse and worse: he also set to talking to them again: but they began to be hardened. They also thought to drive away his distemper by harsh and surly carriages to him; sometimes they would deride, sometimes they would chide, and sometimes they would quite neglect him. Wherefore he began to retire himself to his chamber, to pray for and pity them, and also to condole his own misery; he would also walk solitarily in the fields, sometimes reading, and sometimes praying: and thus for some days he spent his time.

Now I saw, upon a time when he was walking in the fields, that he was, as he was wont, reading in his book, and greatly distressed in his mind; and as he read, he burst out, as he had done before, crying, What shall I do to be saved?

Christian no sooner leaves the world but meets
Evangelist, who lovingly him greets
With tidings of another; and doth show
Him how to mount to that from this below.

I saw also that he looked this way and that way, as if he would run; yet he stood still, because, as I perceived, he could not tell which way to go. I looked then, and saw a man named Evangelist coming to him, who asked, Wherefore dost thou cry?

He answered, Sir, I perceive by the book in my hand that I am condemned to die, and after that to come to judgment, and I find that I am not willing to do the first, nor able to do the second.

Then said Evangelist, Why not willing to die, since this life is attended with so many evils? The man answered, Because I fear that this burden that is upon my back will sink me lower than the grave, and I shall fall into <u>Tophet</u>. And sir, if I be not fit to go to prison, I am not fit to go to judgment, and from thence to execution; and the thoughts of these things make me cry.

Then said Evangelist, If this be thy condition, why standest thou still? He answered, Because I know not whither to go. Then he gave him a parchment <u>roll</u>, and there was written within, "Fly from the wrath to come."

The man therefore read it, and looking upon Evangelist very carefully, said, Whither must I fly? Then said Evangelist, pointing with his finger over a very wide field, Do you see yonder <u>wicket-gate</u>? The man said, No. Then said the other, Do you see yonder <u>shining light</u>? He said, I think I do. Then said Evangelist, Keep that light in your eye, and go up directly thereto: so shalt thou see the gate; at which, when thou knockest, it shall be told thee what thou shalt do. So I saw in my dream that the man began to run. Now, he had not run far from his own door, but his wife and children perceiving it, began to cry after him to <u>return</u>; but the man put his fingers in his ears, and ran on, crying,

Tophet. An Old Testament name for hell (Isaiah 30:33). Tophet was an area outside Jerusalem where some of the wicked kings practiced idolatrous worship (Jeremiah 7:31). Godly King Josiah stopped these evil practices (2 Kings 23:10). The word *Tophet* probably comes from an Aramaic word that means "to burn."

roll. Another picture of the Bible. "Who hath warned you to flee from the wrath to come?" (Matthew 3:7). As a young man seeking salvation, Bunyan was under a constant fear of judgment.

wicket-gate. A small gate for foot-passengers that leads into a field or a road. "Enter ye in at the strait gate: for wide is the gate, and broad is the way, that leadeth to destruction . . ." (Matthew 7:13-14). "Strait," of course, means narrow and confined, and must not be confused with *straight*. In *Paradise Lost* (Book 3, line 484), Milton calls the gate of heaven "Heaven's Wicket." *Paradise Lost* was published in 1667.

shining light. "Thy word is a lamp unto my feet, and a light unto my path" (Psalm 119:105). Evangelist points away from himself and uses the Word of God to guide the burdened sinner. God's Word is "a light that shineth in a dark place" (2 Peter 1:19). If people will obediently follow the light God gives, He will lead them to salvation.

return. "If any man come to me, and hate not his father, and mother, and wife, and children,

23

and brethren, and sisters, yea, and his own life also, he cannot be my disciple" (Luke 14:26). Our desire for God and salvation ought to be so great that even the closest ties on earth cannot hold us.

eternal life. This is God's life shared with those who trust Christ. "For God so loved the world, that he gave his only begotten Son, that whosoever believeth in him should not perish, but have everlasting life" (John 3:16).

looked not behind him. Lot's wife looked back and was judged (Genesis 19:17, 26). The phrase "middle of the plain" also connects this scene with the destruction of Sodom and Gomorrah in Genesis 19.

Obstinate, . . . Pliable. When the sinner begins to seek salvation, well-meaning friends often try to stop him. Bunyan wrote, "They that fly from the wrath to come are a gazing-stock to the world." He probably had Jeremiah 20:10 in mind. Obstinate and Pliable are two opposite characters. Obstinate has great strength of will, but he lacks the insight and values to put it to work in the right way. Pliable seems to have some insight, but he lacks the willpower to act and continue to the end. Bunyan himself was a very stubborn man prior to his conversion, so perhaps he saw himself in this scene.

Life! life! eternal life! So he looked not behind him, but fled towards the middle of the plain.

The neighbours also came out to see him run; and as he ran, some mocked, others threatened, and some cried after him to return; and, among those that did so, there were two that resolved to fetch him back by force. The name of the one

was Obstinate, and the name of the other Pliable. Now by this time the man was got a good distance from them; but, however, they were resolved to pursue him, which they did, and in a little time they overtook him. Then said the man, Neighbours, wherefore are ye come? They said, To persuade you to go back with us. But he said, That can by no means be; you dwell, said he, in the City of Destruction, the place also where I was born: I see it to be so; and dying there, sooner or later, you will sink lower than the grave, into a place that burns with <u>fire and brimstone</u>: be content, good neighbours, and go along with me.

OBST. What! said Obstinate, and leave our friends and our comforts behind us?

CHR. Yes, said <u>Christian</u> (for that was his name), because that ALL which you shall forsake is not worthy to be compared with a little of that which I am seeking to enjoy; and if you will go along with me, and hold it, you shall fare as I myself; for there where I go is <u>enough</u> and to

fire and brimstone. This is what destroyed Sodom and Gomorrah (Genesis 19:24). It is also a description of hell (Revelation 21:8).

Christian. This is the name of our pilgrim; it means "belonging to Christ." Before he started on his pilgrimage to the Holy City, his name was Graceless (page 62). Grace is God's favor to undeserving sinners, and Christian had been without that grace. The word *Christian* is used only three times in the New Testament: Acts 11:26; Acts 26:28; and 1 Peter 4:16. Bunyan himself did not approve of denominational labels. In *A Confession of Faith*, which he published in 1672, Bunyan wrote: "I tell you I would be, and hope I am, a Christian, and choose, if God should count me worthy, to be called a Christian, a believer, or other such name which is approved by the Holy Ghost."

ALL. "While we look not at the things which are seen, but at the things which are not seen: for the things which are seen are temporal; but the things which are not seen are eternal" (2 Corinthians 4:18).

enough. The Prodigal Son said this when he came to himself. "How many hired servants of my father's have bread enough and to spare" (Luke 15:17). God has more to offer than does the world.

25

leave. "For what is a man profited, if he shall gain the whole world, and lose his own soul?" (Matthew 16:26).

inheritance. 1 Peter 1:4-6 and Hebrews 11:6, 16.

Tush. Obstinate's mind is made up; do not confuse him with facts! "But the natural man receiveth not the things of the Spirit of God; for they are foolishness unto him" (1 Corinthians 2:14). The "natural man" is the man who has never been converted.

plough. "No man, having put his hand to the plough, and looking back, is fit for the kingdom of God" (Luke 9:62).

coxcombs. Conceited fools. People thought that Jesus was out of His mind (Mark 3:21), and Festus said that Paul was mad (Acts 26:24).

wiser. "The sluggard is wiser in his own conceit than seven men that can render a reason" (Proverbs 26:16).

Nay, but do thou come. Bunyan's note is, "Christian and Obstinate pull for Pliable's soul." Salvation does not come easy, and some sinners must struggle to decide for Christ.

confirmed. Just as the Old Testament Law was sealed by the blood of the sacrifices, so the New Covenant of grace was sealed by the blood of Jesus Christ. (See Hebrews 9:17-22 and 13:20-21.)

the way. You will note that Pliable is more concerned with the blessings at the destination than the burdens along the way. He is

spare. Come away, and prove my words.

OBST. What are the things you seek, since you leave all the world to find them?

CHR. I seek an inheritance incorruptible, undefiled, and that fadeth not away, and it is laid up in heaven, and safe there, to be bestowed, at the time appointed, on them that diligently seek it. Read it so, if you will, in my book.

OBST. Tush! said Obstinate, away with your book; will you go back with us or no?

CHR. No, not I, said the other, because I have laid my hand to the plough.

OBST. Come then, neighbour Pliable, let us turn again and go home without him; there is a company of these crazed-headed coxcombs, that, when they take a fancy by the end, are wiser in their own eyes than seven men that can render a reason.

PLI. Then said Pliable, Don't revile; if what the good Christian says is true, the things he looks after are better than ours: my heart inclines to go with my neighbour.

OBST. What! more fools still! Be ruled by me, and go back; who knows whither such a brain-sick fellow will lead you? Go back, go back, and be wise.

CHR. Nay, but do thou come with thy neighbour, Pliable; there are such things to be had which I spoke of, and many more glories besides. If you believe not me, read here in this book; and for the truth of what is expressed therein, behold all is confirmed by the blood of Him that made it.

PLI. Well, neighbour Obstinate, said Pliable, I begin to come to a point; I intend to go along with this good man, and to cast in my lot with him; but, my good companion, do you know the way to this desired place?

CHR. I am directed by a man whose name is Evangelist, to speed me to a little gate that is before us, where we shall receive instructions about the way.

26

PLI. Come then, good neighbour, let us be going. Then they went both together.

OBST. And I will go back to my place, said Obstinate; I will be no companion of such misled, fantastical fellows.

Now I saw in my dream that, when Obstinate was gone back, Christian and Pliable went talking over the plain; and thus they began their discourse.

CHR. Come, neighbour Pliable, how do you do? I am glad you are persuaded to go along with me. Had even Obstinate himself but felt what I have felt of the powers and terrors of what is yet unseen, he would not thus lightly have given us the back.

PLI. Come, neighbour Christian, since there are none but us two here, tell me now further what the things are, and how to be enjoyed, whither we are going.

CHR. I can better conceive of them with my mind, than speak of them with my tongue; but yet, since you are desirous to know, I will read of them in my book.

PLI. And do you think that the words of your book are certainly true?

CHR. Yes, verily; for it was made by Him that cannot lie.

PLI. Well said; what things are they?

CHR. There is an endless kingdom to be inhabited, and everlasting life to be given us, that we may inhabit that kingdom for ever.

PLI. Well said; and what else?

CHR. There are crowns of glory to be given us, and garments that will make us shine like the sun in the firmament of heaven.

a picture of many people who want to enjoy the blessings of heaven but want to get there the easy way.

fantastical. Eccentric, foolish.

powers. "And have tasted the good word of God, and the powers of the world to come" (Hebrews 6:5).

enjoyed. Pliable wants to hear nothing about terror; he is interested only in enjoyment. He illustrates the "shallow soil" in Christ's parable of the sower (Matthew 13:1-9 and 18-23). He receives the Word with joy, but he has no roots. When he comes to the Slough of Despond, he decides to turn back.

cannot lie. "In hope of eternal life, which God, that cannot lie, promised before the world began" (Titus 1:2).

what things. Bunyan introduces this description of the heavenly city early in his book for several reasons. The glories of heaven are an encouragement to Christian to keep on his difficult journey and to invite others to share the pilgrimage with him. These glories also help him to keep in perspective the trials that he endures along the way because the glory to come more than compensates for the sufferings (Romans 8:18; 2 Corinthians 4:16-18; 1 Peter 5:10). Jesus Christ was able to endure the cross because of the "joy that was set before him" (Hebrews 12:2). For the Christian, the expectation of heaven is a proper motive for godly living and sacrificial service.

kingdom. Isaiah 65:17; John 10:27-29.

crowns. Matthew 13:43; 2 Timothy 4:8; Revelation 3:4 and 22:5.

crying. Isaiah 25:8; Revelation 7:16-17 and 21:4.

seraphims and cherubims. A special order of angels. The seraphim worship at the throne of God (Isaiah 6:1-8). The cherubim were a part of the Jewish tabernacle and Temple (Exodus 25:17-22). The prophet Ezekiel describes cherubim in Ezekiel 1:4-14. (Note Ezekiel 10:20.) Both Bunyan and the King James Version misspelled the plural form. The plural of *seraph* is *seraphim*; the plural of *cherub* is *cherubim*. The *s* is not needed. The word *seraph* in Hebrew means "to burn."

elders. Revelation 4:4.

holy virgins. The reference is to the 144,000 dedicated Jews described in Revelation 7:1-8 and 14:1-5. The term "virgin" refers to their purity of life and devotion to God.

cut in pieces. See Hebrews 11:33-34.

clothed. "For in this we groan, earnestly desiring to be clothed upon with our house which is from heaven . . ." (2 Corinthians 5:2-4), referring to the new body the believer receives at the resurrection and the return of Christ. Bunyan also refers to John 12:25.

PLI. This is very pleasant; and what else?

CHR. There shall be no more crying nor sorrow; for He that is owner of the place will wipe all tears from our eyes.

PLI. And what company shall we have there?

CHR. There we shall be with seraphims and cherubims, creatures that will dazzle your eyes to look on them. There also you shall meet with thousands and ten thousands that have gone before us to that place; none of them are hurtful, but loving and holy; every one walking in the sight of God, and standing in his presence with acceptance for ever. In a word, there we shall see the elders with their golden crowns; there we shall see the holy virgins with their golden harps, there we shall see men that by the world

were cut in pieces, burnt in flames, eaten of beasts, drowned in the seas, for the love that they bear to the Lord of the place, all well, and clothed with immortality as with a garment.

PLI. The hearing of this is enough to ravish one's heart. But are these things to be enjoyed? How shall we get to be sharers thereof?

CHR. The Lord, the Governor of the country, hath recorded that in this book; the substance of which is, If we be truly willing to have it, he will bestow it upon us freely.

PLI. Well, my good companion, glad am I to hear of these things; come on, let us mend our pace.

CHR. I cannot go so fast as I would, by reason of this burden that is on my back.

Now I saw in my dream, that just as they had ended this talk they drew near to a very miry slough that was in the midst of the plain; and they, being heedless, did both fall suddenly into the bog. The name of the slough was Despond. Here, therefore, they wallowed for a time, being grievously bedaubed with the dirt; and Christian, because of the burden that was on his back, began to sink in the mire.

PLI. Then said Pliable, Ah! neighbour Christian, where are you now?

CHR. Truly, said Christian, I do not know.

PLI. At that Pliable began to be offended, and angrily said to his fellow, Is this the happiness you have told me all this while of? If we have such ill speed at our first setting out, what may we expect betwixt this and our journey's end?

truly willing. God is willing to save if we are willing to receive His gift of eternal life. "All that the Father giveth me shall come to me; and him that cometh to me I will in no wise cast out" (John 6:37). "If any man thirst, let him come unto me, and drink" (John 7:37). "I will give unto him that is athirst of the fountain of the water of life freely" (Revelation 21:6). "And the Spirit and the bride say, Come. And let him that heareth say, Come. And let him that is athirst come. And whosoever will, let him take the water of life freely" (Revelation 22:17). See also Isaiah 55:1-8.

mend our pace. Pliable is in a hurry to get to heaven, but he has no burden for sin to hold him back. He pictures the shallow person who has never felt conviction, and who does not want to face the fact that salvation involves more than the pleasures of heaven.

slough. A swamp. There was such a slough near Bunyan's birthplace in Bedford, England. The rain would fill the streams and turn the area into mire.

heedless. Pliable got Christian so interested in things to come that he became careless about things present. Christian's burden made him sink. Here Bunyan is picturing the despair that can come with conviction of sin, something he himself experienced.

offended. The test proved that Pliable had no true conviction or desire to become a Christian. He endured for a while, then became offended when trouble came (Matthew 13:20-21). People who want to be saved only to avoid trials will always be disappointed.

what may we expect. The rest of the book answers that question, but Pliable never experienced the journey's end. Like many people, he made a brave beginning outwardly, but he lacked inward conviction. He could not keep going.

got out of the mire. People who do not feel a deep burden for their sins find it easy to escape conviction. Christian was carrying a burden. This made it difficult for him to get out.

further. Even if he is in despair, Christian wants to get as far from the City of Destruction as possible.

Help. "I was brought low, and he helped me" (Psalm 116:6). There is a gift of helps in the New Testament church (1 Corinthians 12:28). Help is not an ordained minister, or an evangelist. He represents any believer who assists others in getting out of despair.

steps. The promises of God found in the Word. Later, when Christian finds himself in the dungeon of Doubting Castle, it is the "key of promise" that opens the door and sets him free.

drew him out. "He brought me up also out of an horrible pit, out of the miry clay, and set my

May I get out again with my life, you shall possess the brave country alone for me. And with that he gave a desperate struggle or two, and got out of the mire on that side of the slough which was next to his own house: so away he went, and Christian saw him no more.

Wherefore Christian was left to tumble in the Slough of Despond alone: but still he endeavoured to struggle to that side of the slough that was still further from his own house, and next to the wicket-gate; the which he did, but could not get out, because of the burden that was upon his back: but I beheld in my dream that a man came to him, whose name was Help, and asked him, What he did there?

CHR. Sir, said Christian, I was bid go this way by a man called Evangelist, who directed me also to yonder gate, that I might escape the wrath to come; and as I was going thither I fell in here.

HELP. But why did not you look for the steps?

CHR. Fear followed me so hard that I fled the next way and fell in.

HELP. Then said he, Give me thy hand: so he gave him his hand, and he drew him out, and set him upon sound ground, and bid him go on his way.

Then I stepped to him that plucked him out, and said, Sir, wherefore, since over this place is the way from the City of Destruction to yonder gate, is it that this plat is not mended, that poor travellers might go thither with more security? And he said unto me, This miry slough is such a place as cannot be mended; it is the descent whither the scum and filth that attends conviction for sin doth continually run, and therefore it is called the Slough of Despond; for still, as the sinner is awakened about his lost condition, there ariseth in his soul many fears, and doubts, and discouraging apprehensions, which all of them get together, and settle in this place. And this is the reason of the badness of this ground.

It is not the pleasure of the King that this place should remain so bad. His labourers also have, by the direction of His Majesty's surveyors, been for above these sixteen hundred years employed about this patch of ground, if perhaps it might have been mended: yea, and to my knowledge, said he, here have been swallowed up at least twenty thousand cart-loads, yea, millions of wholesome instructions, that have at all seasons been brought from all places of the King's dominions, and they that can tell, say they are the best materials to make good ground of the place; if so be, it might have been mended, but it is the Slough of Despond still, and so will be when they have done what they can.

True, there are, by the direction of the Lawgiver, certain good and substantial steps, placed even through the very midst of this slough; but at such time as this place doth much spew out its filth, as it doth against change of weather, these steps are hardly seen; or if they be, men through the dizziness of their heads, step beside, and then they are bemired to purpose, notwithstanding the steps be there; but the ground is good when they are once got in at the gate.

Now I saw in my dream that by this time Pliable was got home to his house again, so that his neighbours came to visit him; and some of them called him wise man for coming back, and some

feet upon a rock, and established my goings" (Psalm 40:2). Note that Help did not do all the work for Christian. Christian had to give him his hand. To sit and do nothing is the best way to stay in despair.

Then I stepped. The author, by using the pronoun "I," identifies with Christian. Bunyan ceases to be a spectator at this point, but three paragraphs later he takes up his previous position.

pleasure. "Strengthen ye the weak hands, and confirm the feeble knees. Say to them that are of a fearful heart, Be strong, fear not: behold, your God will come with vengeance, even God with a recompence; he will come and save you . . . And an highway shall be there, and a way, and it shall be called The way of holiness; the unclean shall not pass over it; but it shall be for those: the wayfaring men, though fools, shall not err therein" (Isaiah 35:3-4, 8). God has provided a right way, and no man need fall into the Slough of Despond. Stick to God's highway!

steps. "Moreover as for me, God forbid that I should sin against the LORD in ceasing to pray for you: but I will teach you the good and the right way" (1 Samuel 12:23). These "steps" are the promises God gives of forgiveness and acceptance when we trust Christ.

sneaking. How a person can
both sit and "sneak" at the same
time becomes clear when you
realize that "sneaking" in Bunyan's day meant "cringing."

Mr. Worldly Wiseman. This
character was not in the original
edition of *The Pilgrim's Progress*,
but we are glad Bunyan added
him. He pictures the man of this
world who really has no understanding of spiritual things.
Read 1 Corinthians 1:18-31 for
Paul's estimate of the wisdom of
this world, because this is where
Bunyan got his idea. Mr.
Worldly Wiseman, you will discover, wants to deal with the
symptoms, but not the *causes*. His
counsel is, "Get rid of your
burden!" not, "Deal with the
sins that cause your burden."
He condemns Evangelist for his
counsel, and even condemns the
Bible, because it helped to give
Christian his burden. His only
solution to Christian's problem
is morality: obey the Law of
God and you will lose your burden. He does not understand the
deeper meaning of sin, that
mere outward obedience is no
guarantee of an inward change.

some guess. An estimate, some
idea. Worldly wise persons find
it easy to jump to conclusions.

wife. To the man of this world,
leaving a family behind in order
to find salvation is a foolish
thing. In the second part of *The
Pilgrim's Progress*, published in
1684, Bunyan tells how Christian's wife, Christiana, and the
children made their journey to
heaven.

as if I had none. "But this I say,
brethren, the time is short: it

called him fool for hazarding himself with
Christian: others again did mock at his coward-
liness; saying, Surely, since you began to venture, I would not have been so base to have
given out for a few difficulties. So Pliable sat
sneaking among them. But at last he got more
confidence, and then they all turned their tales,
and began to deride poor Christian behind his
back. And thus much concerning Pliable.

Now as Christian was walking solitarily by
himself, he espied one afar off come crossing
over the field to meet him; and their hap was to
meet just as they were crossing the way of each
other. The gentleman's name that met him was
Mr. Worldly Wiseman: he dwelt in the town of
Carnal Policy, a very great town, and also hard
by from whence Christian came. This man,
then, meeting with Christian, and having some
inkling of him—for Christian's setting forth
from the City of Destruction was much noised
abroad, not only in the town where he dwelt,
but also it began to be the town talk in some
other places—Master Worldly Wiseman, therefore, having some guess of him, by beholding
his laborious going, by observing his sighs and
groans, and the like, began thus to enter into
some talk with Christian.

WORLD. How now, good fellow, whither away
after this burdened manner?

CHR. A burdened manner indeed, as ever, I
think, poor creature had! And whereas you ask
me, Whither away? I tell you, Sir, I am going to
yonder wicket-gate before me; for there, as I am
informed, I shall be put into a way to be rid of
my heavy burden.

WORLD. Hast thou a wife and children?

CHR. Yes; but I am so laden with this burden
that I cannot take that pleasure in them as formerly; methinks I am as if I had none.

WORLD. Wilt thou hearken unto me if I give
thee counsel?

32

CHR. If it be good, I will; for I stand in need of good counsel.

WORLD. I would advise thee, then, that thou with all speed get thyself rid of thy burden; for thou wilt never be settled in thy mind till then; nor canst thou enjoy the benefits of the blessing which God hath bestowed upon thee till then.

CHR. That is that which I seek for, even to be rid of this heavy burden; but get it off myself, I cannot; nor is there any man in our country that can take it off my shoulders; therefore am I going this way, as I told you, that I may be rid of my burden.

WORLD. Who bid thee go this way to be rid of thy burden?

CHR. A man that appeared to me to be a very great and honourable person; his name, as I remember, is Evangelist.

WORLD. I <u>beshrew</u> him for his counsel; there is not a more dangerous and troublesome way in the world than is that unto which he hath directed thee; and that thou shalt find, if thou will be ruled by his counsel. Thou hast met with something, as I perceive, already; for I see the dirt of the Slough of Despond is upon thee; but that slough is the beginning of the sorrows that do attend those that go on in that way. Hear me, I am older than thou; thou are like to meet with, in the way which thou goest, <u>wearisomeness</u>, painfulness, hunger, perils, nakedness, sword, lions, dragons, darkness, and, in a word, death, and what not! These things are certainly true, having been confirmed by many testimonies. And why should a man so carelessly cast away himself, by giving heed to a stranger?

CHR. Why, sir, this burden upon my back is more terrible to me than are all these things which you have mentioned; nay, methinks I care not what I meet with in the way, if so be I can also meet with deliverance from my burden.

WORLD. How camest thou by the burden at first?

remaineth, that both they that have wives be as though they had none" (1 Corinthians 7:29).

beshrew. Condemn, curse. The man of the world has no understanding of the gospel, or no appreciation for those who tell it to others.

wearisomeness. See 2 Corinthians 11:26-27.

33

things too high. "LORD, my heart is not haughty, nor mine eyes lofty: neither do I exercise myself in great matters, or in things too high for me" (Psalm 131:1). Worldly Wiseman suggests that the desire to read and understand the Bible is an evidence of pride. This, of course, was the attitude Bunyan's judges had toward him when he was tried for preaching illegally. They could not understand how an untrained tinker could understand the Bible and preach it to others.

Morality . . . Legality. In his early life, Bunyan went through a period of intense legalism, during which he thought he could be saved by morality. He writes in *Grace Abounding*: "Wherefore I fell to some outward reformation, both in my words and life, and did set the commandments before me for my way to heaven; which commandments I did also strive to keep. . . . Thus I continued about a year; all which time our neighbors did take me to be a very godly man, a new and religious man, and did marvel much to see such a great and famous alteration in my life and manners."

CHR. By reading this book in my hand.

WORLD. I thought so; and it is happened unto thee as to other weak men, who, meddling with things too high for them, do suddenly fall into thy distractions; which distractions do not only unman men, as thine, I perceive, have done thee, but they run them upon desperate ventures to obtain they know not what.

CHR. I know what I would obtain; it is ease for my heavy burden.

WORLD. But why wilt thou seek for ease this way, seeing so many dangers attend it? Especially since, hadst thou but patience to hear me, I could direct thee to the obtaining of what thou desirest, without the dangers that thou in this way wilt run thyself into; yea, and the remedy is at hand. Besides, I will add that instead of those dangers thou shalt meet with much safety, friendship, and content.

CHR. Pray, sir, open this secret to me.

WORLD. Why, in yonder village (the village is named Morality) there dwells a gentleman whose name is Legality, a very judicious man, and a man of a very good name, that has skill to help men off with such burdens as thine are from their shoulders: yea, to my knowledge, he hath done a great deal of good this way; ay, and besides, he hath skill to cure those that are somewhat crazed in their wits with their burdens. To him, as I said, thou mayest go, and be helped presently. His house is not quite a mile from this place, and if he should not be at home himself, he hath a pretty young man to his son, whose name is Civility, that can do it (to speak on) as well as the old gentleman himself; there, I say, thou mayest be eased of thy burden; and if thou art not minded to go back to thy former habitation, as indeed I would not wish thee, thou mayest send for thy wife and children to thee to this village, where there are houses now standing empty, one of which thou mayest have at reasonable rates; provision is there also cheap and good;

34

and that which will make thy life the more happy is, to be sure, there thou shalt live by honest neighbours, in credit and good fashion.

Now was Christian somewhat at a stand; but presently he concluded, If this be true which this gentleman hath said, my wisest course is to take his advice; and with that he thus further spoke.

CHR. Sir, which is my way to this honest man's house?

WORLD. Do you see yonder high hill?

CHR. Yes, very well.

WORLD. By that hill you must go, and the first house you come at is his.

So Christian turned out of his way to go to Mr. Legality's house for help; but behold, when he was got now hard by the hill, it seemed so high, and also that side of it that was next the wayside did hang so much over, that Christian was afraid to venture further, lest the hill should fall on his head; wherefore there he stood still, and wotted not what to do. Also his burden now seemed heavier to him than while he was in his way. There came also flashes of fire out of the hill, that made Christian afraid that he should be burned. Here, therefore, he sweat and did quake for fear.

When Christians unto carnal men give ear,
Out of their way they go, and pay for't dear;
For Master Worldly Wiseman can but show
A saint the way to bondage and to woe.

And now he began to be sorry that he had taken Mr. Worldly Wiseman's counsel. And with that he saw Evangelist coming to meet him; at the sight also of whom he began to blush for shame. So Evangelist drew nearer and nearer; and coming up to him, he looked upon him with a severe and dreadful countenance, and thus began to reason with Christian.

EVAN. What dost thou here, Christian? said

cheap and good. There is no price to pay for worldly morality. But outward conformity to laws does not change the heart.

high hill. This is Mount Sinai, where God gave the Law to Moses. See Exodus 19:16-25 and Hebrews 12:21. Why did Christian's burden become heavier? Because the Law does not remove sin; it only makes our guilt worse. The Puritans made much of the work of the Law to bring sinners to conviction and repentance. This is the first of several hills in *The Pilgrim's Progress.* Christian will meet the Hill Difficulty, the Hill Error, Mount Caution, the Little Hill Lucre, the high hill Clear, and the Holy City set on a high hill.

wotted not. Knew not.

carnal men. Carnal means "fleshly." It is a New Testament word that describes the old nature of the sinner. Mr. Worldly Wiseman was a carnal man; he thought like a mere man, and not like a Christian.

35

What . . . speechless. "What doest thou here, Elijah?" (1 Kings 19:9). Both Elijah and Christian were out of God's will, and were caught. "And he was speechless" (Matthew 22:12). After all, what could he say?

turned aside. "I marvel that ye are so soon removed from him that called you into the grace of Christ unto another gospel" (Galatians 1:6). The Galatian letter was written by Paul to refute the idea that sinners can be saved by keeping the Law of Moses. Evangelist is also referring to Exodus 32:8 — "They have turned aside quickly out of the way which I commanded them." God spoke this to Moses when Israel, because of Moses' absence, made an idol and worshiped it. The Law did not make Israel obedient!

with speed. There is no salvation that is "quick and easy," as Mr. Worldly Wiseman suggested. The Puritans spoke of "heart work" —that is, the deep working of God in the heart to bring the sinner to the light. This takes time.

I believed him. Christian had faith, but not in Christ. Faith is only as good as the object. Faith in worldly wise religion cannot save the sinner.

he: at which words Christian knew not what to answer; wherefore at present he stood speechless before him. Then said Evangelist further, Art not thou the man that I found crying without the walls of the City of Destruction?

CHR. Yes, dear sir, I am the man.

EVAN. Did not I direct thee the way to the little wicket-gate?

CHR. Yes, dear sir, said Christian.

EVAN. How is it, then, that thou art so quickly turned aside? For thou art now out of the way.

CHR. I met with a gentleman so soon as I had got over the Slough of Despond, who persuaded me that I might, in the village before me, find a man that could take off my burden.

EVAN. What was he?

CHR. He looked like a gentleman, and talked much to me, and got me at last to yield, so I came hither; but when I beheld this hill, and how it hangs over the way, I suddenly made a stand, lest it should fall on my head.

EVAN. What said that gentleman to you?

CHR. Why, he asked me whither I was going, and I told him.

EVAN. And what said he then?

CHR. He asked me if I had a family; and I told him. But, said I, I am so loaden with the burden that is on my back, that I cannot take pleasure in them as formerly.

EVAN. And what said he then?

CHR. He bid me with speed get rid of my burden; and I told him 'twas ease that I sought. And, said I, I am therefore going to yonder gate, to receive further direction how I may get to the place of deliverance. So he said that he would show me a better way, and short, not so attended with difficulties as the way, sir, that you set me in; which way, said he, will direct you to a gentleman's house that hath skill to take off these burdens; so I believed him, and turned out of that way into this, if haply I might be soon eased of my burden. But when I came to this place, and beheld things as they are, I stopped for fear (as I said) of danger: but I now know not what to do.

EVAN. Then, said Evangelist, stand still a little, that I may show thee the words of God. So he stood trembling. Then said Evangelist, "See that ye refuse not him that speaketh. For if they escaped not who refused him that spake on earth, much more shall not we escape, if we turn away from him that speaketh from heaven." He said, moreover, "Now the just shall live by faith: but if any man draw back, my soul shall have no pleasure in him." He also did thus apply them: Thou art the man that art running into this misery; thou hast begun to reject the counsel of the Most High, and to draw back thy foot from the way of peace, even almost to the hazarding of thy perdition.

Then Christian fell down at his feet as dead, crying, "Woe is me, for I am undone!" At the sight of which Evangelist caught him by the right hand, saying, "All manner of sin and blasphemies shall be forgiven unto men. Be not faithless, but believing." Then did Christian again a little revive, and stood up trembling, as at first, before Evangelist.

Then Evangelist proceeded, saying, Give more earnest heed to the things that I shall tell thee of. I will now show thee who it was that deluded thee, and who it was also to whom he sent thee. The man that met thee is one Worldly Wiseman, and rightly is he so called; partly, because he savoureth only the doctrine of this world (therefore he always goes to the town of Morality to church): and partly, because he loveth that doctrine best, for it saveth him best from the cross. And because he is of this carnal temper, therefore he seeketh to pervert my ways though right. Now there are three things in this man's counsel that thou must utterly abhor.

1. His turning thee out of the way. 2. His labouring to render the cross odious to thee.

stand still. "Stand thou still a while, that I may shew thee the word of God" (1 Samuel 9:27).

See that ye . . . . The quotation is from Hebrews 12:25.

Now the just . . . . This statement is found originally in Habakkuk 2:4. Bunyan is quoting from Hebrews 10:38. The statement is also quoted in Romans 1:17 and Galatians 3:11. It is an important concept in the Bible, that a person is justified (declared righteous by God) by faith in Christ and not by obeying laws. This was a cardinal doctrine in Puritan theology.

Thou art the man. Nathan the prophet said this to King David when God faced David with his sins (2 Samuel 12:7).

reject. "But the Pharisees and lawyers rejected the counsel of God against themselves" (Luke 7:30). In listening to the counsel of Mr. Worldly Wiseman, Christian rejected God's counsel given to him by faithful Evangelist. See Psalm 1:1.

perdition. Judgment. The reference is Hebrews 10:38-39.

fell down. This happens several times in the Bible: Ezekiel 1:28; Daniel 8:18 and 10:8-19; Revelation 1:17. It is a sign of overwhelming conviction and a sense of unworthiness.

Woe is me. This was Isaiah's response to the vision of God (Isaiah 6:1-8).

All manner . . . . Matthew 12:31.

Be not faithless . . . . John 20:27.

earnest heed. Hebrews 2:1.

doctrine. "They are of the world: therefore speak they of the world, and the world heareth them" (1 John 4:5).

cross. "As many as desire to make a fair shew in the flesh, they constrain you to be circumcised; only lest they should suffer persecution for the cross of Christ" (Galatians 6:12). The false teachers that Paul describes taught that a person becomes a Christian by faith in Christ *plus* keeping the Law of Moses. Circumcision was the "sign of the covenant," proof that a person was seeking to obey the Law. These teachers held to the Law so that they could avoid persecution from the Jews. But there is no salvation apart from the cross. Morality avoids the cross and clings to the Law.

pervert. "But there be some that trouble you, and would pervert the gospel of Christ" (Galatians 1:7). Mixing Law with the gospel perverts the truth.

administration of death. Another name for the Law. See 2 Corinthians 3:1-9. The Law can never give life, because it can only reveal sin, not remove it.

Strive . . . . Luke 13:24, and see Matthew 7:13-14.

Egypt. Moses gave up the treasures of Egypt to "suffer affliction with the people of God . . ." (Hebrews 11:25-26). People who depend on religious morality avoid the doctrine of the cross, because it reveals the sinfulness of sin and the necessity for a Savior.

King of Glory. Psalm 24:7-10.

save his life. Matthew 10:37-39;

3. His setting thy feet in that way that leadeth unto the <u>administration of death</u>.

First, Thou must abhor his turning thee out of the way; yea, and thine own consenting thereto: because this is to reject the counsel of God for the sake of the counsel of a Worldly Wiseman. The Lord says, "<u>Strive</u> to enter in at the strait gate," the gate to which I sent thee; for "strait is the gate that leadeth unto life, and few there be that find it." From this little wicket-gate, and from the way thereto, hath this wicked man turned thee, to the bringing of thee almost to destruction; hate, therefore, his turning thee out of the way, and abhor thyself for hearkening to him.

Secondly, Thou must abhor his labouring to render the cross odious unto thee; for thou art to prefer it before "the treasures of <u>Egypt</u>." Besides, the <u>King of Glory</u> hath told thee that he that "will <u>save his life</u> shall lose it"; and he that comes after him, "and hates not his father, and mother, and wife, and children, and brethren, and sisters, yea, and his own life also, he cannot be my disciple." I say, therefore, for man to labour to persuade thee that that shall be thy death, without which, THE TRUTH hath said, thou canst not have eternal life; this doctrine thou must abhor.

38

Thirdly, Thou must hate his setting of thy feet in the way that leadeth to the ministration of death. And for this thou must consider to whom he sent thee, and also how unable that person was to deliver thee from thy burden.

He to whom thou wast sent for ease, being by name Legality, is the son of the bond-woman which now is, and is in bondage with her children; and is, in a mystery, this Mount Sinai, which thou hast feared will fall on thy head. Now if she, with her children, are in bondage, how canst thou expect by them to be made free? This Legality, therefore, is not able to set thee free from thy burden. No man was as yet ever rid of his burden by him; no, nor ever is like to be: ye cannot be justified by works of the law; for by the deeds of the law no man living can be rid of his burden: therefore, Mr. Worldly Wiseman is an alien, and Mr. Legality is a cheat; and for his son Civility, notwithstanding his simpering looks, he is but a hypocrite and cannot help thee. Believe me, there is nothing in all this noise that thou hast heard of these sottish men, but a design to beguile thee of thy salvation, by turning thee from the way in which I had set thee. After this, Evangelist called aloud to the heavens for confirmation of what he had said: and with that there came words and fire out of the mountain under which poor Christian stood, that made the hair of his flesh stand up. The words were thus pronounced: "As many as are of the works of the law are under the curse; for it is written, Cursed is every one that continueth not in all things which are written in the book of the law to do them."

Now Christian looked for nothing but death, and began to cry out lamentably; even cursing the time in which he met with Mr. Worldly Wiseman; still calling himself a thousand fools for hearkening to his counsel; he also was greatly ashamed to think that this gentleman's arguments, flowing only from the flesh, should

Mark 8:34-38; Luke 14:26-27; John 12:25.

Thirdly. Mr. Worldly Wiseman promised life, but the Law only brings death. The Law can put a man in bondage, but it cannot deliver him. "For if righteousness come by the law, then Christ is dead in vain" (Galatians 2:21).

bond-woman. Galatians 4:21-31 and Genesis 18 and 21:1-21. Abraham ran ahead of God's will and married Hagar, his wife's maid, hoping to beget the son God had promised him. Ishmael was born, and he brought nothing but trouble. Finally, both Ishmael and Hagar had to be cast out when the true heir, Isaac, came on the scene. Hagar represents the Law; she was a bond-woman. Ishmael represents the flesh, the old nature, because he was born out of Abraham's disobedience. Sarah represents God's grace, and Isaac pictures the true believer, born out of promise by the power of God. Ishmael was a slave, because his mother was a bond-woman. Isaac was free because his mother was free. There is no salvation by Law: Hagar and Ishmael were cast out!

mystery. A symbol; a "sacred secret" hidden in the Old Testament and explained in the New Testament.

justified. Justification is the act of God whereby He graciously declares righteous all who trust Jesus Christ. It is a legal term and has to do with our standing

have the prevalency with him as to cause him to
forsake the right way. This done, he applied
himself again to Evangelist in words and sense
as follow:

CHR. Sir, what think you? Is there hope? May
I now go back and go up to the wicket-gate?
Shall I not be abandoned for this, and sent back
from thence ashamed? I am sorry I have hear-
kened to this man's counsel. But may my sin be
forgiven?

EVAN. Then said Evangelist to him, Thy sin is
very great, for by it thou hast committed two
evils: thou hast forsaken the way that is good, to
tread in forbidden paths; yet will the man at the
gate receive thee, for he has good-will for men;
only, said he, take heed that thou turn not aside
again, lest thou perish from the way, when his
wrath is kindled but a little. Then did Christian
address himself to go back; and Evangelist, after
he had kissed him, gave him one smile, and bid
him God-speed. So he went on with haste,
neither spake he to any man by the way; nor, if
any asked him, would he vouchsafe them an answer. He went like one that was all the while
treading on forbidden ground, and could by no
means think himself safe, till again he was got
into the way which he left to follow Mr. Worldly
Wiseman's counsel. So in process of time Christian got up to the gate. Now, over the gate there
was written, "Knock, and it shall be opened
unto you."

> He that will enter in must first without
> Stand knocking at the gate, nor need he doubt
> That is a knocker but to enter in;
> For God can love him and forgive his sin.

He knocked, therefore, more than once or
twice, saying,

> May I now enter here? Will he within
> Open to sorry me, though I have been
> An undeserving rebel? Then shall I
> Not fail to sing his lasting praise on high.

40

At last there came a grave person to the gate, named Good-will, who asked who was there? and whence he came? and what he would have?

CHR. Here is a poor burdened sinner. I come from the City of Destruction, but am going to Mount Zion, that I may be delivered from the wrath to come. I would, therefore, sir, since I am informed that by this gate is the way thither, know if you are willing to let me in?

GOOD-WILL. I am willing with all my heart, said he; and with that he opened the gate.

So when Christian was stepping in, the other gave him a pull. Then said Christian, What means that? The other told him, A little distance from this gate, there is erected a strong castle, of which Beelzebub is the captain; from thence, both he and them that are with him shoot arrows at those that come up to this gate, if haply they may die before they can enter in.

Then said Christian, I rejoice and tremble. So when he was got in, the man of the gate asked him who directed him thither?

CHR. Evangelist bid me come hither and knock (as I did); and said that you, sir, would tell me what I must do.

GOOD-WILL. An open door is set before thee, and no man can shut it.

CHR. Now I begin to reap the benefits of my hazards.

GOOD-WILL. But how is it that you came alone?

CHR. Because none of my neighbours saw their danger, as I saw mine.

who was there. Christian will answer these questions several times during his pilgrimage. The Puritans carefully questioned new converts and candidates for church membership to make certain they were truly converted. "Be ready always to give an answer to every man that asketh you a reason of the hope that is in you with meekness and fear" (1 Peter 3:15).

Mount Zion. A name for the heavenly city (Hebrews 12:22ff.). It applied to the earthly city of Jerusalem (Psalm 2:6), where David reigned (1 Chronicles 11:4-9). See also Psalm 48:2.

wrath to come. Matthew 3:7; 1 Thessalonians 1:10.

willing. "Am I one of God's elect? Is He willing to save me?" These questions plagued the Puritans. "God our Savior . . . who will have all men to be saved, and to come unto the knowledge of the truth" (1 Timothy 2:3-4). "The Lord . . . is longsuffering to us-ward, not willing that any should perish, but that all should come to repentance" (2 Peter 3:9). Bunyan's marginal note here is: "The gate will be opened to broken-hearted sinners," referring to Psalm 51:17.

pull. To get him in quickly before Beelzebub (Satan) can attack him and hinder him. Good-will did not pull Christian in against his will, nor did Christian force his way in. Here Bunyan reconciles God's divine election and man's responsibility to believe. "All that the

41

Father giveth me shall come to me [divine sovereignty]; and him that cometh to me I will in no wise cast out [human responsibility]" (John 6:37).

Beelzebub. One of several names for Satan in the Bible (Matthew 10:25 and 12:24-27). It may mean "lord of the flies" (2 Kings 1:2) or "lord of the house" (Matthew 10:25). It could also mean "the dung god." It speaks of the devil's filthiness of character and works. On shooting arrows, see Ephesians 6:16.

rejoice. "Serve the LORD with fear, and rejoice with trembling" (Psalm 2:11). Later on (page 53) Christian will experience "hope and fear." The Puritans sought to maintain proper balance in their spiritual emotions. If they rejoiced, they also realized the greatness and holiness of God and therefore trembled. Their hope was balanced by godly fear. There is a false joy that is shallow, and a false hope that lacks reality.

open door. "Behold, I have set before thee an open door, and no man can shut it" (Revelation 3:8).

betterment. An old word that means "condition of being better." Christian does not condemn Pliable without accusing himself.

GOOD-WILL Did any of them know of your coming?

CHR. Yes; my wife and children saw me at the first, and called after me to turn again; also some of my neighbours stood crying and calling after me to return; but I put my fingers in my ears, and so came on my way.

GOOD-WILL. But did none of them follow you to persuade you to go back?

CHR. Yes, both Obstinate and Pliable; but when they saw that they could not prevail, Obstinate went railing back, but Pliable came with me a little way.

GOOD-WILL. But why did he not come through?

CHR. We indeed came both together, until we came at the Slough of Despond, into the which we also suddenly fell. And then was my neighbour Pliable discouraged, and would not adventure further. Wherefore, getting out again on that side next to his own house, he told me I should possess the brave country alone for him; so he went his way, and I came mine—he after Obstinate, and I to this gate.

GOOD-WILL. Then said Good-will, Alas, poor man, is the celestial glory of so small esteem with him, that he counteth it not worth running the hazards of a few difficulties to obtain it?

CHR. Truly, said Christian, I have said the truth of Pliable, and if I should also say all the truth of myself, it will appear there is no betterment betwixt him and myself. 'Tis true, he went back to his own house, but I also turned aside to go in the way of death, being persuaded thereto by the carnal arguments of one Mr. Worldly Wiseman.

GOOD-WILL. Oh, did he light upon you? What! he would have had you seek for ease at the hands of Mr. Legality. They are, both of them, a very cheat. But did you take his counsel?

CHR. Yes, as far as I durst; I went to find out

Mr. Legality, until I thought that the mountain that stands by his house would have fallen upon my head; wherefore, there I was forced to stop.

GOOD-WILL. That mountain has been the death of many and will be the death of many more; 'tis well you escaped being by it dashed in pieces.

CHR. Why, truly, I do not know what had become of me there, had not Evangelist happily met me again, as I was musing in the midst of my dumps; but 'twas God's mercy that he came to me again, for else I had never come hither. But now I am come, such a one as I am, more fit indeed for death by that mountain, than thus to stand talking with my Lord; but, oh, what a favour is this to me, that yet I am admitted entrance here!

GOOD-WILL. We make no objections against any, notwithstanding all that they have done before they came hither. They "in no wise are cast out." And therefore, good Christian, come a little way with me, and I will teach thee about the way thou must go. Look before thee; dost thou see this narrow way? THAT is the way thou must go. It was cast up by the patriarchs, prophets, Christ, and his apostles, and it is as straight as a rule can make it. This is the way thou must go.

CHR. But, said Christian, are there no turnings or windings, by which a stranger may lose his way?

GOOD-WILL. Yes, there are many ways butt down upon this, and they are crooked and wide. But thus thou mayest distinguish the right from the wrong, the right only being straight and narrow.

Then I saw in my dream that Christian asked him further if he could not help him off with his burden that was upon his back; for as yet he had not got rid thereof, nor could he by any means get it off without help.

He told him, As to thy burden, be content to bear it until thou comest to the place of deliver-

mercy. God in His mercy does not give us what we deserve. God in His grace gives us what we do not deserve—salvation. The word "favor" means "grace." It is God's favor for the undeserving.

in no wise. John 6:37.

this narrow way. Matthew 7:13-14.

cast up. "And an highway shall be there, and a way, and it shall be called The way of holiness" (Isaiah 35:8). See also Isaiah 19:23 and 40:3.

butt down. Abut. Christian will discover some of these "crooked and wide" detours!

gird up. Since people in Bible days usually wore flowing robes, they had to tie them together in order to be able to run. You find the phrase often in the Bible: 2 Kings 4:29 and 9:1; Luke 12:35; 1 Peter 1:13.

Interpreter. This is the Holy Spirit of God, who interprets the things of God to seekers. "Howbeit when he, the Spirit of truth, is come, he will guide you into all truth" (John 16:13).

candle. "Thy word is a lamp unto my feet, and a light unto my path" (Psalm 119:105). The Holy Spirit uses the Bible to show us God's truth.

picture. The picture is that of the ideal pastor, and Bunyan certainly had his own pastor, John Gifford, in mind. See also Malachi 2:4-7 for a description of God's ideal servant. The Puritans held their pastors in great respect and condemned the careless pastors.

ance; for there it will fall from thy back of itself.

Then Christian began to gird up his loins, and to address himself to his journey. So the other told him, that by that he was gone some distance from the gate, he would come at the house of the Interpreter, at whose door he should knock, and he would show him excellent things. Then Christian took his leave of his friend, and he again bid him God-speed.

Then he went on till he came to the house of the Interpreter, where he knocked over and over; at last one came to the door and asked who was there.

CHR. Sir, here is a traveller, who was bid by an acquaintance of the good-man of this house to call here for my profit; I would therefore speak with the master of the house. So he called for the master of the house, who after a little time came to Christian and asked him what he would have.

CHR. Sir, said Christian, I am a man that am come from the City of Destruction, and am going to the Mount Zion; and I was told by the man that stands at the gate, at the head of this way, that if I called here, you would show me excellent things, such as would be a help to me in my journey.

INTER. Then said the Interpreter, Come in; I will show thee that which will be profitable to thee. So he commanded his man to light the candle, and bid Christian follow him: so he had him into a private room, and bid his man open a door; the which when he had done, Christian saw the picture of a very grave person hung up against the wall; and this was the fashion of it. It had eyes lifted up to heaven, the best of books in his hand, the law of truth was written upon his lips, the world was behind his back. It stood as if it pleaded with men, and crown of gold did hang over his head.

CHR. Then said Christian, What meaneth this?

44

INTER. The man whose picture this is, is one of a thousand; he can beget children, travail in birth with children, and nurse them himself when they are born. And whereas thou seest him with his eyes lift up to heaven, the best of books in his hand, and the law of truth writ on his lips, it is to show thee that his work is to know and unfold dark things to sinners; even as also thou seest him stand as if he pleaded with men; and whereas thou seest the world as cast behind him, and that a crown hangs over his head, that is to show thee that slighting and despising the things that are present, for the love that he hath to his Master's service, he is sure in the world that comes next to have glory for his reward. Now, said the Interpreter, I have showed thee this picture first because the man whose picture this is, is the only man whom the Lord of the place whither thou art going hath authorized to be thy guide in all difficult places thou mayest meet with in the way; wherefore, take good heed to what I have showed thee, and bear well in thy mind what thou hast seen, lest in thy journey thou meet with some that pretend to lead thee right, but their way goes down to death.

Then he took him by the hand and led him into a very large parlour that was full of dust, because never swept; the which, after he had reviewed a little while, the Interpreter called for a man to sweep. Now when he began to sweep, the dust began so abundantly to fly about that Christian had almost therewith been choked. Then said the Interpreter to a damsel that stood by, Bring hither the water and sprinkle the room; the which, when she had done, it was swept and cleansed with pleasure.

CHR. Then said Christian, What means this?

INTER. The Interpreter answered, This parlour is the heart of a man that was never sanctified by the sweet grace of the Gospel; the dust is his original sin and inward corruptions that

beget, . . . travail, . . . nurse. "For in Christ Jesus I have begotten you through the gospel" (1 Corinthians 4:15). "My little children, of whom I travail in birth again until Christ be formed in you" (Galatians 4:19). "But we were gentle among you, even as a nurse cherisheth her children" (1 Thessalonians 2:7). Puritan pastors diligently cared for their "spiritual children."

authorized. The officials of the established church told Bunyan he was not authorized to preach, and this is why they put him in jail. It was necessary for a man to have a license from the government before he could preach and pastor a church. The Puritans were careful to ordain men called of God, and they warned their people about false prophets.

pretend. "Beware of false prophets" (Matthew 7:15; see also verses 13-20). "There is a way which seemeth right unto a man, but the end thereof are the ways of death" (Proverbs 14:12).

sanctified. The word literally means "set apart for God's exclusive use." To the Puritans it meant the process of becoming a holy person. When a sinner trusts Christ, he is *justified* (declared righteous by God), and he should *be sanctified* (reveal that righteousness in daily living). The Law can never sweep the parlor clean; it can only "raise the dust" and reveal how sinful the human heart is. The gospel is like water that keeps the dust down.

original sin. The sin we are born with by nature because we are children of Adam. Note that the water does not completely wash away the dust; it merely keeps it under control. Salvation does not remove the old sinful nature; rather, it gives us a new nature within. This new nature enables us to conquer sin and obey God. Perhaps Ezekiel 36:25-27 is what Bunyan had in mind. However, do not read baptism into this sprinkling. Bunyan did not believe that baptism was essential to salvation.

revive, put strength into. God did not give the Law to save people, but to reveal to us that we need to be saved. "Moreover the law entered, that the offence might abound" (Romans 5:20). In Romans 7:7-11, Paul describes how his trying to keep the Law only increased his desires to sin! "The strength of sin is the law" (1 Corinthians 15:56). Rather than weaken sin, the Law actually gives strength to sin. This explains why Morality and Legality can never save. See John 14:21-23 and 15:3; Acts 15:9; Romans 16:25-26; and Ephesians 5:26.

Passion . . . Patience. The Christian does not receive everything here and now; he must exercise patience and wait for the promised blessings. "Be ye also patient; stablish your hearts: for the coming of the Lord draweth nigh" (James 5:8). The men of this world must have everything now.

have defiled the whole man. He that began to sweep at first is the Law; but she that brought water and did sprinkle it is the Gospel. Now whereas thou sawest that so soon as the first began to sweep, the dust did so fly about that the room by him could not be cleansed, but that thou wast almost choked therewith; this is to show thee that the Law, instead of cleansing the heart (by its working) from sin, doth revive, put strength into, and increase it in the soul, even as it doth discover and forbid it, for it doth not give power to subdue.

Again, as thou sawest the damsel sprinkle the room with water, upon which it was cleansed with pleasure; this is to show thee that when the Gospel comes in the sweet and precious influences thereof to the heart, then, I say, even as thou sawest the damsel lay the dust by sprinkling the floor with water, so is sin vanquished and subdued, and the soul made clean through the faith of it, and consequently fit for the King of glory to inhabit.

I saw, moreover, in my dream, that the Interpreter took him by the hand and had him into a little room, where sat two little children, each one in his chair. The name of the eldest was Passion, and the name of the other Patience. Passion seemed to be much discontented; but Patience was very quiet. Then Christian asked, What is the reason of the discontent of Passion? The Interpreter answered, The Governor of them would have him stay for his best things till the beginning of the next year; but he will have all now: but Patience is willing to wait.

Then I saw that one came to Passion, and brought him a bag of treasure, and poured it down at his feet, the which he took up and rejoiced therein, and withal laughed Patience to scorn. But I beheld but a while, and he had lavished all away, and had nothing left him but rags.

CHR. Then said Christian to the Interpreter,

46

Expound this matter more fully to me.

INTER. So he said, These two lads are figures: Passion, of the men of this world; and Patience, of the men of that which is to come; for, as here thou seest, Passion will have all now this year, that is to say, in this world; so are the men of this world, they must have all their good things now, they cannot stay till next year, that is, until the next world, for their portion of good. That proverb, "A bird in the hand is worth two in the bush," is of more authority with them than are all the Divine testimonies of the good of the world to come. But as thou sawest that he had quickly lavished all away, and had presently left him nothing but rags; so will it be with all such men at the end of this world.

CHR. Then said Christian, Now I see that Patience has the best wisdom, and that upon many accounts. First, Because he stays for the best things. Second, And also because he will have the glory of his, when the other has nothing but rags.

INTER. Nay, you may add another, to wit, the glory of the next world will never wear out; but these are suddenly gone. Therefore Passion had not so much reason to laugh at Patience, because he had his good things first, as Patience will have to laugh at Passion, because he had his best things last; for first must give place to last, because last must have his time to come; but last gives place to nothing, for there is not another to succeed. He, therefore, that hath his portion first, must needs have a time to spend it; but he that hath his portion last, must have it lastingly; therefore it is said of Dives, "Thou in thy lifetime receivedst thy good things, and likewise Lazarus evil things: but now he is comforted, and thou art tormented."

CHR. Then I perceive 'tis not best to covet things that are now, but to wait for things to come.

INTER. You say truth: "For the things that are

bird in the hand. An ancient proverb. The Greek author Plutarch (A.D. 46?-120?) wrote, "He is a fool who lets slip a bird in the hand for a bird in the bush." But martyred missionary Jim Elliot wrote, "He is no fool to give what he cannot keep to gain what he cannot lose." Bunyan would have agreed with Elliot.

first . . . last. "So the last shall be first, and the first last" (Matthew 20:16). At the judgment, those who are first in the eyes of men, or in their own eyes, will be last; while those who humbly are last in their own eyes will be first.

Thou in thy lifetime. Luke 16:25; see also verses 19-31. "Dives" is the traditional name for the rich man. He is not named in the parable.

For the things . . . . 2 Corinthians 4:18.

47

fleshly appetite. See Romans 7:15-25.

fire. "Did not our heart burn within us, while he talked with us by the way . . . ?" (Luke 24:32). "Wherefore I put thee in remembrance that thou stir up the gift of God, which is in thee" (2 Timothy 1:6).

Devil. Bunyan writes in *Grace Abounding*: "Then hath the tempter come upon me with such discouragements as these: You are very hot for mercy, but I will cool you; this frame shall not last always; many have been as hot as you but I have quenched their zeal. Though you be burning hot at present, yet I can pull you from this fire; I shall have you cold before it be long."

oil. The image comes from Zechariah 4:11-14. The oil symbolizes the grace of God given through the Holy Spirit. "Being confident of this very thing, that he which hath begun a good work in you will perform it until the day of Jesus Christ" (Philippians 1:6).

gracious still. "And he said unto me, My grace is sufficient for thee" (2 Corinthians 12:9). Satan attacked Paul, but God's grace sustained him.

palace. This seems to symbolize the rewards God has for those who "fight the good fight

seen are temporal; but the things that are not seen are eternal." But though this be so, yet since things present and our fleshly appetite are such near neighbours one to another; and again, because things to come, and carnal sense, are such strangers one to another; therefore it is that the first of these so suddenly fall into amity, and that distance is so continued between the second.

Then I saw in my dream that the Interpreter took Christian by the hand and led him into a place where was a fire burning against a wall, and one standing by it, always casting much water upon it to quench it; yet did the fire burn higher and hotter.

Then said Christian, What means this?

The Interpreter answered, This fire is the work of grace that is wrought in the heart; he that casts water upon it, to extinguish and put it out, is the Devil; but in that thou seest the fire notwithstanding burn higher and hotter, thou shalt also see the reason of that. So he had him about to the backside of the wall, where he saw a man with a vessel of oil in his hand, of the which he did also continually cast, but secretly, into the fire.

Then said Christian, What means this?

The Interpreter answered, This is Christ, who continually, with the oil of his grace, maintains the work already begun in the heart: by the means of which, notwithstanding what the Devil can do, the souls of his people prove gracious still. And in that thou sawest that the man stood behind the wall to maintain the fire, that is to teach thee that it is hard for the tempted to see how his work of grace is maintained in the soul.

I saw also that the Interpreter took him again by the hand and led him into a pleasant place, where was builded a stately palace, beautiful to behold; at the sight of which Christian was greatly delighted. He saw also, upon the top

48

thereof, certain persons walking, who were clothed all in gold.

Then said Christian, May we go in thither?

Then the Interpreter took him and led him up toward the door of the palace; and behold, at the door stood a great company of men, as desirous to go in, but durst not. There also sat a man at a little distance from the door, at a tableside, with a _book_ and his _inkhorn_ before him, to take the name of him that should enter therein; he saw also that in the doorway stood many men in armour to keep it, being resolved to do the men that would enter what hurt and mischief they could. Now was Christian somewhat in amaze. At last, when every man started back for fear of the armed men, Christian saw a man of a very _stout_ countenance come up to the man that sat there to write, saying, Set down my name, sir: the which when he had done, he saw the man draw his sword, and put an helment upon his head, and _rush_ toward the door upon the armed men, who laid upon him with deadly force; but the man, not at all discouraged, fell to cutting and hacking most fiercely. So after he had received and given many wounds to those that attempted to keep him out, he cut his way through them all, and pressed forward into the palace, at which there was a pleasant voice heard from those that were within, even of those that walked upon the top of the palace, saying,

> Come in, come in;
> Eternal glory thou shalt _win_.

So he went in, and was clothed with such garments as they. Then Christian smiled and said, I think verily I know the meaning of this.

Now, said Christian, let me go hence. Nay, stay, said the Interpreter, till I have showed thee a little more, and after that thou shalt go on thy way. So he took him by the hand again, and led him into a very dark room, where there sat a man in an _iron cage._

of faith" (1 Timothy 6:12). Although salvation is by grace, the rewards are given only to the faithful; and faithfulness involves fighting a battle.

book . . . inkhorn. The image comes from Ezekiel 9, except that the recorder in our text wrote down the names instead of putting a mark on the persons.

stout. Strong, firm, determined.

rush. "The kingdom of heaven suffereth violence, and the violent take it by force" (Matthew 11:12). "We must through much tribulation enter into the kingdom of God" (Acts 14:22). The man in armor balances the picture of Patience given previously. In the Christian life, patience is not merely waiting; it is also bravely enduring and keeping going when things are difficult.

win. The New Testament letters often use military figures of speech to picture the Christian life. Bunyan himself was in the army at one time. Keep in mind that Christian is being shown the difficulties and demands of the pilgrim walk. He will fight many enemies before he reaches the Holy City.

iron cage. A picture of despair, in contrast to the valiant soldier who pressed through to victory. The man himself tells us that he was "a fair and flourishing professor," meaning "one who professed to be a Christian."

even joy. Bunyan refers to Luke 8:13, from the parable of the sower: "They on the rock are they, which, when they hear, receive the word with joy; and these have no root, which for a while believe, and in time of temptation fall away." Feelings alone are no guarantee of salvation.

watch. "Be ye therefore sober, and watch unto prayer" (1 Peter 4:7). The Puritans constantly kept watch over their spiritual lives, lest they should disobey God and sin. They also watched over each other.

grieved the Spirit. "And grieve not the holy Spirit of God, whereby ye are sealed unto the day of redemption" (Ephesians 4:30). When the sinner trusts Christ, he receives the gift of the Holy Spirit and his body becomes God's temple (1 Corinthians 6:19-20). To grieve the Spirit is to sin repeatedly against God and not repent.

none at all. The man is convinced that he has no hope. In *Grace Abounding* Bunyan states that he "was persuaded that those who were once effectually in Christ . . . could never lose him forever." The Interpreter does not say that the man's case is hopeless, nor does Bunyan. It is the man who condemns himself, because he is in such despair.

pitiful. "Full of pity," a quotation from James 5:11. Christian

Now the man, to look on, seemed very sad; he sat with his eyes looking down to the ground, his hands folded together, and he sighed as if he would break his heart. Then said Christian, What means this? At which the Interpreter bid him talk with the man.

Then said Christian to the man, What art thou? The man answered, I am what I was not once.

CHR. What wast thou once?

MAN. The man said, I was once a fair and flourishing professor, both in mine own eyes, and also in the eyes of others; I once was, as I thought, fair for the Celestial City, and had then even joy at the thoughts that I should get thither.

CHR. Well, but what art thou now?

MAN. I am now a man of despair, and am shut up in it, as in this iron cage. I cannot get out. Oh, now I cannot!

CHR. But how camest thou in this condition?

MAN. I left off to watch and be sober; I laid the reins upon the neck of my lusts; I sinned against the light of the Word and the goodness of God; I have grieved the Spirit, and he is gone; I tempted the Devil, and he is come to me; I have provoked God to anger, and he has left me: I have so hardened my heart that I cannot repent.

Then said Christian to the Interpreter, But is there no hope for such a man as this? Ask him, said the Interpreter. Nay, said Christian, pray, sir, do you.

INTER. Then said the Interpreter, Is there no hope, but you must be kept in the iron cage of despair?

MAN. No, none at all.

INTER. Why, the Son of the Blessed is very pitiful.

MAN. I have crucified him to myself afresh, I have despised his person, I have despised his righteousness, I have counted his blood an unholy thing, I have "done despite to the spirit of

50

grace." Therefore I have shut myself out of all the promises, and there now remains to me nothing but threatenings, dreadful threatenings, fearful threatenings of certain judgment and fiery indignation, which shall devour me as an adversary.

INTER. For what did you bring yourself into this condition?

MAN. For the lusts, pleasures, and profits of this world; in the enjoyment of which I did then promise myself much delight: but now every one of those things also bite me and gnaw me like a burning worm.

INTER. But canst thou not now repent and turn?

MAN. God hath denied me repentance. His Word gives me no encouragement to believe; yea, himself hath shut me up in this iron cage; nor can all the men in the world let me out. O eternity! eternity! how shall I grapple with the misery that I must meet with in eternity!

INTER. Then said the Interpreter to Christian, Let this man's misery be remembered by thee and be an everlasting caution to thee.

CHR. Well, said Christian, this is fearful! God help me to watch and be sober, and to pray that I may shun the cause of this man's misery! Sir, is it not time for me to go on my way now?

INTER. Tarry till I shall show thee one thing more, and then thou shalt go on thy way.

So he took Christian by the hand again and led him into a chamber, where there was one rising out of bed; and as he put on his raiment, he shook and trembled. Then said Christian, Why doth this man thus tremble? The Interpreter then bid him tell to Christian the reason of his so doing. So he began and said, This night, as I was in my sleep, I dreamed, and behold the heavens grew exceeding black; also it thundered and lightened in most fearful wise, that it put me into an agony. So I looked up in my dream, and saw the clouds rack at an unusual rate,

assures the despairing man that Christ is ready to forgive and restore him.

I have crucified. Quoted from Hebrews 6:4-6 and 10:28-29. These passages in Hebrews have long been a battleground for theologians. Do they describe the condition of a believer who has abandoned faith in Christ? Or do they describe a professed Christian (Bunyan's "professor") who was not truly converted? Bunyan's previous reference to Luke 8:13 suggests that the man in the cage was not saved at all, because he did not produce the necessary fruits. In any case, the man in despair is a warning that we should "watch and be sober."

despised. "We will not have this man to reign over us" (Luke 19:14).

repent. To repent means to change your mind. True repentance results in an act of the will that causes the sinner to turn from sin and trust Christ. The man in the cage believed that the gift of repentance had been denied him and it was too late. Bunyan may be referring here to Hebrews 12:16-17, the experience of Esau, who begged his father Isaac to give him a blessing. Isaac had already given the blessing to Esau's brother, Jacob, and Isaac could not change his mind. It is Isaac's change of mind that is referred to, not Esau's. See Genesis 27.

shook and trembled. Caused, of course, by the fear of judgment. Bunyan wrote, "Even in my childhood the Lord did scare and affright me with fearful dreams, and did terrify me with dreadful visions." During his period of conviction, he

51

greatly feared God's wrath. "My sins also came into my mind, and my conscience did accuse me on every side."

the heavens. The dream of judgment is a composite of several "judgment passages" in the Bible. See John 5:28-29; 1 Corinthians 15:51-58; 2 Thessalonians 1:7-10; Jude 14-15; and Revelation 20:11-15.

rack. An old English word meaning "drive, rush and collide." It is a vivid word to describe judgment clouds rolling in the heavens.

sound. 1 Thessalonians 4:16.

man sit upon a cloud. Matthew 26:64.

rocks rent. See Matthew 27:50-53.

hide themselves. Psalm 50:1-3, 22; Isaiah 26:20-21; Micah 7:16-17; Revelation 6:12-17.

flame. Daniel 7:10. Fire is a symbol of the holy judgment of God. See also Malachi 3:2-3.

Gather together the tares . . . . See the parable of the wheat and tares in Matthew 13:24-30 and 36-43. The wheat pictures the true children of God; the tares picture imitation believers, counterfeits. You cannot distinguish them until the harvest. At the judgment, the tares will be burned. See also Malachi 4:2; Matthew 3:12; and Luke 3:17.

pit. Revelation 9:1, 2, 11; 11:7; 17:8; 20:1, 3. "Abyss" is the correct word. It seems to be a pit within the confines of hell.

catched up. This is the "rapture" of God's people when Jesus Christ returns. It is de-

upon which I heard a great sound of a trumpet, and saw also a man sit upon a cloud, attended with the thousands of heaven; they were all in flaming fire: also the heavens were in a burning flame. I heard then a voice saying, "Arise, ye dead, and come to judgment"; and with that the rocks rent, the graves opened, and the dead that were therein came forth. Some of them were exceeding glad, and looked upward; and some sought to hide themselves under the mountains. Then I saw the man that sat upon the cloud open the book, and bid the world draw near. Yet there was, by reason of a fierce flame which issued out and came from before him, a convenient distance betwixt him and them, as betwixt the judge and the prisoners at the bar. I heard it also proclaimed to them that attended on the man that sat on the cloud, "Gather together the tares, the chaff, and stubble, and cast them into the burning lake." And with that the bottomless pit opened, just whereabout I stood; out of the mouth of which there came, in an abundant manner, smoke and coals of fire, with hideous noises. It was also said to the same persons, "Gather my wheat into the garner." And with that I saw many catched up and carried away into the clouds, but I was left behind. I also sought to hide myself, but I could not, for the man that sat upon the cloud still kept his eye upon me: my sins also came into my mind; and my conscience did accuse me on every side. Upon this I awaked from my sleep.

CHR. But what was it that made you so afraid of this sight?

MAN. Why, I thought that the day of judgment was come, and that I was not ready for it: but this frighted me most, that the angels gathered up several, and left me behind; also the pit of hell opened her mouth just where I stood. My conscience, too, afflicted me; and, as I thought, the Judge had always his eye upon me, showing indignation in his countenance.

52

Then said the Interpreter to Christian, Hast thou considered all these things?

CHR. Yes, and they put me in hope and fear.

INTER. Well, keep all things so in thy mind that they may be as a goad in thy sides, to prick thee forward in the way thou must go. Then Christian began to gird up his loins, and to address himself to his journey. Then said the Interpreter, The Comforter be always with thee, good Christian, to guide thee in the way that leads to the City. So Christian went on his way, saying,

Here I have seen things rare and profitable;
Things pleasant, dreadful,
      things to make me stable
In what I have begun to take in hand;
Then let me think on them, and understand
Wherefore they showed me were, and let me be
Thankful, O good Interpreter, to thee.

Now I saw in my dream that the highway up which Christian was to go was fenced on either side with a wall, and that wall was called Salvation. Up this way, therefore, did burdened Christian run, but not without great difficulty, because of the load on his back.

He ran thus till he came at a place somewhat ascending, and upon that place stood a cross, and a little below, in the bottom, a sepulchre. So I saw in my dream that just as Christian came up with the cross, his burden loosed from off his shoulders, and fell from off his back, and began to tumble, and so continued to do, till it came to the mouth of the sepulchre. where it fell in, and I saw it no more.

Then was Christian glad and lightsome, and said, with a merry heart, "He hath given me rest by his sorrow, and life by his death." Then he stood still awhile to look and wonder; for it was very surprising to him that the sight of the cross should thus ease him of his burden. He looked, therefore, and looked again, even till the

scribed in 1 Thessalonians 4:13-18. Christians will suddenly be caught up to meet Christ in the air.

accuse me. Romans 2:14-15. Conscience is the inner judge, given by God, that accuses us when we have done wrong, and approves when we have done right. The word "conscience" was important in the Puritan vocabulary. If a man was right with God, he was also right with himself and others, and had a good conscience that did not disturb him.

hope and fear. See the note on "rejoice and tremble," page 42.

goad. The sharp stick used to prod oxen. All that Christian had seen in the house of the Interpreter should motivate him to continue his pilgrimage, no matter the cost. The image comes from Ecclesiastes 12:11—"The words of the wise are as goads"; and see Acts 9:5.

Comforter. One of the names of the Holy Spirit; see John 14:16-26. The Greek word means "one called to your side to help." The English word comes from the Latin meaning "with strength." The Holy Spirit gives us the strength we need to do God's will.

highway . . . wall. "Salvation will God appoint for walls and bulwarks" (Isaiah 26:1). See also Isaiah 35:8.

cross . . . sepulchre. The death of Christ, and His resurrection, are the heart of the Christian gospel. "Christ died for our sins, . . . he was buried, . . . he rose again the third day according to the scriptures" (1 Corinthians 15:3-4). Christian lost his burden of sin because he trusted Christ. See page 65 where Christian explains his experience to Piety. This had been Bunyan's own experience, as he relates it in *Grace Abounding*: "I remember that one day, as I was musing on the wickedness of my heart, . . . that Scripture came into my mind, He hath 'made peace by the blood of His cross,' by which I was made to see both again and again that God and my soul were friends by His blood. This was a good day to me; I hope I shall never forget it." It is worth noting that there was a stone cross at Elstow, near which Bunyan often played games. The stump of the cross remains.

rest . . . life. The paradox of the Christian faith: Christ dies that we might have life; Christ sorrows that we might have joy and rest.

waters. Bunyan's reference is to Zechariah 12:10, a description of true repentance.

Shining Ones. Angels. This scene is one of the most important in the book, for it presents Bunyan's beliefs about salvation. When he trusted Christ at the cross, Christian received peace ("Therefore being justified by faith, we have peace with God"—Romans 5:1); forgiveness (Mark 2:5); a clean garment, representing salvation (Isaiah 64:6 and Zechariah 3:4); a mark on his forehead (the seal of God—Ephesians 1:13); and a roll, or scroll (the assurance of salvation, see page 61). The three angels symbolize the Trinity: The Father forgives; the Son clothes; the Spirit seals and gives assurance. See Ephesians 1:3-14

springs that were in his head sent the waters down his cheeks. Now, as he stood looking and weeping, behold, three Shining Ones came to him and saluted him with "Peace be to thee." So the first said to him, "Thy sins be forgiven"; the second stripped him of his rags, and clothed him "with change of raiment"; the third also set a mark on his forehead, and gave him a roll with a seal upon it, which he bade him look on as he ran, and that he should give it in at the Celestial Gate. So they went their way.

> Who's this? the Pilgrim. How! 'tis very true,
> Old things are passed away, all's become new.
> Strange! he's another man, upon my word,
> They be fine feathers that make a fine bird.

Then Christian gave three leaps for joy, and went on, singing,

> Thus far did I come laden with my sin;
> Nor could aught ease the grief that I was in
> Till I came hither: What a place is this!
> Must here be the beginning of my bliss?
> Must here the burden fall from off my back?
> Must here the strings that bound it to me crack?
> Blest cross! blest sepulchre! blest rather be
> The Man that there was put to shame for me!

I saw then in my dream that he went on thus, even until he came at a bottom, where he saw, a little out of the way, three men fast asleep, with fetters upon their heels. The name of the one was Simple, another Sloth, and the third Presumption.

Christian then seeing them lie in this case, went to them, if peradventure he might awake them, and cried, You are like them that sleep on the top of a mast, for the Dead Sea is under you—a gulf that hath no bottom. Awake, therefore, and come away; be willing also, and I will help you off with your irons. He also told them, If he that goeth about like "a roaring lion" comes by, you will certainly become a prey to his teeth. With that they looked upon him, and began to reply in this sort: Simple said, "I see no danger"; Sloth said, "Yet a little more sleep"; and Presumption said, "Every vat must stand upon its own bottom; what is the answer else that I should give thee?" And so they lay down to sleep again, and Christian went on his way.

Yet was he troubled to think that men in that danger should so little esteem the kindness of him that so freely offered to help them, both by awakening of them, counselling of them, and proffering to help them off with their irons. And as he was troubled thereabout, he espied two men come tumbling over the wall, on the left hand of the narrow way; and they made up apace to him. The name of the one was Formalist, and the name of the other Hypocrisy. So, as I said, they drew up unto him, who thus entered with them into discourse.

CHR. Gentlemen, whence came you, and whither do you go?

FORM. and HYP. We were born in the land of Vain-glory, and are going for praise to Mount Zion.

CHR. Why came you not in at the gate which standeth at the beginning of the way? Know you not that it is written, that he that cometh not in

for this trinitarian view of salvation. The mark on the forehead speaks of ownership and protection; see Revelation 14:1 and 22:4.

Old things. Quoted from 2 Corinthians 5:17.

The Man. Bunyan's emphasis is on Christ, not on "religious places" such as the cross and the empty tomb.

out of the way. The first of the dangerous "detours" that "butt down" upon the true way. See page 43.

three men. We go from three shining ones to three careless ones. Filled with the joy of his salvation experience, Christian wants to witness to them and try to help them. Bunyan wrote that he would have told God's love and mercy "even to the very crows that sat upon the ploughed lands." The three men represent different kinds of religious indifference. Simple and Sloth depend on false security and false peace (see Proverbs 1:22, 32); and Presumption depends on false self-reliance.

mast. Quoted from Proverbs 23:34.

lion. Satan (1 Peter 5:8).

sleep. Proverbs 24:30-34.

vat. An old proverb that simply means, "I can make it myself without any help from you!" In other words, "God helps those who help themselves."

troubled. The new believer has a concern for those who are lost and cannot understand their ignorance.

Formalist . . . Hypocrisy. A "formalist" is a person who practices religious forms but does not possess real salvation. He may be very sincere, but his religion is vain. "Having a form of godliness, but denying the power there of" (2 Timothy 3:5). A hypocrite, however, deliberately deceives. At one time, Bunyan was quite taken up with the rituals of the church and thought that, through them, he would find salvation.

Vain-glory. Empty glory. The glory of man is vain because it does not endure. "All the glory of man [is] as the flower of grass" (1 Peter 1:24).

for praise. "For the purpose of doing a praiseworthy thing." Their motive for going to Mount Zion is all wrong. Both ritualists and hypocrites enjoy the praise of men.

the door. John 10:1

custom. Ancient customs were the authority for their religion. The Puritans rejected tradition and held that only the Bible could dictate to their conscience. Bunyan wrote in *Grace Abounding*, "Because I knew no better, I fell in very eagerly with the religion of the times. . . . I was so overrun with the spirit of superstition that I adored . . . even all things, both the high place, priest, clerk, vestment, service, and what else belonged to the church." Formalist and Hypocrisy depended on ancient tradition to support their approach to the Heavenly City

at the end. If we do not make the right beginning, we cannot expect the right ending. To come

by the door, "but climbeth up some other way, the same is a thief and a robber"?

FORM. and HYP. They said, That to go to the gate for entrance was by all their countrymen counted too far about; and that therefore their usual way was to make a short cut of it, and to climb over the wall, as they had done.

CHR. But will it not be counted a trespass against the Lord of the city whither we are bound, thus to violate his revealed will?

FORM. and HYP. They told him, that, as for that, he needed not to trouble his head thereabout; for what they did they had custom for; and could produce, if need were, testimony that would witness it for more than a thousand years.

CHR. But, said Christian, will your practice stand a trial at law?

FORM. and HYP. They told him, That custom, it being of so long a standing as above a thousand years, would doubtless now be admitted as a thing legal by an impartial judge; and besides, said they, if we get into the way, what's matter which way we get in? if we are in, we are in; thou art but in the way, who, as we perceive, came in at the gate; and we are also in the way that came tumbling over the wall; wherein now is thy condition better than ours?

CHR. I walk by the rule of my Master; you walk by the rude working of your fancies. You are counted thieves already by the Lord of the way; therefore I doubt you will not be found true men at the end of the way. You come in by yourselves without his direction, and shall go out by yourselves without his mercy.

To this they made him but little answer; only they bid him look to himself. Then I saw that they went on every man in his way, without much conference one with another; save that these two men told Christian, that as to laws and ordinances, they doubted not but they should as conscientiously do them as he; therefore, said they, we see not wherein thou differest from us but by the coat that is on thy back, which was, as we trow, given thee by some of thy neighbours, to hide the shame of thy nakedness.

CHR. By laws and ordinances you will not be saved, since you came not in by the door. And as for this coat that is on my back, it was given me by the Lord of the place whither I go; and that, as you say, to cover my nakedness with. And I take it as a token of his kindness to me; for I had nothing but rags before. And besides, thus I comfort myself as I go: Surely, think I, when I come to the gate of the city, the Lord thereof will know me for good, since I have his coat on my back—a coat that he gave me freely in the day that he stripped me of my rags. I have, moreover, a mark in my forehead, of which perhaps you have taken no notice, which one of my Lord's most intimate associates fixed there in the day that my burden fell off my shoulders. I will tell you, moreover, that I had then given me a roll, sealed, to comfort me by reading as I go on the way; I was also bid to give it in at the Celestial Gate, in token of my certain going in after it; all which things, I doubt, you want, and want them because you came not in at the gate.

To these things they gave him no answer; only they looked upon each other and laughed. Then I saw that they went on all, save that Christian kept before, who had no more talk but with himself, and that sometimes sighingly and sometimes comfortably; also he would be often reading in the roll that one of the Shining Ones gave him, by which he was refreshed.

I beheld then that they all went on till they came to the foot of the Hill Difficulty; at the bottom of which was a spring. There were also in the same place two other ways besides that which came straight from the gate; one turned to the left hand, and the other to the right, at the bottom of the hill; but the narrow way lay right up the hill, and the name of the going up the

into the way by some other entrance than the right door is to be a thief and a robber. Again, the reference is to John 10.

differest. The coat symbolizes the righteousness of Christ received by faith. There is a difference between God's righteousness and mere morality that is religious. Christian goes on to explain that there are other differences: he bears God's mark on his forehead, and he possesses the roll which assures him of his salvation. Formalist and Hypocrisy have none of these things.

laws. "Knowing that a man is not justified by the works of the law, but by the faith of Jesus Christ" (Galatians 2:16).

Hill Difficulty. The second of seven hills named in the book. Early in the Christian life, difficulties come to test our faith and to prove the reality of conversion. The true way leads up the hill; the false ways lead around the hill and end in judgment.

spring. "For he that hath mercy on them shall lead them, even by the springs of water shall he guide them. And I will make all my mountains a way, and my highways shall be exalted" (Isaiah 49:10-11).

those ways. "There is a way which seemeth right unto a man, but the end thereof are the ways of death" (Proverbs 14:12).

stumbled. "Give glory to the LORD your God, before he cause darkness, and before your feet stumble upon the dark mountains" (Jeremiah 13:16).

going. Old English for "walking." The way was so difficult that he went from running to walking to crawling on his hands and knees.
arbour. "And my people shall dwell in a peaceable habitation, and in sure dwellings, and in quiet resting places" (Isaiah 32:18). "They that wait upon the LORD shall renew their strength" (Isaiah 40:31).

side of the hill is called Difficulty. Christian now went to the spring, and drank thereof, to refresh himself, and then began to go up the hill, saying,

The hill, though high, I covet to ascend,
The difficulty will not me offend;
For I perceive the way to life lies here.
Come, pluck up heart,
    let's neither faint nor fear;
Better, though difficult, the right way to go,
Than wrong, though easy,
    where the end is woe.

The other two also came to the foot of the hill; but when they saw that the hill was steep and high, and that there were two other ways to go, and supposing also that these two ways might meet again with that up which Christian went, on the other side of the hill, therefore they were resolved to go in those ways. Now the name of one of those ways was Danger, and the name of the other Destruction. So the one took the way which is called Danger, which led him into a great wood, and the other took directly up the way to Destruction, which led him into a wide field, full of dark mountains, where he stumbled and fell, and rose no more.

Shall they who wrong begin yet rightly end?
Shall they at all have safety for their friend?
No, no; in headstrong manner they set out,
And headlong will they fall at last, no doubt.

I looked then after Christian, to see him go up the hill, where I perceived he fell from running to going, and from going to clambering upon his hands and his knees, because of the steepness of the place. Now about the midway to the top of the hill was a pleasant arbour, made by the Lord of the hill for the refreshing of weary travellers; thither, therefore, Christian got, where also he sat down to rest him. Then he pulled his roll out of his bosom, and read therein to his comfort; he also now began afresh to take a review of the coat or garment that was

58

given him as he stood by the cross. Thus pleasing himself awhile, he at last fell into a slumber, and thence into a fast sleep, which detained him in that place until it was almost night; and in his sleep, his roll fell out of his hand. Now as he was sleeping, there came one to him and awaked him, saying "Go to the ant, thou sluggard; consider her ways, and be wise." And with that Christian suddenly started up, and sped him on his way, and went apace, till he came to the top of the hill.

Now when he was got up to the top of the hill, there came two men running against him amain; the name of the one was Timorous, and of the other, Mistrust; to whom Christian said, Sirs, what's the matter? You run the wrong way. Timorous answered, that they were going to the City of Zion, and had got up that difficult place; but, said he, the further we go, the more danger we meet with; wherefore we turned, and are going back again.

Yes, said Mistrust, for just before us lie a couple of lions in the way, whether sleeping or waking we know not, and we could not think, if we came within reach, but they would presently pull us in pieces.

CHR. Then said Christian, You make me afraid, but whither shall I fly to be safe? If I go back to mine own country, *that* is prepared for fire and brimstone, and I shall certainly perish there. If I can get to the Celestial City, I am sure to be in safety there. I must venture. To go back is nothing but death; to go forward is fear of death, and life everlasting beyond it. I will yet go forward. So Mistrust and Timorous ran down the hill, and Christian went on his way. But, thinking again of what he had heard from the men, he felt in his bosom for his roll, that he might read therein and be comforted; but he felt, and found it not. Then was Christian in great distress, and knew not what to do; for he wanted that which used to relieve him, and that

slumber. Times of spiritual refreshment are to prepare us for the demands of life, not to lead us into careless lethargy. Bunyan refers to Proverbs 6:6 — "Go to the ant, thou sluggard; consider her ways, and be wise."

amain. At full speed.

Timorous . . . Mistrust. Fear and unbelief usually go together and try to escape difficulty and danger.

lions. Satan is pictured as a lion (1 Peter 5:8), but he does not sleep. These men are imagining the worst because they cannot trust God for the best. Perhaps Bunyan wants us to see the lions as symbolic of the religious persecution of his day, promoted by the king. Many people would not openly confess Christ for fear of persecution.

mine own country. Hebrews 11:14-16.

which should have been his pass into the Celestial City. Here, therefore, he began to be much perplexed, and knew not what to do. At last he bethought himself that he had slept in the arbour that is on the side of the hill; and, falling down upon his knees, he asked God's <u>forgiveness</u> for that his foolish act, and then went back to look for his roll. But all the way he went back, who can sufficiently set forth the sorrow of Christian's heart? Sometimes he sighed, sometimes he wept, and oftentimes he <u>chid</u> himself for being so foolish to fall asleep in that place which was erected only for a little refreshment for his weariness. Thus, therefore, he went back, carefully looking on this side and on that, all the way as he went, if happily he might find his roll, that had been his comfort so many times in his journey. He went thus till he came again within sight of the arbour where he sat and slept; but that sight renewed his sorrow the more by bringing again, even afresh, his evil of sleeping into his mind. Thus, therefore, he now went on bewailing his sinful sleep, saying, "O <u>wretched</u> man that I am!" that I should sleep in the <u>day-time</u>! that I should sleep in the midst of difficulty! that I should so indulge the flesh, as to use that rest for ease to my flesh, which the Lord of the hill hath erected only for the relief of the spirits of pilgrims! How many steps have I took in vain! (Thus it happened to <u>Israel,</u> for their sin; they were sent back again by the way of the Red Sea) and I am made to tread those steps with sorrow, which I might have trod with delight, had it not been for this sinful sleep. How far might I have been on my way by this time! I am made to tread those steps thrice over, which I needed not to have trod but once; yea, now also I am like to be <u>benighted,</u> for the day is almost spent. Oh, that I had not slept!

Now by this time he was come to the arbour again, where for a while he sat down and wept; but at last, as <u>Christian</u> would have it, looking

forgiveness. Christian's sin was forgiven because he confessed it to God. "If we confess our sins, he is faithful and just to forgive us our sins, and to cleanse us from all unrighteousness" (1 John 1:9). He did not need to return to the cross and be converted over again.

chid. Rebuked, blamed. Today we would say "chided."

wretched. The quotation is from Romans 7:24.

day-time. "For they that sleep sleep in the night; and they that be drunken are drunken in the night. But let us, who are of the day, be sober" (1 Thessalonians 5:7-8). Bunyan also refers to Revelation 2:4-5—"thou hast left thy first love. Remember therefore from whence thou art fallen, and repent, and do the first works."

Israel. The nation failed at Kadesh-barnea, did not enter the promised land, and wandered for the next forty years in the wilderness. See Numbers 14.

benighted. Deprived of light. He had to go through dangerous places in the darkness because

sorrowfully down under the settle, there he espied his roll; the which he with trembling and haste catched up, and put it into his bosom. But who can tell how joyful this man was when he had gotten his roll again! for this roll was the assurance of his life, and acceptance at the desired haven. Therefore he laid it up in his bosom, gave thanks to God for directing his eye to the place where it lay, and with joy and tears betook himself again to his journey. But oh, how nimbly now did he go up the rest of the hill! Yet before he got up the sun went down upon Christian; and this made him again recall the vanity of his sleeping to his remembrance; and thus he again began to condole with himself. O thou sinful sleep: how for thy sake am I like to be benighted in my journey! I must walk without the sun; darkness must cover the path of my feet; and I must hear the noise of the doleful creatures, because of my sinful sleep. Now also he remembered the story that Mistrust and Timorous told him of, how they were frighted with the sight of the lions. Then said Christian to himself again, These beasts range in the night for their prey; and if they should meet with me in the dark, how should I shift them? How should I escape being by them torn in pieces? Thus he went on his way. But while he was thus bewailing his unhappy miscarriage, he lift up his eyes, and behold there was a very stately palace before him, the name of which was Beautiful; and it stood just by the highway side.

So I saw in my dream that he made haste and went forward, that if possible he might get lodging there. Now before he had gone far, he entered into a very narrow passage, which was about a furlong off the porter's lodge; and looking very narrowly before him as he went, he espied two lions in the way. Now, thought he, I see the dangers that Mistrust and Timorous were driven back by. (The lions were chained, but he saw not the chains.) Then he was afraid,

of his disobedience. Though God forgives the sin, He does not change the consequences.

Christian. Some editions read, "As God would have it."

settle. A wooden bench.

doleful creatures. Isaiah 13:21.

palace . . . Beautiful. Bunyan's picture of the church. "Beautiful for situation, the joy of the whole earth, is mount Zion. . . . Mark ye well her bulwarks, consider her palaces" (Psalm 48:2, 13). Note that the palace is "by the highway side" and not on the highway itself. It is not necessary to be a member of a church to be a Christian, but fellowship in the church strengthens the Christian for his difficult pilgrimage. Bunyan himself was not a denominationalist, although several groups would like to claim him.

very narrow. The Puritans did not make church membership an easy thing. A person had to give evidence of true salvation before he was received into fellowship.

lions. Timorous and Mistrust had run from lions that were already chained! Christian is afraid, but he keeps going. It is this spiritual perseverance that proves he is a true believer. See Proverbs 22:13 and 26:13.

Watchful. The porter illustrates the work of the faithful pastor in watching for souls and helping them enter the fellowship. See Hebrews 13:17—"Obey them that have the rule over you, and submit yourselves: for they watch for your souls." See also Revelation 3:2.

strength. Bunyan refers to Mark 4:40—"Why are ye so fearful? how is it that ye have no faith?" "If thou faint in the day of adversity, thy strength is small" (Proverbs 24:10).

trial. "Knowing this, that the trying of your faith worketh patience" (James 1:3). See also 1 Peter 1:7.

Japheth. Noah had three sons, Shem, Ham, and Japheth. God promised the spiritual blessings to Shem (ancestor of the Jews), and said that the descendants of Japheth (the Gentiles) would "dwell in the tents of Shem" (Genesis 9:27)—that is, share in the spiritual blessings of Israel. It is through Abraham that all the Gentile nations are blessed (Genesis 12:1-3). This was fulfilled in Christ (Galatians 3:1-18).

so late. Because Christian lost his roll, he was delayed on his journey. But the statement was also autobiographical. Bunyan was twenty-five years old before he united with the local church in Bedford, pastored by John Gifford.

wretched. Another reference to Romans 7:24. Paul's experience in Romans 7 parallels Bunyan's own experience of frustration,

and thought also himself to go back after them, for he thought nothing but death was before him. But the porter at the lodge, whose name is Watchful, perceiving that Christian made a halt as if he would go back, cried unto him, saying, Is thy strength so small? Fear not the lions, for they are chained, and are placed there for trial of faith where it is, and for discovery of those that have none. Keep in the midst of the path, and no hurt shall come unto thee.

> Difficulty is behind, fear is before,
> Though he's got on the hill, the lions roar;
> A Christian man is never long at ease,
> When one fright's gone,
>   another doth him seize.

Then I saw that he went on, trembling for fear of the lions, but taking good heed to the directions of the porter; he heard them roar, but they did him no harm. Then he clapped his hands, and went on till he came and stood before the gate where the porter was. Then said Christian to the porter, Sir, what house is this? And may I lodge here to-night? The porter answered, This house was built by the Lord of the hill, and he built it for the relief and security of pilgrims. The porter also asked whence he was, and whither he was going.

CHR. I am come from the City of Destruction, and am going to Mount Zion; but because the sun is now set, I desire, if I may, to lodge here to-night.

POR. What is your name?

CHR. My name is now Christian, but my name at the first was Graceless; I came of the race of Japheth, whom God will persuade to dwell in the tents of Shem.

POR. But how doth it happen that you come so late? The sun is set.

CHR. I had been here sooner, but that, "wretched man that I am!" I slept in the arbour that stands on the hill-side; nay, I had, notwithstanding that, been here much sooner, but that in my sleep I lost my evidence, and came without it to the brow of the hill; and then feeling for it and finding it not, I was forced with sorrow of heart to go back to the place where I slept my sleep, where I found it, and now I am come.

POR. Well, I will <u>call</u> out one of the <u>virgins</u> of this place, who will, if she likes your talk, bring you in to the rest of the family, according to the rules of the house. So Watchful, the porter, rang a bell, at the sound of which came out at the door of the house a grave and beautiful damsel, named <u>Discretion</u>, and asked why she was called.

The porter answered, This man is in a journey from the City of Destruction to Mount Zion, but being weary and benighted, he asked me if he might lodge here to-night; so I told him I would call for thee, who, after discourse had with him, mayest do as seemeth thee good, even according to the law of the house.

Then she asked him whence he was and whither he was going; and he told her. She asked him also how he got into the way; and he told her. Then she asked him what he had seen and met with in the way; and he told her. And last she asked his name; so he said, It is Christian, and I have so much the more a desire to lodge here to-night, because, by what I perceive, this place was built by the Lord of the hill, for the relief and security of pilgrims. So she smiled, but the water stood in her eyes; and after a little pause she said, I will call forth two or three more of the family. So she ran to the door and called out <u>Prudence, Piety,</u> and <u>Charity</u>, who after a little more discourse with him had him into the family; and many of them, meeting him at the threshold of the house, said, "<u>Come in</u>, thou blessed of the Lord"; this house was <u>built</u> by the Lord of the hill, on purpose to entertain such pilgrims in. Then he bowed his head and followed them into the

defeat, and eventual victory in Christ.

call . . . virgins. The church is a family, and the members of the family interview Christian to discover the reality of his profession. For the Puritans, church membership was not automatic; the candidate had to prove himself. By calling these persons virgins, Bunyan may be referring to Psalm 45:14, Song of Solomon 1:3, and Matthew 25:1-13, where virgins are closely associated with the church and Christ. The word also speaks of their moral purity. **Discretion.** "Discretion shall preserve thee, understanding shall keep thee" (Proverbs 2:11).

Prudence, Piety, Charity. These virtues should belong to all Christians. "Charity" means "love," and not merely the giving of aid to the needy.

Come in . . . . This is the way Laban greeted Abraham's servant in Genesis 24:31.

built. "I will build my church" (Matthew 16:18). The church is often pictured in the New Testament as a house or temple built by the Lord. See 1 Corinthians 3:9-17; Ephesians 2:19-22; 1 Peter 2:5-10.

discourse. "Spiritual discourse" was a common practice among the Puritans. It was the spiritual conversation of some women in Bedford, overheard by Bunyan, that helped to lead him to salvation. "Then they that feared the LORD spake often one to another" (Malachi 3:16). This conversation also pictures the kind of personal examination that was given to candidates for church membership in that day.

What moved you . . . . Piety asks questions that deal with Christian's outward actions, and Christian tells what he heard, felt, and saw. Later, Prudence will ask him about the inner motives of his decision; and Charity will focus on his love for his home. Generally speaking, Piety deals with the events of his life, Prudence with the motives, and Charity with how he overcame the obstacles in the way.

house. So when he was come in and sat down, they gave him something to drink, and consented together that until supper was ready some of them should have some particular discourse with Christian, for the best improvement of time; and they appointed Piety, and Prudence, and Charity to discourse with him; and thus they began:

PIETY. Come, good Christian, since we have been so loving to you, to receive you in our house this night, let us, if perhaps we may better ourselves thereby, talk with you of all things that have happened to you in your pilgrimage.

CHR. With a very good will, and I am glad that you are so well disposed.

PIETY. What moved you at first to betake yourself to a pilgrim's life?

CHR. I was driven out of my native country by a dreadful sound that was in mine ears: to wit, that unavoidable destruction did attend me, if I abode in that place where I was.

PIETY. But how did it happen that you came out of your country this way?

CHR. It was as God would have it; for when I was under the fears of destruction, I did not know whither to go; but by chance there came a man, even to me, as I was trembling and weeping, whose name is Evangelist, and he directed me to the wicket-gate, which else I should never have found, and so set me into the way that hath led me directly to this house.

PIETY. But did you not come by the house of the Interpreter?

CHR. Yes, and did see such things there, the remembrance of which will stick by me as long as I live; especially three things: to wit, how Christ, in despite of Satan, maintains his work of grace in the heart; how the man had sinned himself quite out of hope of God's mercy; and also the dream of him that thought in his sleep the day of judgment was come.

PIETY. Why, did you hear him tell his dream?

CHR. Yes, and a dreadful one it was. I thought it made my heart ache as he was telling of it; but yet I am glad I heard it.

PIETY. Was that all that you saw at the house of the Interpreter?

CHR. No; he took me and had me where he showed me a stately palace, and how the people were clad in gold that were in it; and how there came a venturous man and cut his way through the armed men that stood in the door to keep him out, and how he was bid to come in, and win eternal glory. Methought those things did ravish my heart! I would have stayed at that good-man's house a twelvemonth, but that I knew I had further to go.

PIETY. And what saw you else in the way?

CHR. Saw! why, I went but a little further, and I saw one, as I thought in my mind, hang bleeding upon the tree; and the very sight of him made my burden fall off my back (for I groaned under a very heavy burden), but then it fell down from off me. It was a strange thing to me, for I never saw such a thing before; yea, and while I stood looking up, for then I could not forbear looking, three Shining Ones came to me. One of them testified that my sins were forgiven me; another stripped me of my rags and gave me this broidered coat which you see; and the third set the mark which you see in my forehead, and gave me this sealed roll. (And with that he plucked it out of his bosom.)

PIETY. But you saw more than this, did you not?

CHR. The things that I have told you were the best; yet some other matters I saw, as, namely—I saw three men, Simple, Sloth, and Presumption, lie asleep a little out of the way, as I came, with irons upon their heels; but do you think I could awake them? I also saw Formality and Hypocrisy come tumbling over the wall, to go, as they pretended, to Zion, but they were quickly lost, even as I myself did tell them; but

broidered. The Jewish high priest wore a beautiful embroidered coat (Exodus 28:4). All who have trusted Jesus Christ as Savior are God's priests (1 Peter 2:5, 9). In Ezekiel 16:10, 13, and 18, the "broidered coat" symbolizes God's love for His people as He covers their shame and forgives them.

65

mindful. Hebrews 11:15.

bear away. In other words, "You are not yet perfect, are you?" Salvation does not mean that the Christian is perfect in himself, but only that he is accepted in Christ. There are still areas of weakness and sin that must be overcome.

best . . . worst. An allusion to Romans 7:15-21.

what means. Here Bunyan gives us his views of sanctification—that is, how a Christian can live a godly life. He names four encouragements to godly living: the cross, his justification (the coat), the assurance of salvation (the roll), and the prospects of heaven. These four encouragements are definitely a part of Puritan theology.

they would not believe. But above all, I found it hard work to get up this hill, and as hard to come by the lions' mouths; and truly if it had not been for the goodman, the porter that stands at the gate, I do not know but that after all I might have gone back again; but now I thank God I am here, and I thank you for receiving of me.

Then Prudence thought good to ask him a few questions, and desired his answer to them.

PRUD. Do you not think sometimes of the country from whence you came?

CHR. Yes, but with much shame and detestation: "Truly, if I had been <u>mindful</u> of that country from whence I came out, I might have had opportunity to have returned; but now I desire a better country, that is, an heavenly."

PRUD. Do you not yet <u>bear away</u> with you some of the things that then you were conversant withal?

CHR. Yes, but greatly against my will; especially my inward and carnal cogitations, with which all my countrymen, as well as myself, were delighted; but now all those things are my grief; and might I but choose mine own things, I would choose never to think of those things more; but when I would be doing of that which is <u>best</u>, that which is <u>worst</u> is with me.

PRUD. Do you not <u>find</u> sometimes as if those things were vanquished, which at other times are your perplexity?

CHR. Yes, but that is seldom; but they are to me golden hours in which such things happen to me.

PRUD. Can you remember by <u>what means</u> you find your annoyances, at times, as if they were vanquished?

CHR. Yes, when I think what I saw at the cross, that will do it; and when I look upon my broidered coat, that will do it; also when I look into the roll that I carry in my bosom, that will do it; and when my thoughts wax warm about whither I am going, that will do it.

PRUD. And what is it that makes you so desirous to go to Mount Zion?

CHR. Why, there I hope to see him alive that did hang dead on the cross; and there I hope to be rid of all those things that to this day are in me an annoyance to me; there, they say, there is no death; and there I shall dwell with such company as I like best. For to tell you truth, I love him, because I was by him eased of my burden; and I am weary of my inward sickness. I would fain be where I shall die no more, and with the company that shall continually cry, "Holy, Holy, Holy!"

Then said Charity to Christian, Have you a family? Are you a married man?

CHR. I have a wife and four small children.

CHAR. And why did you not bring them along with you?

CHR. Then Christian wept and said, Oh, how willingly would I have done it, but they were all of them utterly averse to my going on pilgrimage.

CHAR. But you should have talked to them, and have endeavoured to have shown them the danger of being behind.

CHR. So I did; and told them also what God had showed to me of the destruction of our city; but I seemed to them "as one that mocked," and they believed me not.

CHAR. And did you pray to God that he would bless your counsel to them?

CHR. Yes, and that with much affection: for you must think that my wife and poor children were very dear unto me.

CHAR. But did you tell them of your own sorrow and fear of destruction? for I suppose that destruction was visible enough to you.

CHR. Yes, over, and over, and over. They might also see my fears in my countenance, in my tears, and also in my trembling under the apprehension of the judgment that did hang over our heads; but all was not sufficient to pre-

death. "And there shall be no more death" (Revelation 21:4; see also Isaiah 25:8).

cry. Isaiah 6:3; Revelation 4:8.

family. When *The Pilgrim's Progress* was published, Bunyan had a wife, two sons, and two daughters.

mocked. When Lot tried to warn his family that Sodom would be destroyed, he "seemed as one that mocked" (Genesis 19:14).

vail with them to come with me.

CHAR. But what could they say for themselves, why they came not?

CHR. Why, my wife was afraid of losing this world, and my children were given to the foolish delights of youth: so what by one thing, and what by another, they left me to wander in this manner alone.

CHAR. But did you not with your vain life damp all that you by words used by way of persuasion to bring them away with you?

CHR. Indeed, I cannot commend my life; for I am conscious to myself of many failings therein; I know also that a man by his <u>conversation</u> may soon overthrow what by argument or persuasion he doth labour to fasten upon others for their good. Yet this I can say, I was very wary of giving them occasion, by any unseemly action, to make them averse to going on pilgrimage. Yea, for this very thing they would tell me I was too precise, and that I denied myself of things, for their sakes, in which they saw no evil. Nay, I think I may say that if what they saw in me did hinder them, it was my great tenderness in sinning against God, or of doing any wrong to my neighbour.

CHAR. Indeed <u>Cain</u> hated his brother, "because his own works were evil, and his brother's righteous"; and if thy wife and children have been offended with thee for this, they thereby show themselves to be <u>implacable</u> to good, and "thou hast <u>delivered</u> thy soul" from their blood.

Now I saw in my dream that thus they sat talking together until <u>supper</u> was ready. So when they had made ready, they sat down to meat. Now the table was furnished with <u>fat things</u>, and with wine that was well refined: and all their talk at the table was about the Lord of the hill; as, namely, about what he had done, and wherefore he did what he did, and why he had built that house. And by what they said I

conversation. In that day, conversation meant behavior. Today it means talk. A Christian, by his bad behavior, can do damage to his witness.

Cain. 1 John 3:12, and see Genesis 4:1-15.

implacable. They cannot be pleased.

delivered. "Yet if thou warn the wicked, and he turn not from his wickedness, nor from his wicked way, he shall die in his iniquity; but thou hast delivered thy soul" (Ezekiel 3:19).

supper. This pictures the Lord's Supper, or the Communion, practiced in Puritan churches. It was considered a simple meal, not a ritual or a sacrament. Its purpose was to remember the Lord and glorify Him. "This do in remembrance of me" (Luke 22:19; 1 Corinthians 11:24). The Puritans did not teach that participation in the Communion was necessary for salvation.

fat things. "And in this mountain shall the LORD of hosts make unto all people a feast of fat things, . . . of fat things full of marrow" (Isaiah 25:6).

68

perceived that he had been a great warrior, and had fought with and slain "him that had the power of death," but not without great danger to himself, which made me love him the more.

For, as they said, and as I believe (said Christian), he did it with the loss of much blood; but that which put glory of grace into all he did, was, that he did it out of pure love to his country. And besides, there were some of them of the household that said they had been and spoke with him since he did die on the cross; and they have attested that they had it from his own lips, that he is such a lover of poor pilgrims, that the like is not to be found from the east to the west.

They, moreover, gave an instance of what they affirmed, and that was, he had stripped himself of his glory, that he might do this for the poor; and that they heard him say and affirm that he would not dwell in the mountain of Zion alone. They said, moreover, that he had made many pilgrims princes, though by nature they were beggars born, and their original had been the dunghill.

Thus they discoursed together till late at night; and after they had committed themselves to their Lord for protection, they betook themselves to rest: the pilgrim they laid in a large upper chamber, whose window opened towards the sun-rising: the name of the chamber was Peace, where he slept till break of day, and then he awoke and sang,

> Where am I now? Is this the love and care
> Of Jesus for the men that pilgrims are?
> Thus to provide that I should be forgiven!
> And dwell already the next door to heaven!

So in the morning they all got up; and after some more discourse they told him that he should not depart till they had shown him the rarities of that place. And first they had him into the study, where they showed him records of the greatest antiquity; in which, as I remember in

slain. Hebrews 2:14-15.

stripped. An allusion to Philippians 2:5-11.

beggars. "He raiseth up the poor out of the dust, and lifteth up the beggar from the dunghill" (1 Samuel 2:8; see also Psalm 113:7).

large upper chamber. "And he will shew you a large upper room furnished and prepared: there make ready for us" (Mark 14:15).

Peace. Christian had received "peace with God" when he came to the cross (page 54). Now he experiences "the peace of God" as he rests in the upper chamber. See Philippians 4:6-7.

rarities. The various rooms in the palace illustrate various aspects of the Christian life. The visit begins in the study because the knowledge of the Word of God is basic to everything else. Bunyan was a great lover of his Bible.

69

Ancient of Days. A name for the Lord. See Daniel 7:9, 13, 22.

eternal generation. A theological term referring to the relationship between Jesus Christ and God the Father. If Jesus is eternal God, then how can He also be the Son of God? When was He begotten? The orthodox reply is that He was "eternally generated" by the Father, not created; and therefore is both eternal God and God the Son. The Puritans were careful theologians, and Bunyan could debate with the best of them!

subdued. Quoted from Hebrews 11:33-34.

armoury. There are many New Testament references to the Christian life as that of a soldier: 1 Corinthians 9:7; Ephesians 6:13ff.; and 2 Timothy 2:1-4 are but a few. Bunyan himself had been a soldier.

furniture. "Equipment." This is based on Ephesians 6:13ff. and Deuteronomy 29:5.

engines. Tools, agents, implements. Moses' rod (Exodus 4:2ff.); Jael (Judges 4:18ff.); Gideon (Judges 6-7); Shamgar (Judges 3:31); jaw-bone (Judges 15:15); David (1 Samuel 17).

my dream, they showed him first the pedigree of the Lord of the hill, that he was the son of the Ancient of Days, and came by that eternal generation. Here also was more fully recorded the acts that he had done, and the names of many hundreds that he had taken into his service; and how he had placed them in such habitations that could neither by length of days nor decays of nature be dissolved.

Then they read to him some of the worthy acts that some of his servants had done: as, how they had "subdued kingdoms, wrought righteousness, obtained promises, stopped the mouths of lions, quenched the violence of fire, escaped the edge of the sword, out of weakness were made strong, waxed valiant in fight, and turned to flight the armies of the aliens."

They then read again, in another part of the records of the house, where it was showed how willing their Lord was to receive into his favour any, even any, though they in time past had offered great affronts to his person and proceedings. Here also were several other histories of many other famous things, of all which Christian had a view; as of things both ancient and modern; together with prophecies and predictions of things that have their certain accomplishment, both to the dread and amazement of enemies, and the comfort and solace of pilgrims.

The next day they took him and had him into the armoury, where they showed him all manner of furniture, which their Lord had provided for pilgrims, as sword, shield, helmet, breastplate, *all-prayer*, and shoes that would not wear out. And there was here enough of this to harness out as many men for the service of their Lord as there be stars in heaven for multitude.

They also showed him some of the engines with which some of his servants had done wonderful things. They showed him Moses' rod; the hammer and nail with which Jael slew Sisera; the pitchers, trumpets, and lamps too, with which Gideon put to flight the armies of Midian. Then they showed him the ox's goad wherewith Shamgar slew six hundred men. They showed him also the jaw-bone with which Samson did such mighty feats. They showed him, moreover, the sling and stone with which David slew Goliath of Gath; and the sword also with which their Lord will kill the Man of Sin, in the day that he shall rise up to the prey. They showed him besides many excellent things, with which Christian was much delighted. This done, they went to their rest again.

Then I saw in my dream that on the morrow he got up to go forward; but they desired him to stay till the next day also; and then, said they, we will, if the day be clear, show you the Delectable Mountains, which, they said, would yet further add to his comfort, because they were nearer the desired haven than the place where at present he was; so he consented and stayed. When the morning was up, they had him to the top of the house, and bade him look south; so he did: and behold at a great distance he saw a most pleasant mountainous country, beautified with woods, vineyards, fruits of all sorts, flowers also, with springs and fountains, very delectable to behold. Then he asked the name of the country. They said it was Immanuel's Land; and it is as common, said they, as this hill is, to and for all the pilgrims. And when thou comest there, from thence, said they, thou mayest see to the gate of the Celestial City, as the shepherds that live there will make appear.

Now he bethought himself of setting forward, and they were willing he should. But first, said they, let us go again into the armoury. So they did; and when they came there, they harnessed him from head to foot with what was of proof, lest perhaps he should meet with assaults in the way. He being therefore thus accoutred, walketh out with his friends to the gate, and there he

sword . . . Man of Sin. The "man of sin" is described in 2 Thessalonians 2 and Revelation 13:1-10. He is Satan's future "world dictator," who will fight Christ. The Lord will defeat Him with His sword, just as David slew Goliath with a sword (Revelation 19:15). In Bunyan's day, the phrase "man of sin" also referred to the pope, because of Roman persecution of believers. You find this statement in the preface to the King James Bible.

Delectable Mountains. The vision of future blessing encourages the believer in the trials of life.

desired haven. Psalm 107:30.

look south . . . Immanuel's Land. "Thine eyes shall see the king in his beauty: they shall behold the land that is very far off" (Isaiah 33:17). "Immanuel" means "God with us" (Matthew 1:23). "Immanuel's Land" refers to the Holy Land (Isaiah 8:8); Bunyan uses it as a name for heaven.

accoutred. Clad.

71

asked the porter if he saw any pilgrims pass by. Then the porter answered, Yes.

CHR. Pray, did you know him? said he.

POR. I asked him his name, and he told me it was Faithful.

CHR. Oh, said Christian, I know him; he is my townsman, my near neighbour; he comes from the place where I was born. How far do you think he may be before?

POR. He is got by this time below the hill.

CHR. Well, said Christian, good Porter, the Lord be with thee, and add to all thy blessings much increase, for the kindness that thou hast showed to me.

Then he began to go forward; but Discretion, Piety, Charity, and Prudence would accompany him down to the foot of the hill. So they went on together, reiterating their former discourses, till they came to go down the hill. Then said Christian, As it was difficult coming up, so, so far as I can see, it is dangerous going down. Yes, said Prudence, so it is, for it is a hard matter for a man to go down into the Valley of Humiliation, as thou art now, and to catch no slip by the way; therefore, said they, are we come out to accompany thee down the hill. So he began to go down, but very warily; yet he caught a slip or two.

Then I saw in my dream that these good companions, when Christian was gone to the bottom of the hill, gave him a loaf of bread, a bottle of wine, and a cluster of raisins; and then he went on his way.

But now in this Valley of Humiliation poor Christian was hard put to it; for he had gone but a little way before he espied a foul fiend coming over the field to meet him; his name is Apollyon. Then did Christian begin to be afraid, and to cast in his mind whether to go back or to stand his ground. But he considered again that he had no armour for his back; and therefore thought that to turn the back to him might give

Faithful. He will be Christian's companion until they reach Vanity Fair. There Faithful will be martyred. It is interesting that Faithful did not stop at the Palace Beautiful. Bunyan suggests by this that not all Christians unite with local churches.

dangerous. It is not easy for us to humble ourselves and go "down the hill." Christians must help one another and remind one another of what God has taught them. The Valley of Humiliation represents the special trials and difficulties that come to us from Satan.

gave him. See 1 Samuel 30:11-12. After Christian defeats Apollyon, he eats of this food. Bread and wine remind us of the Lord's Supper; they are symbols of His death. The Christian gets his spiritual strength from "feeding on the Lord."

Apollyon. "The Destroyer" (see Revelation 9:11). This is the third of the traditional enemies (the world, the flesh, the devil). Christian encountered the world at Hill Difficulty, and the flesh when he slept at the arbor. Now he must battle the forces of Satan.

no armour. The spiritual armor listed in Ephesians 6:13ff. Bunyan saw here the importance of standing against the devil and not running away. When he was first arrested, Bunyan could have avoided prosecution; but he chose to stand true to the Lord.

him the greater advantage with ease to pierce him with his darts. Therefore he resolved to venture and stand his ground; for, thought he, had I no more in mine eye than the saving of my life, it would be the best way to stand.

So he went on, and Apollyon met him. Now the monster was hideous to behold; he was clothed with scales like a fish (and they are his pride), he had wings like a dragon, feet like a bear, and out of his belly came fire and smoke, and his mouth was as the mouth of a lion. When he was come up to Christian, he beheld him with a disdainful countenance, and thus began to question with him.

APOL. Whence come you, and whither are you bound?

CHR. I am come from the City of Destruction, which is the place of all evil, and am going to the City of Zion.

APOL. By this I perceive thou art one of my subjects, for all that country is mine, and I am the prince and god of it. How is it then that thou hast run away from thy king? Were it not that I hope thou mayest do me more service, I would strike thee now at one blow to the ground.

CHR. I was born indeed in your dominions, but your service was hard, and your wages such as a man could not live on, "for the wages of sin is death"; therefore, when I was come to years, I did, as other considerate persons do, look out if perhaps I might mend myself.

APOL. There is no prince that will thus lightly lose his subjects, neither will I as yet lose thee; but since thou complainest of thy service and wages, be content to go back: what our country will afford, I do here promise to give thee.

CHR. But I have let myself to another, even to the King of princes; and how can I with fairness go back with thee?

APOL. Thou hast done in this, according to the proverb, "Changed a bad for a worse"; but it is ordinary for those that have professed

darts. "Above all, taking the shield of faith, wherewith ye shall be able to quench all the fiery darts of the wicked [one]" (Ephesians 6:16).

hideous. Bunyan borrowed this composite creature from Job 41:15; Daniel 7:5; 1 Peter 5:8; Revelation 9:17; 12:3ff; and Revelation 13:2. Christian's song (page 77) indicates that Apollyon is not Satan, but was sent by "Great Beelzebub." Revelation 9:11 states that Apollyon is "the angel of the bottomless pit," which suggests that he is Satan.

question. Apollyon uses every argument he can muster to win back Christian's allegiance. First he claims him as a subject of his kingdom. Then he makes promises to him and asks him to reconsider. When these attempts fail, Apollyon accuses him of being unfaithful to the Lord because of his past failures. Finally, he attacks him physically. First Satan comes as the serpent to deceive (2 Corinthians 11:3); then he comes as the dragon and lion to devour (1 Peter 5:8).

prince and god. Satan is called the "prince of this world" in John 12:31; 14:30; and 16:11; and the "god of this world" in 2 Corinthians 4:4.

born. See Ephesians 2:1-3.

wages. "For the wages of sin is death" (Romans 6:23).

lightly lose. In Bunyan's day, a citizen needed a license in order to leave the realm. No king gives up his people carelessly, for they mean to him taxes and service.

themselves his servants, after a while to give him the slip, and return again to me. Do thou so too, and all shall be well.

CHR. I have given him my faith, and sworn my allegiance to him; how then can I go back from this, and not be hanged as a traitor?

APOL. Thou didst the same to me, and yet I am willing to pass by all, if now thou wilt yet turn again and go back.

CHR. What I promised thee was in my nonage; and besides, I count that the Prince under whose banner now I stand is able to absolve me; yea, and to pardon also what I did as to my compliance with thee; and besides, O thou destroying Apollyon! to speak truth, I like his service, his wages, his servants, his government, his company and country, better than thine; and therefore leave off to persuade me further; I am his servant, and I will follow him.

APOL. Consider again when thou art in cool blood, what thou art like to meet with in the way that thou goest. Thou knowest that, for the most part, his servants come to an ill end, because they are transgressors against me and my ways. How many of them have been put to shameful deaths! and, besides, thou countest his service better than mine, whereas he never came yet from the place where he is to deliver any that served him out of their hands; but as for me, how many times, as all the world very well knows, have I delivered, either by power or fraud, those that have faithfully served me from him and his, though taken by them; and so I will deliver thee.

CHR. His forbearing at present to deliver them is on purpose to try their love, whether they will cleave to him to the end; and as for the ill end thou sayest they come to, that is most glorious in their account; for, for present deliverance, they do not much expect it, for they stay for their glory, and then they shall have it

nonage. Youth, innocence, immaturity.

his service. This list of advantages reminds us of the Queen of Sheba's admiration for Solomon and his court (1 Kings 10:1-10).

74

when their Prince comes in his and the glory of the angels.

APOL. Thou hast already been unfaithful in thy service to him; and how dost thou think to receive wages of him?

CHR. Wherein, O Apollyon, have I been unfaithful to him?

APOL. Thou didst faint at first setting out, when thou wast almost choked in the Gulf of Despond; thou didst attempt wrong ways to be rid of thy burden, whereas thou shouldest have stayed till thy Prince had taken it off; thou didst sinfully sleep and lose thy choice thing; thou wast also almost persuaded to go back at the sight of the lions; and when thou talkest of thy journey, and of what thou hast heard and seen, thou art inwardly desirous of vain-glory in all that thou sayest or dost.

CHR. All this is true, and much more which thou hast left out; but the Prince whom I serve and honour is merciful and ready to forgive; but besides, these infirmities possessed me in thy country, for there I sucked them in; and I have groaned under them, been sorry for them, and have obtained pardon of my Prince.

APOL. Then Apollyon broke out into a grievous rage, saying, I am an enemy to this Prince; I hate his person, his laws, and people; I am come out on purpose to withstand thee.

CHR. Apollyon, beware what you do; for I am in the King's highway, the way of holiness; therefore take heed to yourself.

APOL. Then Apollyon straddled quite over the whole breadth of the way, and said, I am void of fear in this matter: prepare thyself to die; for I swear by my infernal den that thou shalt go no further; here will I spill thy soul.

And with that he threw a flaming dart at his breast; but Christian had a shield in his hand, with which he caught it, and so prevented the danger of that.

Then did Christian draw, for he saw 'twas

Prince comes. "When the Son of man shall come in his glory, and all the holy angels with him" (Matthew 25:31).

Thou didst faint. Satan is the accuser who reminds us of our past sins (Zechariah 3:1-5; Revelation 12:10-11).

merciful. "For thou, Lord, art good, and ready to forgive; and plenteous in mercy unto all them that call upon thee" (Psalm 86:5).

highway. "The king's highway" was an important trade route mentioned in the Bible (Numbers 20:17-19 and 21:22; Deuteronomy 2:27). It was the route Israel wanted to use in its wilderness wandering. "The way of holiness" comes from Isaiah 35:8. The fact that Christian was on the King's highway meant that he was under the protection of the Lord; therefore, Satan was warned to be careful.

spill thy soul. Shed thy blood.

wounded. The head=the understanding; the hand=faith in God; the foot=behavior, walk. We wonder if Christian lost his helmet and shoes so that those areas were vulnerable. Satan wants to attack the believer in those three important areas.

despair. "We were pressed out of measure, above strength, insomuch that we despaired even of life" (2 Corinthians 1:8).

Rejoice not . . . . Quoted from Micah 7:8. The sword is the Word of God (Ephesians 6:17). When Satan tempted our Lord, Jesus used the Word to defeat him (Matthew 4:1-11).

mortal wound. The great dragon described in Revelation 13 suffered mortal wounds (vv. 3, 12, 14).

Nay, in all . . . . Quoted from Romans 8:37-39. "Resist the devil, and he will flee from you" (James 4:7).

for a season. "And when the devil had ended all the temptation, he departed from him [Jesus] for a season" (Luke 4:13). Literally it reads "until a season"—that is, until a more appropriate time. Satan patiently waits for the right hour to attack.

dragon. See Revelation 13:11.

two-edged sword. "For the word of God is [living], and powerful, and sharper than any twoedged sword" (Hebrews 4:12).

time to bestir him; and Apollyon as fast made at him, throwing darts as thick as hail; by the which, notwithstanding all that Christian could do to avoid it, Apollyon wounded him in his head, his hand, and foot. This made Christian give a little back; Apollyon therefore followed his work amain, and Christian again took courage, and resisted as manfully as he could. This sore combat lasted for above half a day, even till Christian was almost quite spent; for you must know that Christian, by reason of his wounds, must needs grow weaker and weaker.

Then Apollyon, espying his opportunity, began to gather up close to Christian, and wrestling with him, gave him a dreadful fall; and with that Christian's sword flew out of his hand. Then said Apollyon, I am sure of thee now. And with that he had almost pressed him to death, so that Christian began to despair of life: but as God would have it, while Apollyon was fetching of his last blow, thereby to make a full end of this good man, Christian nimbly reached out his hand for his sword and caught it, saying, "Rejoice not against me, O mine enemy; when I fall I shall arise"; and with that gave him a deadly thrust, which made him give back, as one that had received his mortal wound. Christian perceiving that, made at him again, saying, "Nay, in all these things we are more than conquerors through him that loved us." And with that Apollyon spread forth his dragon's wings and sped him away, that Christian for a season saw him no more.

In this combat no man can imagine, unless he had seen and heard as I did, what yelling and hideous roaring Apollyon made all the time of the fight—he spake like a dragon; and on the other side, what sighs and groans burst from Christian's heart. I never saw him all the while give so much as one pleasant look, till he perceived he had wounded Apollyon with his twoedged sword; then indeed he did smile and look upward; but 'twas the dreadfulest sight that ever I saw.

> A more unequal match can hardly be —
> Christian must fight an angel; but you see,
> The valiant man by handling sword and shield,
> Doth make him, though a dragon,
> > quit the field.

So when the battle was over, Christian said, I will here give thanks to him that hath delivered me out of the mouth of the lion, to him that did help me against Apollyon. And so he did, saying,

> Great Beelzebub, the captain of this fiend,
> Designed my ruin; therefore to this end
> He sent him harnessed out: and he with rage
> That hellish was, did fiercely me engage.
> But blessed Michael helped me, and I
> By dint of sword did quickly make him fly.
> Therefore to him let me give lasting praise,
> And thank and bless his holy name always.

Then there came to him a hand with some of the leaves of the tree of life, the which Christian took, and applied to the wounds that he had received in the battle, and was healed immediately. He also sat down in that place to eat bread, and to drink of the bottle that was given him a little before; so being refreshed, he addressed himself to his journey, with his sword drawn in his hand; for he said, I know not but some other enemy may be at hand. But he met with no other affront from Apollyon quite through this valley.

Now at the end of this valley was another, called the Valley of the Shadow of Death, and Christian must needs go through it, because the way to the Celestial City lay through the midst of it. Now this valley is a very solitary place. The prophet Jeremiah thus describes it: "A wilderness, a land of deserts and of pits, a land of drought, and of the shadow of death, a land that no man" (but a Christian) "passed through, and where no man dwelt."

mouth. "Notwithstanding the Lord stood with me, and strengthened me; . . . and I was delivered out of the mouth of the lion" (2 Timothy 4:17).

Beelzebub. See page 41.

Michael. The reference is to a future war in heaven, during which Satan and Michael the archangel will battle. See Daniel 10:13 and 21; Revelation 12:7-12.

leaves. Revelation 22:2.

Valley of the Shadow of Death. See Psalm 23:4; Isaiah 9:2; Jeremiah 2:6. This is not death itself, but the experience of fear and horror that Christians sometimes have in this life. The road to the Celestial City often takes Christians through deep valleys of difficulty.

77

Now here Christian was worse put to it than in his fight with Apollyon: as by the sequel you shall see.

I saw then in my dream that when Christian was got to the borders of the Shadow of Death, there met him two men, children of them that brought up an <u>evil report</u> of the good land, making haste to go back; to whom Christian spake as follows:

CHR. Whither are you going?

MEN. They said, Back, back; and we would have you to do so too, if either life or peace is prized by you.

CHR. Why, what's the matter? said Christian.

MEN. Matter! said they; we were going that way as you are going, and went as far as we durst; and indeed we were almost past coming back; for had we gone a little further, we had not been here to bring the news to thee.

CHR. But what have you met with? said Christian.

MEN. Why, we were almost in the Valley of the Shadow of <u>Death;</u> but that by good hap we looked before us, and saw the danger before we came to it.

CHR. But what have you seen? said Christian.

MEN. Seen! Why, the valley itself, which is as dark as pitch; <u>we also saw</u> there the hobgoblins, satyrs, and dragons of the pit; <u>we heard</u> also in that valley a continual howling and yelling, as of a people under unutterable misery, who there sat <u>bound</u> in affliction and irons; and over that valley hang the discouraging <u>clouds</u> of confusion. Death also doth always spread his wings over it. In a word, it is every whit dreadful, being utterly without order.

CHR. Then said Christian, I perceive not yet, by what you have said, but that this is my way to the desired <u>haven</u>.

MEN. Be it thy way; we will not choose it for ours. So they parted, and Christian went on his way, but still with his sword drawn in his hand,

78

for fear lest he should be assaulted.

I saw then in my dream, so far as this valley reached, there was on the right hand a very deep ditch; that ditch is it into which the blind have led the blind in all ages, and have both there miserably perished. Again, behold, on the left hand, there was a very dangerous quag, into which, if even a good man falls, he can find no bottom for his foot to stand on. Into that quag King David once did fall, and had no doubt therein been smothered, had not he that is able plucked him out.

blind. "Let them alone: they be blind leaders of the blind" (Matthew 15:14).

David. "Deliver me out of the mire, and let me not sink" (Psalm 69:14).

The pathway was here also exceeding narrow, and therefore good Christian was the more put to it; for when he sought in the dark to shun the ditch on the one hand, he was ready to tip over into the mire on the other; also when he sought to escape the mire, without great carefulness he would be ready to fall into the ditch. Thus he went on, and I heard him here sigh bitterly; for, besides the dangers mentioned above, the pathway was here so dark that ofttimes, when he lift up his foot to set forward, he knew not where or upon what he should set it next.

foot. "He will keep the feet of his saints, and the wicked shall be silent in darkness" (1 Samuel 2:9).

Poor man! where art thou now?
thy day is night.
Good man, be not cast down, thou yet art right,
Thy way to heaven lies by the gates of hell;
Cheer up, hold out, with thee it shall go well.

About the midst of this valley I perceived the mouth of hell to be, and it stood also hard by the wayside. Now, thought Christian, what shall I do? And ever and anon the flame and smoke would come out in such abundance, with sparks and hideous noises (things that cared not for Christian's sword, as did Apollyon before), that he was forced to put up his sword, and betake himself to another weapon, called *all-prayer*. So he cried in my hearing, "O Lord, I beseech thee, deliver my soul!" Thus he went on a great while, yet still the flames would be reaching towards him. Also he heard doleful voices, and

mouth of hell. Christian will discover several ways to hell as he continues his journey, including one at the very gate of heaven!

all-prayer. "Praying with all prayer and supplication in the Spirit" (Ephesians 6:18). His prayer is from Psalm 116:4. The Christian must use the right weapons in his spiritual warfare.

79

mire. See 2 Samuel 22:43; Isaiah 10:6; and Micah 7:10.

rushings to and fro, so that sometimes he thought he should be torn in pieces, or trodden down like <u>mire</u> in the streets. This frightful sight was seen and these dreadful noises were heard by him for several miles together; and coming to a place where he thought he heard a company of fiends coming forward to meet him, he stopped, and began to muse what he had best to do. Sometimes he had half a thought to go back; then again he thought he might be half way through the valley; he remembered also how he had already vanquished many a danger, and that the danger of going back might be much more than for to go forward; so he resolved to go on. Yet the fiends seemed to come nearer and nearer; but when they were come even almost at him, he cried out with a most

I will walk . . . . Psalm 71:16.

vehement voice, "<u>I will walk</u> in the strength of the Lord God!" so they gave back, and came no further.

One thing I would not let slip; I took notice that now poor Christian was so confounded that he did not know his own voice; and thus I perceived it. Just when he was come over against the mouth of the burning pit, one of the wicked ones got behind him, and stepped up softly to

suggested. Bunyan himself experienced times when his mind was filled with blasphemous thoughts. He writes in *Grace Abounding*: "While I was in this temptation, I should often find my mind suddenly put upon it, to curse and swear, or to speak some grievous thing against God, or Christ his Son, and of the Scripture. Now I thought, surely I am possessed of the devil."

him, and whisperingly <u>suggested</u> many grievous blasphemies to him, which he verily thought had proceeded from his own mind. This put Christian more to it than anything that he met with before, even to think that he should now blaspheme him that he loved so much before; yet if he could have helped it, he would not have done it; but he had not the discretion either to stop his ears, or to know from whence these blasphemies came.

When Christian had travelled in this disconsolate condition some considerable time, he thought he heard the voice of a man, as going

Though I walk . . . . Quoted from Psalm 23:4.

before him, saying, "<u>Though I walk</u> through the Valley of the Shadow of Death, I will fear no evil, for thou art with me."

Then he was glad, and that for these reasons:

First, Because he gathered from thence that some who feared God were in this valley as well as himself.

Secondly, For that he perceived God was with them, though in that dark and dismal state; and why not, thought he, with me? though, by reason of the impediment that attends this place, I cannot perceive it.

perceive. "Lo, he goeth by me, and I see him not: he passeth on also, but I perceive him not" (Job 9:11).

Thirdly, For that he hoped, could he overtake them, to have company by and by. So he went on and called to him that was before; but he knew not what to answer; for that he also thought himself to be alone. And by and by the day broke; then said Christian, He hath turned "the shadow of death into the morning."

turned. Amos 5:8.

Now morning being come, he looked back, not out of desire to return, but to see by the light of the day what hazards he had gone through in the dark. So he saw more perfectly the ditch that was on the one hand and the quag that was on the other; also how narrow the way was which led betwixt them both; also now he saw the hobgoblins, and satyrs, and dragons of the pit, but all afar off (for after break of day they came not nigh); yet they were discovered to him, according to that which is written, "He discovereth deep things out of darkness, and bringeth out to light the shadow of death."

He discovereth . . . . Quoted from Job 12:22. Christians learn lessons in the valley, and even the darkness brings blessing.

Now was Christian much affected with his deliverance from all the dangers of his solitary way; which dangers, though he feared them more before, yet he saw them more clearly now, because the light of the day made them conspicuous to him. And about this time the sun was rising, and this was another mercy to Christian; for you must note that though the first part of the Valley of the Shadow of Death was dangerous, yet this second part which he was yet to go was, if possible, far more dangerous: for from the place where he now stood, even to the end of the valley, the way was all along set so

snares, traps. A list of various kinds of traps for catching game. "Shelvings down" are slopes.

His candle . . . . Quoted from Job 29:3.

Pope and Pagan. Since Foxe's *Book of Martyrs* was Bunyan's second Bible, and since England in that day was threatened by Rome (through alliances with Catholic nations), it is understandable that Bunyan would take this attitude. Puritan theology had no room for a Pope, traditions, or sacraments. However, Bunyan personally did not refuse to fellowship with true Christians who happened to be in the Church of Rome. In his book *Communion and Fellowship of Christians*, Bunyan wrote: "I hold therefore to what I said at first: That if there be any saints in the anti-christian church, my heart, and the door of our congregation is open to receive them, into closest fellowship with us." Bunyan obviously made a distinction between the Roman system of doctrine and practice, and individual believers. He allies Pagan with Pope because he believed that most of Rome's converts were still pagan, even though they were joined to a religious system.

full of snares, traps, gins, and nets here, and so full of pits, pitfalls, deep holes, and shelvings down there, that, had it now been dark, as it was when he came the first part of the way, had he had a thousand souls, they had in reason been cast away; but, as I said just now, the sun was rising. Then said he, "His candle shineth on my head, and by his light I go through darkness."

In this light, therefore, he came to the end of the valley. Now I saw in my dream that at the end of this valley lay blood, bones, ashes, and mangled bodies of men, even of pilgrims that had gone this way formerly; and while I was musing what should be the reason, I espied a little before me a cave, where two giants, Pope and Pagan, dwelt in old time, by whose power and tyranny the men whose bones, blood, ashes, etc., lay there, were cruelly put to death. But by this place Christian went without much danger, whereat I somewhat wondered; but I have learnt since that Pagan has been dead many a day; and as for the other, though he be yet alive, he is, by reason of age, and also of the many shrewd brushes that he met with in his younger days, grown so crazy and stiff in his joints, that he can now do little more than sit in his cave's mouth, grinning at pilgrims as they go by, and biting his nails because he cannot come at them.

So I saw that Christian went on his way; yet at the sight of the Old Man that sat in the mouth of the cave, he could not tell what to think, especially because he spake to him, though he could not go after him, saying, You will never mend till more of you be burned. But he held his peace and set a good face on it, and so went by and catched no hurt. Then sang Christian,

O world of wonders! (I can say no less)
That I should be preserved in that distress
That I have met with here! O blessed be
That hand that from it hath delivered me!
Dangers in darkness, devils, hell, and sin

Did compass me, while I this vale was in:
Yea, snares and pits, and traps, and nets, did lie
My path about, that worthless, silly I
Might have been catched, entangled,
   and cast down;
But since I live, let JESUS wear the crown.

Now as Christian went on his way, he came to a little ascent, which was cast up on purpose that pilgrims might see before them. Up there, therefore, Christian went, and looking forward, he saw Faithful before him upon his journey. Then said Christian aloud, Ho! ho! So-ho! stay, and I will be your companion. At that Faithful looked behind him; to whom Christian cried again, Stay, stay, till I come up to you. But Faithful answered, No, I am upon my life, and the <u>avenger</u> of blood is behind me.

At this, Christian was somewhat moved, and putting to all his strength, he quickly got up with Faithful and did also overrun him; so the <u>last</u> was first. Then did Christian vain-gloriously smile, because he had gotten the start of his brother; but not taking good heed to his feet, he suddenly <u>stumbled</u> and fell, and could not rise again until Faithful came up to <u>help</u> him.

Then I saw in my dream they went very lovingly on together, and had sweet discourse of all things that had happened to them in their pilgrimage; and thus Christian began:

CHR. My honoured and well-beloved brother Faithful, I am glad that I have overtaken you; and that God has so tempered our spirits that we can walk as companions in this so pleasant a path.

FAITH. I had thought, dear friend, to have had your company quite from our town; but you did get the start of me, wherefore I was forced to come thus much of the way alone.

CHR. How long did you stay in the City of Destruction before you set out after me on your pilgrimage?

FAITH. Till I could stay no longer; for there

avenger. There was no police system in Israel. Each family and clan had to avenge the blood of those who were murdered. See Numbers 35:9ff.; and Deuteronomy 19:6ff. God appointed cities of refuge where the slayer might flee and get a fair trial. Faithful was in a hurry to escape the avenger of blood, which in this case means the consequences of his own sins.

last. "But many that are first shall be last; and the last shall be first" (Matthew 19:30).

stumbled. "Pride goeth before destruction, and an haughty spirit before a fall" (Proverbs 16:18). "Wherefore let him that thinketh he standeth take heed lest he fall" (1 Corinthians 10:12).

help. Keep in mind that Christian was wearing armor. Bunyan is here illustrating how much believers need each other as they go through life. "Two are better than one . . . . For if they fall, the one will lift up his fellow" (Ecclesiastes 4:9-10). "Brethren, if a man be overtaken in a fault, ye which are spiritual, restore such an one in the spirit of meekness" (Galatians 6:1).

was great talk presently after you were gone out, that our city would in short time with fire from heaven be burned down to the ground.

CHR. What! did your neighbours talk so?

FAITH. Yes, it was for a while in everybody's mouth.

CHR. What! and did no more of them but you come out to escape the danger?

FAITH. Though there was, as I said, a great talk therefore, yet I do not think they did firmly believe it. For in the heat of the discourse I heard some of them deridingly speak of you and of your desperate journey (for so they called this your pilgrimage), but I did believe, and do still, that the end of our city will be with fire and brimstone from above; and therefore I have made my escape.

CHR. Did you hear no talk of neighbour Pliable?

FAITH. Yes, Christian, I heard that he followed you till he came at the Slough of Despond, where, as some said, he fell in; but he would not be known to have so done; but I am sure he was soundly bedabbled with that kind of dirt.

CHR. And what said the neighbours to him?

FAITH. He hath since his going back been had greatly in derision, and that among all sorts of people; some do mock and despise him; and scarce will any set him on work. He is now seven times worse than if he had never gone out of the city.

CHR. But why should they be so set against him, since they also despise the way that he forsook?

FAITH. Oh, they say, hang him, he is a turncoat! he was not true to his profession. I think God has stirred up even his enemies to hiss at him and make him a proverb, because he hath forsaken the way.

CHR. Had you no talk with him before you came out?

seven times. Jesus uses a similar idea in his parable about the unclean spirit in Matthew 12:43-45.

forsaken. The reference is to Jeremiah 29:18-19.

84

FAITH. I met him once in the streets, but he leered away on the other side, as one ashamed of what he had done; so I spake not to him.

CHR. Well, at my first setting out I had hopes of that man; but now I fear he will perish in the overthrow of the city; for "it is happened to him according to the true proverb, The dog is turned to his own vomit again, and the sow that was washed to her wallowing in the mire."

FAITH. These are my fears of him too; but who can hinder that which will be?

CHR. Well, neighbour Faithful, said Christian, let us leave him and talk of things that more immediately concern ourselves. Tell me now, what you have met with in the way as you came; for I know you have met with some things, or else it may be writ for a wonder.

FAITH. I escaped the Slough that I perceived you fell into, and got up to the gate without that danger; only I met with one whose name was Wanton, who had like to have done me a mischief.

CHR. It was well you escaped her net; Joseph was hard put to it by her, and he escaped her as you did; but it had like to have cost him his life. But what did she do to you?

FAITH. You cannot think, but that you know something, what a flattering tongue she had; she lay at me hard to turn aside with her, promising me all manner of content.

CHR. Nay, she did not promise you the content of a good conscience.

FAITH. You know what I mean; all carnal and fleshly content.

CHR. Thank God you have escaped her: the "abhorred of the Lord shall fall" into her ditch.

FAITH. Nay, I know not whether I did wholly escape her or no.

CHR. Why, I trow, you did not consent to her desires?

FAITH. No, not to defile myself; for I remembered an old writing that I had seen, which

true proverb. Quoted from 2 Peter 2:22. True Christians are sheep, not dogs and swine. Pliable was not a true believer.

what you have met with. Faithful's experiences were different from those of Christian. He escaped some of the trials, and he faced a different set of temptations. Bunyan is showing here that each believer must follow the Lord and not measure himself with other Christians. Faithful met with Wanton, the First Adam, Moses, Discontent, and Shame, none of whom were encountered by his companion.

Wanton. A temptation to sensual sin. Joseph was tempted by his master's wife and fled from her (Genesis 39:11-13). Bunyan himself was very shy with women; this particular temptation did not beset him.

flattering. "To keep thee from the evil woman, from the flattery of the tongue of a strange woman" (Proverbs 6:24). In Proverbs 7 you have a graphic description of this temptation.

abhorred. Quoted from Proverbs 22:14.

trow. Trust, believe.

writing. Proverbs 5:5.

eyes. "I made a covenant with mine eyes; why then should I think upon a maid? (Job 31:1).

said, "Her steps take hold on hell." So I shut mine eyes, because I would not be bewitched with her looks. Then she railed on me, and I went my way.

CHR. Did you meet with no other assault as you came?

FAITH. When I came to the foot of the hill called Difficulty, I met with a very aged man, who asked me what I was and whither bound. I told him that I was a pilgrim going to the Celestial City. Then said the old man, Thou lookest like an honest fellow; wilt thou be content to dwell with me for the wages that I shall give thee? Then I asked him his name and where he dwelt. He said his name was Adam the First, and that he dwelt in the town of Deceit. I asked him then what was his work and what the wages that he would give. He told me that his work was many delights; and his wages that I should be his heir at last. I further asked him what house he kept and what other servants he had. So he told me that his house was maintained with all the dainties in the world; and that his servants were those of his own begetting. Then I asked how many children he had. He said that he had but three daughters: The Lust of the Flesh, The Lust of the Eyes, and The Pride of Life, and that I should marry them all if I would. Then I asked how long time he would have me live with him. And he told me, As long as he lived himself.

Adam the First. Jesus Christ is the Last Adam; the first man is Adam the First (1 Corinthians 15:45). All are born children of the First Adam. Christ by His obedient death on the cross reversed the consequences of Adam's sin and made slavation possible. See Romans 5:6-21. Adam the First can still oppose Christians because they have the old nature yet with them.

Deceit. "That ye put off concerning the former conversation the old man, which is corrupt according to the deceitful lusts" (Ephesians 4:22).

daughters. Quoted from 1 John 2:15-17.

CHR. Well, and what conclusion came the old man and you to at last?

FAITH. Why, at first I found myself somewhat inclinable to go with the man, for I thought he spake very fair; but looking in his forehead, as I talked with him, I saw there written, "Put off the old man with his deeds."

CHR. And how then?

FAITH. Then it came burning hot into my mind, whatever he said and however he flattered, when he got me home to his house, he

Put off. Quoted from Colossians 3:9. Just as Jesus left His grave clothes behind at His resurrection, so the Christian leaves "the old man" behind because of his union with Christ in His resurrection. Salvation means the believer now belongs to the Last Adam, Christ, and not the First Adam.

would sell me for a slave. So I bid him forbear to talk, for I would not come near the door of his house. Then he reviled me and told me that he would send such a one after me that should make my way bitter to my soul. So I turned to go away from him; but just as I turned myself to go thence, I felt him take hold of my flesh and give me such a deadly twitch back that I thought he had pulled part of me after himself. This made me <u>cry,</u> "O wretched man!" So I went on my way up the hill.

Now when I had got about half way up, I looked behind and saw <u>one coming</u> after me swift as the wind; so he overtook me just about the place where the settle stands.

CHR. Just there, said Christian, did I sit down to rest me; but being overcome with sleep, I there lost this roll out of my bosom.

FAITH. But, good brother, hear me out. So soon as the man overtook me, he was but a word and a blow, for down he knocked me and laid me for dead. But when I was a little come to myself again, I asked him wherefore he served me so. He said, because of my secret inclining to Adam the First; and with that he struck me another deadly blow on the breast and beat me down backward; so I lay at his foot as dead as before. So when I came to myself again, I cried him mercy; but he said, I know not how to show <u>mercy;</u> and with that knocked me down again. He had doubtless made an end of me, but that one came by and bid him forbear.

CHR. Who was that that bid him forbear?

FAITH. I did not know him at first, but as he went by I perceived the <u>holes</u> in his hands and in his side; then I concluded that he was our Lord. So I went up the hill.

CHR. That man that overtook you was Moses. He spareth none, neither knoweth he how to show mercy to those that transgress his law.

FAITH. I know it very well; it was not the first time that he has met with me. It was he that

cry. Bunyan's favorite cry again, from Romans 7:24. He does not want us to forget that the old nature can still cause trouble for the Christian.

one coming. This is Moses, representing the Law. Because Faithful was interested in Adam the First (the old nature), Moses disciplined him. All of this is an illustration of Romans 7:7-12. The Puritans believed that the Law had a ministry in the Christian life. It can still convict the believer of his sins.

mercy. The Law cannot grant mercy; it can only pronounce judgment. Christ is the only one who can grant mercy and meet the righteous demands of the Law.

holes. The wounds in our Lord's body (John 20:24-29).

87

came to me when I dwelt securely at home, and that told me he would burn my house over my head if I stayed there.

CHR. But did you not see the house that stood there on the top of the hill on the side of which Moses met you?

FAITH. Yes, and the lions too, before I came at it: but for the lions, I think they were asleep, for it was about noon; and because I had so much of the day before me, I passed by the porter and came down the hill.

passed by. Faithful did not fellowship in the local church family as did Christian. Again, each believer's experience is different. While Bunyan strongly believed in the local church, and even pastored one, he did not make it essential to salvation. Note, however, that Christian tells Faithful how much he missed by passing by!

CHR. He told me, indeed, that he saw you go by, but I wish you had called at the house, for they would have showed you so many rarities that you would scarce have forgot them to the day of your death. But pray tell me, did you meet nobody in the Valley of Humility?

FAITH. Yes, I met with one Discontent, who would willingly have persuaded me to go back again with him; his reason was, for that the valley was altogether without honour. He told me, moreover, that there to go was the way to disobey all my friends, as Pride, Arrogancy, Self-conceit, Worldly-glory, with others, who he knew, as he said, would be very much offended if I made such a fool of myself as to wade through this valley.

CHR. Well, and how did you answer him?

FAITH. I told him that although all these that he named might claim kindred of me, and that rightly, for indeed they were my relations according to the flesh; yet since I became a pilgrim they have disowned me, as I also have rejected them; and therefore they were to me now no more than if they had never been of my lineage. I told him, moreover, that as to this valley, he had quite misrepresented the thing; for "before honour is humility, and a haughty spirit before a fall." Therefore, said I, I had rather go through this valley to the honour that was so accounted by the wisest, than choose that which he esteemed most worthy our affections.

before honour. Proverbs 15:33; 16:18; 18:12. Faithful desires the honor that comes only from God.

88

CHR. Met you with nothing else in that valley?

FAITH. Yes, I met with Shame; but of all the men that I met with in my pilgrimage, he, I think, bears the wrong name. The other would be said nay after a little argumentation, and somewhat else, but this bold-faced Shame would never have done.

CHR. Why, what did he say to you?

FAITH. What! why, he objected against religion itself; he said it was a pitiful, low, sneaking business for a man to mind religion; he said that a tender conscience was an unmanly thing; and that for a man to watch over his words and ways, so as to tie up himself from that hectoring liberty that the brave spirits of the times accustom themselves unto, would make him the ridicule of the times. He objected also that but few of the mighty, rich, or wise, were ever of my opinion; nor any of them neither before they were persuaded to be fools, and to be of a voluntary fondness, to venture the loss of all for nobody knows what. He, moreover, objected the base and low estate and condition of those that were chiefly the pilgrims of the times in which they lived: also their ignorance and want of understanding in all natural science. Yea, he did hold me to it at that rate also about a great many more things than here I relate; as that it was a *shame* to sit whining and mourning under a sermon, and a *shame* to come sighing and groaning home; that it was a *shame* to ask my neighbour forgiveness for petty faults, or to make restitution where I have taken from any. He said also that religion made a man grow strange to the great because of a few vices, which he called by finer names, and made him own and respect the base, because of the same religious fraternity. And is not this, said he, a *shame*?

CHR. And what did you say to him?

FAITH. Say! I could not tell what to say at the first. Yea, he put me so to it that my blood came up in my face; even this Shame fetched it up

Shame. "Whosoever therefore shall be ashamed of me and of my words . . . of him also shall the Son of man be ashamed, when he cometh in the glory of his Father with the holy angels" (Mark 8:38). Shame argues that religion is not a manly thing, that few great people follow it, and that it causes people to act in shameful ways.

hectoring. Bullying.

few of the mighty. "For ye see your calling, brethren, how that not many wise men after the flesh, not many mighty, not many noble, are called" (1 Corinthians 1:26). "If any man among you seemeth to be wise in this world, let him become a fool, that he may be wise" (1 Corinthians 3:18). "Have any of the rulers or of the Pharisees believed on him?" (John 7:48). See also Philippians 3:7-9.

89

highly esteemed. Quoted from Luke 16:15.

and had almost beat me quite off. But at last I began to consider that "that which is <u>highly esteemed</u> among men, is had in abomination with God." And I thought again, this Shame tells me what men are; but it tells me nothing what God or the Word of God is. And I thought, moreover, that at the day of doom we shall not be doomed to death or life according to the hectoring spirits of the world, but according to the wisdom and law of the Highest. Therefore, thought I, what God says is best, indeed is best, though all the men in the world are against it. Seeing, then, that God prefers his religion; seeing God prefers a tender conscience; seeing

fools. "We are fools for Christ's sake" (1 Corinthians 4:10); and see 1 Corinthians 1:18-25.

they that make themselves <u>fools</u> for the kingdom of heaven are wisest; and that the poor man that loveth Christ is richer than the greatest man in the world that hates him; Shame, depart, thou art an enemy to my salvation! Shall I entertain thee against my sovereign Lord? How then shall I look in the face at his coming? Should I now

ashamed. Mark 8:38.

be <u>ashamed</u> of his ways and servants, how can I expect the blessing? But indeed this Shame was a bold villain; I could scarce shake him out of my company; yea, he would be haunting of me and continually whispering me in the ear, with some one or other of the infirmities that attend religion; but at last I told him it was but in vain to attempt further in this business; for those things that he disdained, in those did I see most glory; and so at last I got past this importunate one. And when I had shaken him off, then I began to sing:

> The trials that those men do meet withal,
> That are obedient to the heavenly call,
> Are manifold, and suited to the flesh,
> And come, and come, and come again afresh;
> That now, or sometimes else, we by them may
> Be taken, overcome, and cast away.
> Oh, let the pilgrims, let the pilgrims then
> Be vigilant, and <u>quit</u> themselves like men.

quit. "Quit you like men, be strong" (1 Corinthians 16:13). "Quit" is short for "acquit" = "conduct yourselves."

CHR. I am glad, my brother, that thou didst

90

withstand this villain so bravely; for of all, as thou sayest, I think he has the wrong name; for he is so bold as to follow us in the streets and to attempt to put us to shame before all men: that is, to make us ashamed of that which is good; but if he was not himself audacious, he would never attempt to do as he does. But let us still resist him; for notwithstanding all his bravadoes he promoteth the fool and none else. "The wise shall inherit glory," said Solomon, "but shame shall be the promotion of fools."

FAITH. I think we must cry to Him for help against Shame, that would have us be valiant for truth upon the earth.

CHR. You say true; but did you meet nobody else in that valley?

FAITH. No, not I; for I had sunshine all the rest of the way through that, and also through the Valley of the Shadow of Death.

CHR. 'Twas well for you. I am sure it fared far otherwise with me. I had for a long season, as soon almost as I entered into that valley, a dreadful combat with that foul fiend Apollyon; yea, I thought verily he would have killed me, especially when he got me down and crushed me under him, as if he would have crushed me to pieces; for as he threw me, my sword flew out of my hand; nay, he told me he was sure of me: but I cried to God, and he heard me, and delivered me out of all my troubles. Then I entered into the Valley of the Shadow of Death, and had no light for almost half the way through it. I thought I should have been killed there, over and over; but at last day broke and the sun rose, and I went through that which was behind with far more ease and quiet.

Moreover, I saw in my dream that as they went on, Faithful, as he chanced to look on one side, saw a man whose name is Talkative, walking at a distance beside them (for in this place there was room enough for them all to walk). He was a tall man and something more comely

wise. Quoted from Proverbs 3:35.

valiant for truth. Taken from Jeremiah 9:3—"but they are not valiant for the truth upon the earth." Bunyan used this as the name of one of the most important characters in the second part of *The Pilgrim's Progress*, which was published in 1684 and tells how Christian's wife and children journeyed to the heavenly city.

I cried. An allusion to Psalm 34:6.

Talkative. "Should not the multitude of words be answered? and should a man full of talk be justified?" (Job 11:2). "In the multitude of words there wanteth not sin: but he that refraineth his lips is wise" (Proverbs 10:19). Talkative pictures the person who can discuss religious themes but whose personal life is completely without religious character. "For there are many unruly and vain talkers and deceivers" (Titus 1:10). "They profess that they know God; but in works they deny him" (Titus 1:16).

at a distance than at hand. To this man Faithful addressed himself in this manner:

FAITH. Friend, whither away? Are you going to the heavenly country?

TALK. I am going to the same place.

FAITH. That is well; then I hope we may have your good company.

TALK. With a very good will will I be your companion.

FAITH. Come on then, and let us go together, and let us spend our time in discoursing of things that are profitable.

TALK. To talk of things that are good, to me is very acceptable, with you or with any other; and I am glad that I have met with those that incline to so good a work; for to speak the truth, there are but few that care thus to spend their time (as they are in their travels), but choose much rather to be speaking of things to no profit, and this hath been a trouble to me.

no profit. "Charging them before the Lord that they strive not about words to no profit" (2 Timothy 2:14).

FAITH. That is indeed a thing to be lamented; for what things so worthy of the use of the tongue and mouth of men on earth, as are the things of the God of heaven?

TALK. I like you wonderful well, for your sayings are full of conviction; and I will add, what thing is so pleasant, and what so profitable, as to talk of the things of God? What things so pleasant (that is, if a man hath any delight in things that are wonderful)? For instance, if a man doth delight to talk of the history or the mystery of things; or if a man doth love to talk of miracles, wonders, or signs, where shall he find things recorded so delightful and so sweetly penned as in the Holy Scripture?

FAITH. That is true; but to be profited by such things in our talk should be that which we design.

TALK. That is it that I said; for to talk of such things is most profitable; for by so doing, a man may get knowledge of many things; as of the vanity of earthly things, and the benefit of things above. Thus, in general, but more particularly, by this a man may learn the necessity of the new birth, the insufficiency of our works, the need of Christ's righteousness, etc. Besides, by this a man may learn, by talk, what it is to repent, to believe, to pray, to suffer, or the like; by this also a man may learn what are the great promises and consolations of the gospel, to his own comfort. Further, by this a man may learn to refute false opinions, to vindicate the truth, and also to instruct the ignorant.

FAITH. All this is true, and glad am I to hear these things from you.

TALK. Alas! the want of this is the cause why so few understand the need of faith and the necessity of a work of grace in their soul, in order to eternal life; but ignorantly live in the works of the law, by which a man can by no means obtain the kingdom of heaven.

FAITH. But by your leave, heavenly knowledge of these is the gift of God; no man attaineth to them by human industry, or only by the talk of them.

TALK. All this I know very well; for a man can receive nothing except it be given him from heaven; all is of grace, not of works. I could give you a hundred scriptures for the confirmation of this.

FAITH. Well then, said Faithful, what is that one thing that we shall at this time found our discourse upon?

TALK. What you will. I will talk of things heavenly, or things earthly; things moral, or things evangelical; things sacred, or things profane; things past, or things to come; things foreign, or things at home, things more essential, or things circumstantial; provided that all be done to our profit.

FAITH. Now did Faithful begin to wonder; and stepping to Christian (for he walked all this while by himself), he said to him (but softly), What a brave companion have we got! Surely

learn. Talkative thinks that learning comes primarily from talking. He is ignorant of what Christian and Faithful later call "heart-work"—the working of the Spirit of God in the heart, convicting and teaching.

receive. Quoted from John 3:27.

grace. Ephesians 2:8-9. Note that Talkative is quick to quote the Bible and use the correct language, but he is deficient in personal experience. It is all in his head, and not in his heart.

Surely. Faithful is deceived by Talkative because he judged him by his words alone. "Not every one that saith unto me, Lord, Lord, shall enter into the kingdom of heaven; but he that doeth the will of my Father which is in heaven" (Matthew 7:21).

this man will make a very excellent pilgrim.

CHR. At this Christian modestly smiled and said, This man with whom you are so taken will beguile with this tongue of his twenty of them that know him not.

FAITH. Do you know him then?

CHR. Know him! Yes, better than he knows himself.

FAITH. Pray what is he?

CHR. His name is Talkative; he dwelleth in our town. I wonder that you should be a stranger to him, only I consider that our town is large.

FAITH. Whose son is he? And whereabout doth he dwell?

CHR. He is the son of one Say-well; he dwelt in Prating Row; and is known of all that are acquainted with him, by the name of Talkative in Prating Row; and notwithstanding his fine tongue he is but a sorry fellow.

FAITH. Well, he seems to be a very pretty man.

CHR. That is, to them who have not thorough acquaintance with him; for he is best abroad; near home he is ugly enough. Your saying that he is a pretty man brings to my mind what I have observed in the work of the painter, whose pictures show best at a distance, but, very near, more unpleasing.

FAITH. But I am ready to think you do but jest, because you smiled.

CHR. God forbid that I should jest (although I smiled) in this matter, or that I should accuse any falsely! I will give you a further discovery of him. This man is for any company and for any talk; as he talketh now with you, so will he talk when he is on the ale-bench; and the more drink he hath in his crown, the more of these things he hath in his mouth; religion hath no place in his heart, or house, or conversation; all he hath lieth in his tongue, and his religion is to make a noise therewith.

Prating. Idle chatter, empty talk.

Talkative

94

FAITH. Say you so! Then am I in this man greatly deceived.

CHR. Deceived! you may be sure of it; remember the proverb, "They say and do not." But "the kingdom of God is not in word, but in power." He talketh of prayer, of repentance, of faith, and of the new birth; but he knows but only to talk of them. I have been in his family and have observed him both at home and abroad; and I know what I say of him is the truth. His house is as empty of religion as the white of an egg is of savour. There is there neither prayer, nor sign of repentance for sin; yea, the brute in his kind serves God far better than he. He is the very stain, reproach, and shame of religion to all that know him; it can hardly have a good word in all that end of the town where he dwells, through him. Thus say the common people that know him, A saint abroad and a devil at home. His poor family finds it so; he is such a churl, such a railer at and so unreasonable with his servants, that they neither know how to do for, or speak to him. Men that have any dealings with him say it is better to deal with a Turk than with him; for fairer dealing they shall have at their hands. This Talkative (if it be possible) will go beyond them, defraud, beguile, and overreach them. Besides, he brings up his sons to follow his steps; and if he findeth in any of them a foolish timorousness (for so he calls the first appearance of a tender conscience), he calls them fools and blockheads, and by no means will employ them in much, or speak to their commendations before others. For my part, I am of opinion that he has by his wicked life caused many to stumble and fall; and will be, if God prevent not, the ruin of many more.

FAITH. Well, my brother, I am bound to believe you; not only because you say you know him, but also because like a Christian you make your reports of men. For I cannot think that you

proverb. Quoted from Christ's indictment of the Pharisees, Matthew 23:3.

kingdom. Quoted from 1 Corinthians 4:20.

egg. "Can that which is unsavoury be eaten without salt? or is there any taste in the white of an egg?" (Job 6:6).

stain. "For the name of God is blasphemed among the Gentiles through you" (Romans 2:24).

Turk. A general name for all barbarians and foreigners who could not be trusted.

speak these things of ill-will, but because it is even so as you say.

CHR. Had I known him no more than you, I might perhaps have thought of him as at the first you did; yea, had he received this report at their hands only that are enemies to religion, I should have thought it had been a slander—a lot that often falls from bad men's mouths upon good men's names and professions; but all these things, yea, and a great many more as bad, of my own knowledge I can prove him guilty of. Besides, good men are ashamed of him; they can neither call him brother nor friend; the very naming of him among them makes them blush, if they know him.

saying. See Matthew 23:1-4.

FAITH. Well, I see that saying and doing are two things, and hereafter I shall better observe this distinction.

CHR. They are two things indeed, and are as diverse as are the soul and the body; for as the

body. Quoted from James 2:26.

body without the soul is but a dead carcass, so saying, if it be alone, is but a dead carcass also.

Pure religion. Quoted from James 1:27.

The soul of religion is the practical part: "Pure religion and undefiled, before God and the Father, is this, To visit the fatherless and widows in their affliction, and to keep himself unspotted from the world." This Talkative is not aware of; he thinks that hearing and saying will make a good Christian, and thus he de-

deceiveth. "If any man among you seem to be religious, and bridleth not his tongue, but deceiveth his own heart, this man's religion is vain" (James 1:26).

fruits. "Ye shall know them by their fruits" (Matthew 7:16). And see Matthew 13:23.

doers. "But be ye doers of the word, and not hearers only, deceiving your own selves" (James 1:22).

harvest. Matthew 13:30.

ceiveth his own soul. Hearing is but as the sowing of the seed; talking is not sufficient to prove that fruit is indeed in the heart and life; and let us assure ourselves that at the day of doom men shall be judged according to their fruits. It will not be said then, Did you believe? but, Were you doers or talkers only? and accordingly shall they be judged. The end of the world is compared to our harvest; and you know men at harvest regard nothing but fruit. Not that anything can be accepted that is not of faith, but I speak this to show you how insignificant the profession of Talkative will be at that day.

FAITH. This brings to my mind that of Moses, by which he describeth the <u>beast</u> that is clean. He is such a one that parteth the hoof and cheweth the cud; not that parteth the hoof only, or that cheweth the cud only. The hare cheweth the cud, but yet is unclean, because he parteth not the hoof. And this truly resembleth Talkative; he cheweth the cud, he seeketh knowledge, he cheweth upon the word; but he divideth not the hoof, he parteth not with the way of sinners; but as the hare, he retaineth the foot of a dog or bear, and therefore he is unclean.

CHR. You have spoken, for aught I know, the true gospel sense of those texts. And I will add another thing. <u>Paul</u> calleth some men, yea, and those great talkers too, "sounding brass and tinkling cymbals"; that is, as he expounds them in another place, "things without life, giving sound." Things without life, that is, without the true faith and grace of the gospel; and consequently, things that shall never be placed in the kingdom of heaven among those that are the children of life; though their sound, by their talk, be as if it were the tongue or voice of an angel.

FAITH. Well, I was not so fond of his company at first, but I am as sick of it now. What shall we do to be rid of him?

CHR. Take my advice and do as I bid you, and you shall find that he will soon be sick of your company too, except God shall touch his heart and turn it.

FAITH. What would you have me to do?

CHR. Why, go to him and enter into some serious discourse about the power of religion; and ask him plainly (when he has approved of it, for that he will) whether this thing be set up in his heart, house, or <u>conversation.</u>

FAITH. Then Faithful stepped forward again and said to Talkative, Come, what cheer? How is it now?

TALK. Thank you, well. I thought we should

beast. See Leviticus 11 and Deuteronomy 14. This is a fine example of how the Puritans "spiritualized" the Old Testament Scriptures to find practical guidance for daily life.

Paul. A series of allusions to 1 Corinthians 13:1-3 and 14:7.

conversation. Behavior, not talk.

have had a great deal of talk by this time.

FAITH. Well, if you will, we will fall to it now; and since you left it with me to state the question, let it be this: How doth the saving grace of God discover itself, when it is in the heart of man?

TALK. I perceive then that our talk must be about the power of things. Well, it is a very good question, and I shall be willing to answer you. And take my answer in brief, thus: First, Where the grace of God is in the heart, it causeth there a great outcry against sin. Secondly—

FAITH. Nay hold, let us consider of one at once. I think you should rather say, It shows itself by inclining the soul to abhor its sin.

TALK. Why, what difference is there between crying out against, and abhorring of sin?

FAITH. Oh, a great deal. A man may cry out against sin, of policy, but he cannot abhor it but by virtue of a godly antipathy against it. I have heard many cry out against sin in the pulpit, who yet can abide it well enough in the heart, house, and conversation. Joseph's <u>mistress</u> cried out with a loud voice, as if she had been very holy; but she would willingly, notwithstanding that, have committed uncleanness with him. Some cry out against sin even as the mother cries out against her child in her lap, when she calleth it <u>slut</u> and naughty girl, and then falls to hugging and kissing it.

TALK. You <u>lie at the catch,</u> I perceive.

FAITH. No, not I; I am only for setting things right. But what is the second thing whereby you would prove a discovery of a work of grace in the heart?

TALK. Great knowledge of gospel mysteries.

FAITH. This sign should have been first; but first or last, it is also false; for knowledge, great knowledge, may be obtained in the mysteries of the gospel, and yet no work of grace in the soul. Yea, if a man have <u>all knowledge,</u> he may yet be

mistress. The word simply means she was his master's wife.

slut. The word refers to an untidy and even immoral woman; but here it is used playfully. No mother would seriously call a child a slut!

lie at the catch. "You lie in wait to catch me."

all knowledge. 1 Corinthians 13:2.

nothing, and so consequently be no child of God. When Christ said, "Do you know all these things?" and the disciples had answered, "Yes"; he addeth, "Blessed are ye if ye do them." He doth not lay the blessing in the knowing of them, but in the doing of them. For there is a knowledge that is not attended with doing: "He that knoweth his master's will, and doth it not." A man may know like an angel, and yet be no Christian; therefore your sign of it is not true. Indeed, *to know* is a thing that pleaseth talkers and boasters; but *to do* is that which pleaseth God. Not that the heart can be good without knowledge; for without that the heart is naught. There is, therefore, knowledge and knowledge. Knowledge that resteth in the bare speculation of things; and knowledge that is accompanied with the grace of faith and love; which puts a man upon doing even the will of God from the heart: the first of these will serve the talker; but without the other the true Christian is not content. "Give me understanding, and I shall keep thy law; yea, I shall observe it with my whole heart."

TALK. You lie at the catch again; this is not for edification.

FAITH. Well, if you please, propound another sign how this work of grace discovereth itself where it is.

TALK. Not I, for I see we shall not agree.

FAITH. Well, if you will not, will you give me leave to do it?

TALK. You may use your liberty.

FAITH. A work of grace in the soul discovereth itself either to him that hath it, or standers by.

To him that hath it, thus: It gives him conviction of sin, especially of the defilement of his nature and the sin of unbelief (for the sake of which he is sure to be damned, if he findeth not mercy at God's hand by faith in Jesus Christ). This sight and sense of things worketh in him

---

Christ said. Referring to John 13:12-17.

doing of them. See Ephesians 6:6.

He that knoweth . . . . Quoted from Luke 12:41-48.

Give me . . . . Psalm 119:34.

for edification. "To build up spiritually." "Let every one of us please his neighbour for his good to edification" (Romans 15:2).

mercy. Bunyan lists these references: Mark 16:16; John 16:8-9; Romans 7:24.

99

sorrow and shame for sin; he findeth, moreover, revealed in him the Saviour of the world, and the absolute necessity of closing with him for life, at the which he findeth hungerings and thirstings after him; to which hungerings, etc., the promise is made. Now, according to the strength or weakness of his faith in his Saviour, so is his joy and peace, so is his love to holiness, so are his desires to know him more, and also to serve him in this world. But though I say it discovereth itself thus unto him, yet it is but seldom that he is able to conclude that this is a work of grace; because his corruptions now, and his abused reason, make his mind to misjudge in this matter; therefore in him that hath this work, there is required a very sound judgment before he can with steadiness conclude that this is a work of grace.

To others, it is thus discovered:

1. By an experimental confession of his faith in Christ.

2. By a life answerable to that confession; to wit, a life of holiness, heart-holiness, family-holiness (if he hath a family), and by conversation-holiness in the world, which in the general teacheth him inwardly to abhor his sin, and himself for that in secret; to suppress it in his family, and to promote holiness in the world; not by talk only, as a hypocrite or talkative person may do, but by a practical subjection, in faith and love, to the power of the Word. And now, sir, as to this brief description of the work of grace, and also the discovery of it, if you have aught to object, object; if not, then give me leave to propound to you a second question.

TALK. Nay, my part is not now to object, but to hear; let me therefore have your second question.

FAITH. It is this: Do you experience this first part of this description of it? and doth your life and conversation testify the same? or standeth your religion in word or in tongue, and not in deed and truth? Pray, if you incline to answer me in this, say no more than you know the God above will say Amen to; and also nothing but what your conscience can justify you in; "for not he that commendeth himself is approved, but whom the Lord commendeth." Besides, to say I am thus and thus, when my conversation and all my neighbours tell me I lie, is great wickedness.

for not he that. Quoted from 2 Corinthians 10:18.

TALK. Then Talkative at first began to blush; but recovering himself, thus he replied: You come now to experience, to conscience, and God; and to appeal to him for justification of what is spoken. This kind of discourse I did not expect; nor am I disposed to give an answer to such questions, because I count not myself bound thereto, unless you take upon you to be a catechiser; and, though you should so do, yet I may refuse to make you my judge. But I pray, will you tell me why you ask me such questions?

FAITH. Because I saw you forward to talk, and because I knew not that you had aught else but notion. Besides, to tell you all the truth, I have heard of you, that you are a man whose religion lies in talk, and that your conversation gives this your mouth-profession the lie. They say, you are a spot among Christians; and that religion fareth the worse for your ungodly conversation; that some have already stumbled at your wicked ways, and that more are in danger of being destroyed thereby; your religion, and an ale-house, and covetousness, and uncleanness, and swearing, and lying, and vain-company keeping, etc., will stand together. The proverb is true of you which is said of a whore, to wit, that she is a shame to all women; so are you a shame to all professors.

spot. "These are spots in your feasts of charity" (Jude 12). Professed Christians who can talk, but who do not obey, bring defilement and disgrace to the people of God.

TALK. Since you are ready to take up reports and to judge so rashly as you do, I cannot but conclude you are some peevish or melancholy man, not fit to be discoursed with; and so adieu.

CHR. Then came up Christian and said to his

brother, I told you how it would happen: your words and his lusts could not agree; he had rather leave your company than reform his life. But he is gone, and I said; let him go, the loss is no man's but his own; he has saved us the trouble of going from him; for he continuing (as I suppose he will do) as he is, he would have been but a blot in our company: besides, the apostle says, "From such withdraw thyself."

FAITH. But I am glad we had this little discourse with him; it may happen that he will think of it again: however, I have dealt plainly with him, and so am clear of his blood, if he perisheth.

CHR. You did well to talk so plainly to him as you did; there is but little of this faithful dealing with men nowadays, and that makes religion to stink so in the nostrils of many, as it doth; for they are these talkative fools whose religion is only in word, and are debauched and vain in their conversation, that (being so much admitted into the fellowship of the godly) do puzzle the world, blemish Christianity, and grieve the sincere. I wish that all men would deal with such as you have done: then should they either be made more conformable to religion, or the company of saints would be too hot for them. Then did Faithful say,

> How Talkative at first lifts up his plumes!
> How bravely doth he speak! How he presumes
> To drive down all before him! But so soon
> As Faithful talks of heart-work, like the moon
> That's past the full, into the wane he goes.
> And so will all, but he that heart-work knows.

Thus they went on talking of what they had seen by the way, and so made that way easy which would otherwise, no doubt, have been tedious to them; for now they went through a wilderness.

Now when they were got almost quite out of this wilderness, Faithful chanced to cast his eye back, and espied one coming after them, and he

From such . . . . Quoted from 1 Timothy 6:5. The Puritans practiced church discipline and withdrew fellowship from sinning members.

clear. "Wherefore I take you to record this day, that I am pure from the blood of all men" (Acts 20:26). See also Ezekiel 33:1-9.

little of this. The Puritans feared shallow conversions and sham religious experiences. If there was a lack of "faithful dealing" in Bunyan's day, what must the situation be today!

admitted. Christian remembers the interviews at the Palace Beautiful, when he had to give an account of his conversion and Christian life. The Puritans looked with disfavor upon "easy church membership."

heart-work. The work of God in the human heart. Talkative had the right words on his lips, but he lacked a heart experience of God's grace.

knew him. Oh! said Faithful to his brother, who comes yonder? Then Christian looked, and said, It is my good friend Evangelist. Ay, and my good friend too, said Faithful, for 'twas he that set me the way to the gate. Now was Evangelist come up to them, and thus saluted them:

EVAN. Peace be with you, dearly beloved; and peace be to your helpers.

CHR. Welcome, welcome, my good Evangelist: the sight of thy countenance brings to my remembrance thy ancient kindness and unwearied labouring for my eternal good.

FAITH. And a thousand times welcome, said good Faithful. Thy company, O sweet Evangelist, how desirable it is to us poor pilgrims!

EVAN. Then said Evangelist, How hath it fared with you, my friends, since the time of our last parting? What have you met with, and how have you behaved yourselves?

Then Christian and Faithful told him of all things that had happened to them in the way; and how, and with what difficulty, they had arrived to that place.

EVAN. Right glad am I, said Evangelist, not that you have met with trials, but that you have been victors; and for that you have (notwithstanding many weaknesses) continued in the way to this very day.

I say, right glad am I of this thing, and that for mine own sake and yours. I have sowed, and you have reaped: and the day is coming when both he that sowed and they that reaped shall rejoice together; that is, if you hold out: for in due time ye shall reap, if ye faint not. The crown is before you, and it is an incorruptible one; so run that you may obtain it. Some there be that set out for this crown, and after they have gone far for it, another comes in and takes it from them: hold fast therefore that you have; let no man take your crown. You are not yet out of the gun-shot of the devil; you have not re-

Evangelist. This is his third appearance. He met Christian at the beginning of the pilgrimage to instruct him in the way to the cross. He met him after Christian's failure at the Hill Legality to correct his errors. Now he meets the two pilgrims to prepare them for the trials they will endure in Vanity Fair. Bunyan sees the evangelist not only as one who wins the lost, but also as one who teaches and helps guide believers in the right way.

ancient. Former.

continued. "Having therefore obtained help of God, I continue unto this day" (Acts 26:22). Continuing in the faith is proof of true salvation.

sowed . . . due time. "He that soweth and he that reapeth may rejoice together" (John 4:36). "For in due season we shall reap, if we faint not" (Galatians 6:9).

crown. In 1 Corinthians 9:24-27, Paul compares himself to an athlete who must discipline himself and obey the rules if he is to win the prize. The Greek athletes won an olive branch crown that faded. The obedient Christian wins a crown that will never perish. "Behold, I come quickly: hold that fast which thou hast, that no man take thy crown" (Revelation 3:11).

resisted. "Ye have not yet resisted unto blood, striving against sin" (Hebrews 12:4).

invisible. 2 Corinthians 4:18; Hebrews 11:27.

deceitful. "The heart is deceitful above all things, and desperately wicked" (Jeremiah 17:9).

faces. "Therefore have I set my face like a flint, and I know that I shall not be ashamed" (Isaiah 50:7). "He steadfastly set his face to go to Jerusalem" (Luke 9:51).

all power. Quoted from Matthew 28:18.

tribulations. Acts 14:22.

every city. This was Paul's testimony in Acts 20:23.

hardly beset. Harshly attacked.

faithful unto death. "Be thou faithful unto death, and I will give thee a crown of life" (Revelation 2:10). This statement all but announces that Faithful is the one who will lay down his life.

sisted unto blood, striving against sin; let the kingdom be always before you, and believe steadfastly concerning things that are invisible. Let nothing that is on this side the other world get within you; and above all, look well to your own hearts and to the lusts thereof, for they are deceitful above all things and desperately wicked; set your faces like a flint; you have all power in heaven and earth on your side.

CHR. Then Christian thanked him for his exhortation; but told him withal that they would have him speak further to them for their help the rest of the way, and the rather, for that they well knew that he was a prophet, and could tell them of things that might happen unto them, and also how they might resist and overcome them. To which request Faithful also consented. So Evangelist began as followeth:

EVAN. My sons, you have heard, in the words of the truth of the gospel, that you must through many tribulations enter into the kingdom of heaven. And, again, that in every city bonds and afflictions abide in you; and therefore you cannot expect that you should go long on your pilgrimage without them, in some sort or other. You have found something of the truth of these testimonies upon you already, and more will immediately follow; for now, as you see, you are almost out of this wilderness, and therefore you will soon come into a town that you will by and by see before you; and in that town you will be hardly beset with enemies who will strain hard but they will kill you; and be you sure that one or both of you must seal the testimony which you hold with blood; but be you faithful unto death, and the King will give you a crown of life. He that shall die there, although his death will be unnatural, and his pain perhaps great, he will yet have the better of his fellow; not only because he will be arrived at the Celestial City soonest, but because he will escape many miseries that the other will meet with in the rest of

104

his journey. But when you are come to the town, and shall find fulfilled what I have here related, then remember your friend, and quit yourselves like men, and commit the keeping of your souls to your God in well-doing, as unto a faithful Creator.

Then I saw in my dream that when they were got out of the wilderness, they presently saw a town before them, and the name of that town is Vanity; and at the town there is a fair kept, called Vanity Fair: it is kept all the year long; it beareth the name of Vanity Fair, because the town where it is kept is lighter than vanity; and also because all that is there sold, or that cometh thither, is vanity. As is the saying of the wise, "all that cometh is vanity."

This fair is no new-erected business, but a thing of ancient standing; I will show you the original of it.

Almost five thousand years agone there were pilgrims walking to the Celestial City, as these two honest persons are, and Beelzebub, Apollyon, and Legion, with their companions, perceiving by the path that the pilgrims made that their way to the city lay through this town of Vanity, they contrived here to set up a fair; a fair wherein should be sold all sorts of vanity, and that it should last all the year long: therefore at this fair are all such merchandise sold, as houses, lands, trades, places, honours, preferments, titles, countries, kingdoms, lusts, pleasures, and delights of all sorts, as whores, bawds, wives, husbands, children, masters, servants, lives, blood, bodies, souls, silver, gold, pearls, precious stones, and what not.

And, moreover, at this fair there are at all times to be seen jugglings, cheats, games, plays, fools, apes, knaves, and rogues, and that of every kind.

Here are to be seen too, and that for nothing, thefts, murders, adulteries, false swearers, and that of a blood-red colour.

commit. Quoted from 1 Peter 4:19.

Vanity Fair. The vanity, or emptiness, of human life apart from God is stated in Psalm 62:9; Ecclesiastes 1:2, 14; 2:11, 17; 11:8; and Isaiah 40:17. When Bunyan was a young man, he visited the great fair held at Stourbridge. The Moot Hall, still standing in Elstow, was also the scene of much buying and selling in Bunyan's day. Vanity Fair represents the world and all its activities apart from God.

Beelzebub . . . . All names for Satan and his helpers. "Legion" comes from Mark 5:9, the "legion" of demons that lived in the man. Since Satan is the god and prince of this world, he is the originator and the director of Vanity Fair.

merchandise. The things that unconverted people live for. Bunyan is drawing upon the apostle John's description of "Babylon the great" in Revelation 18:11-14.

apes. Not animals, but people who impersonate others for entertainment.

blood-red. See Revelation 17:3-4 and 18:12, 16 for the significance of this color.

Rome. Bunyan is referring to England's break with Rome during the reign of Henry VIII.

go out. Quoted from 1 Corinthians 5:10.

Prince. Jesus Christ was offered the kingdoms and glory of the world, but refused them (Matthew 4:8-10). Satan promised to make him "lord of the fair," but He obeyed His Father and resisted Satan. See Luke 4:5-7.

clothed. God's righteousness makes believers stand out from the crowd. "We are fools for Christ's sake" (see 1 Corinthians 4:9-10). "I am as one mocked of his neighbour . . . : the just upright man is laughed to scorn" (Job 12:4).

And as in other fairs of less moment there are the several rows and streets under their proper names, where such and such wares are vended; so here likewise you have the proper places, rows, streets (viz. countries and kingdoms), where the wares of this fair are soonest to be found. Here is the Britain Row, the French Row, the Italian Row, the Spanish Row, the German Row, where several sorts of vanities are to be sold. But as in other fairs some one commodity is as the chief of all the fair, so the ware of Rome and her merchandise is greatly promoted in this fair; only our English nation, with some others, have taken a dislike thereat.

Now, as I said, the way to the Celestial City lies just through this town where this lusty fair is kept; and he that will go to the city, and yet not go through this town, must needs "go out of the world." The Prince of princes himself, when here, went through this town to his own country, and that upon a fair day too; yea, and as I think, it was Beelzebub, the chief lord of this fair, that invited him to buy of his vanities; yea, would have made him lord of the fair, would he but have done him reverence as he went through the town. Yea, because he was such a person of honour, Beelzebub had him from street to street, and showed him all the kingdoms of the world in a little time, that he might, if possible, allure the Blessed One to cheapen and buy some of his vanities; but he had no mind to the merchandise, and therefore left the town without laying out so much as one farthing upon these vanities. This fair therefore is an ancient thing, of long standing, and a very great fair. Now these pilgrims, as I said, must needs go through this fair. Well, so they did: but behold, even as they entered into the fair, all the people in the fair were moved, and the town itself as it were in a hubbub about them; and that for several reasons: for,

First, The pilgrims were clothed with such

kind of raiment as was diverse for the raiment of any that traded in that fair. The people therefore of the fair made a great gazing upon them: some said they were fools, some they were bedlams, and some they are outlandish men.

Secondly, And as they wondered at their apparel, so they did likewise at their speech; for few could understand what they said; they naturally spoke the language of Canaan, but they that kept the fair were the men of this world; so that from one end of the fair to the other they seemed barbarians each to the other.

Thirdly, But that which did not a little amuse the merchandisers was that these pilgrims set very light by all their wares; they cared not so much as to look upon them; and if they called upon them to buy, they would put their fingers in their ears and cry, "Turn away mine eyes from beholding vanity," and look upwards, signifying that their trade and traffic was in heaven.

One chanced mockingly, beholding the carriage of the men, to say unto them, What will ye buy? But they, looking gravely upon him, answered, "We buy the truth." At that there was an occasion taken to despise the men the more; some mocking, some taunting, some speaking reproachfully, and some calling upon others to smite them. At last things came to a hubbub and great stir in the fair, insomuch that all order was confounded. Now was word presently brought to the great one of the fair, who quickly came down and deputed some of his most trusty friends to take these men into examination, about whom the fair was almost overturned. So the men were brought to examination, and they that sat upon them asked them whence they came, whither they went, and what they did there in such an unusual garb? The men told them that they were pilgrims and strangers in the world, and that they were going to their own country, which was the heavenly Jerusalem, and

bedlams . . . outlandish. "Bedlams" were madmen. Bethlehem Hospital in London was used to house mental patients, and "bedlam" is a contraction of Bethlehem. "Outlandish" means from outside the land," therefore different from us and not as good as we are!

speech. The "language of Canaan" is the language of God's people (see Nehemiah 13:24). "They are of the world: therefore speak they of the world, and the world heareth them. We are of God: he that knoweth God heareth us; he that is not of God heareth not us" (1 John 4:5-6).

barbarians. See 1 Corinthians 2:7-8 and 14:11.

wares. The Christian is not attracted by, or interested in, the things of this world (1 John 2:15-17).

Turn away . . . . Quoted from Psalm 119:37.

upwards. "For our conversation [that is, our citizenship] is in heaven." (see Philippians 3:20-21).

carriage. Conduct, the way they carried themselves.

We buy . . . . "Buy the truth, and sell it not" (Proverbs 23:23).

great stir. "And the same time there arose no small stir about that way" (Acts 19:23). The entire scene in the fair is based on the riot in Ephesus caused by Paul's ministry and the opposition of the silversmiths (Acts 19:23-41).

examination. These examinations are based on Bunyan's many court trials, as well as the trials of the Puritans in general.

pilgrims. The Old Testament saints (Hebrews 11:13-16) and the New Testament believers (1 Peter 2:11) looked upon themselves as strangers to this world and pilgrims on the way to the heavenly city.

spectacle. "For we are made a spectacle unto the world" (1 Corinthians 4:9).

railing. They were obeying 1 Peter 3:9—"Not rendering evil for evil, or railing for railing: but contrariwise blessing." "To rail" means "to denounce bitterly, to use abusive language."

baser sort. "Certain lewd fellows of the baser sort" (Acts 17:5), just the kind to start a riot.

that they had given no occasion to the men of the town, nor yet to the merchandisers, thus to abuse them, and to let them in their journey, except it was for that, when one asked them what they would buy, they said they would buy the truth. But they that were appointed to examine them did not believe them to be any other than bedlams and mad, or else such as came to put all things into a confusion in the fair. Therefore they took them and beat them, and besmeared them with dirt, and then put them into the cage, that they might be made a spectacle to all men of the fair.

> Behold Vanity Fair! the pilgrims there
> Are chained and stoned beside;
> Even so it was our Lord passed here,
> And on Mount Calvary died.

There therefore they lay for some time and were made the objects of any man's sport, or malice, or revenge, the great one of the fair laughing still at all that befell them. But the men being patient and not rendering railing for railing, but contrariwise blessing, and giving good words for bad and kindness for injuries done, some men in the fair that were more observing and less prejudiced than the rest, began to check and blame the baser sort for their continual abuses done by them to the men; they therefore in angry manner let fly at them again, counting them as bad as the men in the cage, and telling them that they seemed confederates and should be made partakers of their misfortunes. The other replied that for aught they could see, the men were quiet, and sober, and intended nobody any harm; and that there were many that traded in their fair that were more worthy to be put into the cage, yea, and pillory too, than were the men they had abused. Thus after divers words had passed on both sides (the men behaving themselves all the while very wisely and soberly before them) they fell to some blows among themselves and did harm one to another. Then were these two poor men brought before their examiners again, and there charged as being guilty of the late hubbub that had been in the fair. So they beat them pitifully, and hanged irons upon them, and led them in chains up and down the fair, for an example and a terror to others, lest any should speak in their behalf or join themselves unto them. But Christian and Faithful behaved themselves yet more wisely, and received the ignominy and shame that was cast upon them with so much meekness and patience that it won to their side (though but few in comparison of the rest) several of the men in the fair. This put the other party yet into greater rage, insomuch that they concluded the death of these two men. Wherefore they threatened that neither cage nor irons should serve their turn, but that they should die for the abuse they had done and for deluding the men of the fair.

Then were they remanded to the cage again, until further order should be taken with them. So they put them in and made their feet fast in the stocks.

stocks. Paul and Silas experienced this in Philippi (Acts 16:24). Bunyan sees Christian and Faithful sharing the experiences of the first apostles.

Here also they called again to mind what they had heard from their faithful friend Evangelist, and were the more confirmed in their way and sufferings by what he told them would happen to them. They also now comforted each other that whose lot it was to suffer, even he should have the best of it; therefore each man secretly wished that he might have that preferment: but committing themselves to the all-wise disposal of him that ruleth all things, with much content they abode in the condition in which they were, until they should be otherwise disposed of.

Then a convenient time being appointed, they brought them forth to their trial in order to their condemnation. When the time was come, they were brought before their enemies and arraigned. The judge's name was Lord Hate-good. Their indictment was one and the same in

Lord Hate-good. Probably patterned after the judges who tried Bunyan and the other Puritans. Judge George Jeffreys was one of the worst. Bunyan himself was tried by Sir John Keelynge. The king's courts were not favorable to the Puritan position.

disturbers of their trade. A reference to the revolt of the silversmiths in Ephesus, who were in danger of losing their trade (Acts 19:25).

commotions. Because the Puritans would not conform to the state church, they were considered heretics and causes of division. Bunyan's indictment in 1661 was that he was a disturber who refused to cooperate with the established religion.

won a party. Hopeful was converted through their witness.

Envy. "For he knew that for envy they had delivered him" (Matthew 27:18).

Pickthank. The word means to win favor by flattery and talebearing.

law nor custom. The early apostles were accused of breaking Roman law and custom (Acts 16:20-21 and 17:7).

substance, though somewhat varying in form; the contents whereof were this:

"That they were enemies to and <u>disturbers of their trade</u>; that they had made <u>commotions</u> and divisions in the town, and had <u>won a party</u> to their own most dangerous opinions, in contempt of the law of their prince."

> Now, Faithful, play the man,
>   speak for thy God:
> Fear not the wickeds' malice; nor their rod!
> Speak boldly, man, the truth is on thy side:
> Die for it, and to life in triumph ride.

Then Faithful began to answer, that he had only set himself against that which hath set itself against Him that is higher than the highest. And, said he, as for disturbance, I make none, being myself a man of peace; the parties that were won to us were won by beholding our truth and innocence, and they are only turned from the worse to the better. And as to the king you talk of, since he is Beelzebub, the enemy of our Lord, I defy him and all his angels.

Then proclamation was made that they had aught to say for their lord the king against the prisoner at the bar should forthwith appear and give in their evidence. So there came in three witnesses to wit, <u>Envy,</u> Superstition, and <u>Pickthank</u>. They were then asked if they knew the prisoner at the bar, and what they had to say for their lord the king against him.

Then stood forth Envy and said to this effect: My Lord, I have known this man a long time, and will attest upon my oath before this honourable bench that he is—

JUDGE. Hold, give him his oath. (So they sware him.)

Then he said, My Lord, this man, notwithstanding his plausible name, is one of the vilest men in our country. He neither regardeth prince nor people, <u>law nor custom</u>; but doth all that he can to possess all men with certain of his

110

disloyal notions, which he in the general calls principles of faith and holiness. And, in particular, I heard him once myself affirm that Christianity and the customs of our town of Vanity were diametrically opposite and could not be reconciled. By which saying, my Lord, he doth at once not only condemn all our laudable doings, but us in the doing of them.

JUDGE. Then did the judge say to him, Hast thou any more to say?

ENVY. My Lord, I could say much more, only I would not be tedious to the court. Yet, if need be, when the other gentlemen have given in their evidence, rather than anything shall be wanting that will dispatch him, I will enlarge my testimony against him. So he was bid to stand by.

tedious. A quotation from Acts 24:4 (Paul's trial).

Then they called Superstition, and bid him look upon the prisoner. They also asked what he could say for their lord the king against him. Then they sware him; so he began.

SUPER. My Lord, I have no great acquaintance with this man, nor do I desire to have further knowledge of him; however, this I know, that he is a very pestilent fellow, from some discourse that the other day I had with him in this town; for then talking with him, I heard him say that our religion was naught, and such by which a man could by no means please God. Which sayings of his, my Lord, your Lordship very well knows what necessarily thence will follow, to wit, that we do still worship in vain, are yet in our sins, and finally shall be damned; and this is that which I have to say.

pestilent. Paul was accused of this (Acts 24:5).

worship in vain. When Paul preached at Lystra, he told the people that they should "turn from these vanities unto the living God" The result was that the mob stoned Paul (Acts 14:8ff.). The result here is that Faithful is slain.

Then was Pickthank sworn and bid say what he knew in behalf of their lord the king against the prisoner at the bar.

PICK. My Lord, and you gentlemen all, this fellow I have known of a long time, and have heard him speak things that ought not to be spoke; for he hath railed on our noble prince Beelzebub, and hath spoken contemptibly of his

111

honourable friends, whose names are the Lord Old Man, the Lord Carnal Delight, the Lord Luxurious, the Lord Desire of Vain-glory, my old Lord Lechery, Sir Having Greedy, with all the rest of our nobility; and he hath said, moreover, that if all men were of his mind, if possible, there is not one of these noblemen should have any longer a being in this town. Besides, he hath not been afraid to rail on you, my Lord, who are now appointed to be his judge, calling you an ungodly villain, with many other such like vilifying terms, with which he hath bespattered most of the gentry of our town.

When this Pickthank had told his tale, the judge directed his speech to the prisoner at the bar, saying, Thou runagate, heretic, and traitor, hast thou heard what these honest gentlemen have witnessed against thee?

FAITH. May I speak a few words in my own defence?

JUDGE. Sirrah, sirrah, thou deservest to live no longer, but to be slain immediately upon the place; yet that all men may see our gentleness towards thee, let us hear what thou, vile runagate, hast to say.

FAITH. 1. I say then in answer to what Mr. Envy hath spoken, I never said aught but this, That what rule, or laws, or custom, or people, were flat against the Word of God, are diametrically opposite to Christianity. If I have said amiss in this, convince me of my error, and I am ready here before you to make my recantation.

2. As to the second, to wit, Mr. Superstition, and his charge against me, I said only this, That in the worship of God there is required a Divine faith; but there can be no Divine faith without a Divine revelation of the will of God. Therefore whatever is thrust into the worship of God that is not agreeable to Divine revelation cannot be done but by a human faith, which faith will not be profitable to eternal life.

runagate. An old form of renegade—a deserter, an apostate.

defence. Paul said this when facing the Jewish mob (Acts 22:1)

deservest. This was the mob's sentence on Paul: "Away with such a fellow from the earth: for it is not fit that he should live" (Acts 22:22). The judge is prejudiced before the trial is ended.

convince. Jesus answered him, "If I have spoken evil, bear witness of the evil" (John 18:23). Bunyan in this trial scene combines elements from the trials of Jesus and of Paul.

112

3. As to what Mr. Pickthank hath said, I say (avoiding terms, as that I am said to rail and the like) that the prince of this town, with all the rabblement, his attendants, by this gentleman named, are more fit for a being in hell, than in this town and country; and so the Lord have mercy upon me!

Then the judge called to the jury (who all this while stood by, to hear and observe): Gentlemen of the jury, you see this man about whom so great an uproar hath been made in this town. You have also heard what these worthy gentlemen have witnessed against him. Also you have heard his reply and confession. It lieth now in your breasts to hang him or save his life; but yet I think meet to instruct you into our law.

uproar. There was a citywide uproar in Ephesus (Acts 19:28ff.).

instruct you. The judge uses the Bible to try to prove his case! Pharaoh ordered the Jewish baby boys drowned (Exodus 1); Nebuchadnezzar commanded a unified worship (Daniel 3); and Darius demanded all prayer to be offered to him (Daniel 6). The Puritans lived at a time when the king wanted a uniform religion, and they refused to conform. The judge uses only those facts that prove his case; he does not mention that in all three examples, it was the minority of dissenters who won!

There was an Act made in the days of Pharaoh the Great, servant to our prince, that lest those of a contrary religion should multiply and grow too strong for him, their males should be thrown into the river. There was also an Act made in the days of Nebuchadnezzar the Great, another of his servants, that whosoever would not fall down and worship his golden image should be thrown into a fiery furnace. There was also an Act made in the days of Darius, that whoso for some time called upon any god but him should be cast into the lions' den. Now the substance of these laws this rebel has broken, not only in thought (which is not to be borne), but also in word and deed; which must therefore needs be intolerable.

For that of Pharaoh, his law was made upon a supposition, to prevent mischief, no crime being yet apparent; but here is a crime apparent. For the second and third, you see he disputeth against our religion; and for the treason he hath confessed, he deserveth to die the death.

Then went the jury out, whose names were, Mr. Blind-man, Mr. No-good, Mr. Malice, Mr. Love-lust, Mr. Live-loose, Mr. Heady, Mr. High-mind, Mr. Enmity, Mr. Liar, Mr. Cruelty,

Heady . . . Highmind. Taken from 2 Timothy 3:4. It is a packed jury to say the least!

113

Away. Acts 22:22.

scrub. Insignificant person.

according to their law. See John 18:31 and 19:7.

scourged . . . buffeted. Matthew 26:67 and 27:26. This is the way the Lord was treated.

lanced. A reference to 1 Kings 18:28.

chariot. This is the way the prophet Elijah went to heaven (2 Kings 2:11). For the Christian, suffering only leads to glory.

Mr. Hate-light, and Mr. Implacable; who every one gave in his private verdict against him among themselves, and afterwards unanimously concluded to bring him in guilty before the judge. And first, among themselves, Mr. Blind-man, the foreman, said, I see clearly that this man is a heretic. Then said Mr. No-good, Away with such a fellow from the earth. Ay, said Mr. Malice, for I hate the very looks of him. Then said Mr. Love-lust, I could never endure him. Nor I, said Mr. Live-loose, for he would always be condemning my way. Hang him, hang him, said Mr. Heady. A sorry scrub, said Mr. High-mind. My heart riseth against him, said Mr. Enmity. He is a rogue, said Mr. Liar. Hanging is too good for him, said Mr. Cruelty. Let us dispatch him out of the way, said Mr. Hate-light. Then said Mr. Implacable, Might I have all the world given me, I could not be reconciled to him; therefore let us forthwith bring him in guilty of death. And so they did; therefore he was presently condemned to be had from the place where he was, to the place from whence he came, and there to be put to the most cruel death that could be invented.

They therefore brought him out, to do with him according to their law; and first they scourged him, then they buffeted him, then they lanced his flesh with knives; after that they stoned him with stones, then pricked him with their swords; and last of all they burned him to ashes at the stake. Thus came Faithful to his end. Now I saw that there stood behind the multitude a chariot and a couple of horses, waiting for Faithful, who (so soon as his adversaries had dispatched him) was taken up into it, and straightway was carried up through the clouds, with sound of trumpet, the nearest way to the Celestial Gate.

> Brave Faithful, bravely done in word and deed;
> Judge, witnesses, and jury have, instead
> Of overcoming thee, but shown their rage;

114

When they are dead,
thou'lt live from age to age.

But as for Christian, he had some respite, and was remanded back to prison. So he there remained for a space; but He that overrules all things, having the power of their rage in his own hand, so wrought it about that Christian for that time escaped them and went his way; and as he went he sang, saying,

Well, Faithful, thou hast faithfully professed
Unto thy Lord; with whom thou shalt be blest,
When faithless ones,
with all their vain delights,
Are crying out under their hellish plights:
Sing, Faithful, sing, and let thy name survive;
For though they killed thee, thou art yet alive.

Now I saw in my dream that Christian went not forth alone, for there was one whose name was Hopeful (being made so by the beholding of Christian and Faithful in their words and behaviour, in their sufferings at the fair), who joined himself unto him, and entering into a brotherly covenant, told him that he would be his companion. Thus one died to bear testimony to the truth, and another rises out of his ashes to be a companion with Christian in his pilgrimage. This Hopeful also told Christian that there were many more of the men in the fair, that would take their time and follow after.

So I saw that quickly after they were got out of the fair, they overtook one that was going before them, whose name was By-ends: so they said to him, What countryman, sir? and how far go you this way? He told them that he came from the town of Fair-speech, and he was going to the Celestial City, but told them not his name.

From Fair-speech, said Christian; is there any good that lives there?

By-ENDS. Yes, said By-ends, I hope.

CHR. Pray, sir, what may I call you? said Christian.

rage. "Surely the wrath of man shall praise thee: the remainder of wrath shalt thou restrain" (Psalm 76:10). Faithful's death praised God and won Hopeful. God restrained the men so that they did not kill Christian but permitted him to go.

Hopeful. Christian now has a new, and different, companion. Again, Bunyan reminds us that not all conversions are alike, nor are all Christians alike. However, the personalities and experiences of the two men are complementary, not contradictory.

By-ends. One who uses base means to achieve his purposes. The end justifies the means. Just as Pliable and Obstinate left the City of Destruction but did not succeed, so By-ends leaves Vanity Fair but fails to reach the heavenly city. Bunyan keeps reminding us that there are "professors" of religion who are not true possessors.

Fair-speech. "When he speaketh fair, believe him not: for there are seven abominations in his heart (Proverbs 26:25). "And by good words and fair speeches [they] deceive the hearts of the simple" (Romans 16:18).

By-ends. I am a stranger to you, and you to me: if you be going this way, I shall be glad of your company; if not, I must be content.

Chr. This town of Fair-speech, said Christian, I have heard of it; and as I remember, they say it's a wealthy place.

By-ends. Yes, I will assure you that it is; and I have very many rich kindred there.

Chr. Pray, who are your kindred there? if a man may be so bold.

By-ends. Almost the whole town; and in particular, my Lord Turn-about, my Lord Time-server, my Lord Fair-speech (from whose ancestors that town first took its name), also Mr. Smooth-man, Mr. Facing-both-ways, Mr. Anything; and the parson of our parish, Mr. Two-tongues, was my mother's own brother by father's side; and to tell you the truth, I am become a gentleman of good quality, yet my great-grandfather was but a waterman, looking one way and rowing another, and I got most of my estate by the same occupation.

Chr. Are you a married man?

By-ends. Yes, and my wife is a very virtuous woman, the daughter of a virtuous woman; she was my Lady Feigning's daughter, therefore she came of a very honourable family, and is arrived to such a pitch of breeding that she knows how to carry it to all, even to prince and peasant. 'Tis true, we somewhat differ in religion from those of the stricter sort, yet but in two small points: first, we never strive against wind and tide; secondly, we are always most zealous when religion goes in his silver slippers; we love much to walk with him in the street, if the sun shines and the people applaud him.

Then Christian stepped a little aside to his fellow Hopeful, saying, It runs in my mind that this is one By-ends of Fair-speech; and if it be he, we have as very a knave in our company as dwelleth in all these parts. Then said Hopeful, Ask him; methinks he should not be ashamed of his name. So Christian came up with him again and said, Sir, you talk as if you knew something more than all the world doth; and if I take not my mark amiss, I deem I have half a guess of you: Is not your name Mr. By-ends of Fair-speech?

BY-ENDS. This is not my name, but indeed it is a nickname that is given me by some that cannot abide me: and I must be content to bear it as a reproach, as other good men have borne theirs before me.

CHR. But did you never give an occasion to men to call you by this name?

BY-ENDS. Never, never! The worst that ever I did to give them an occasion to give me this name was that I had always the luck to jump in my judgment with the present way of the times, whatever it was, and my chance was to get thereby; but if things are thus cast upon me, let me count them a blessing; but let not the malicious load me therefore with reproach.

CHR. I thought indeed that you were the man that I heard of; and to tell you what I think, I fear this name belongs to you more properly than you are willing we should think it doth.

BY-ENDS. Well, if you will thus imagine, I cannot help it; you shall find me a fair company-keeper, if you will still admit me your associate.

CHR. If you will go with us, you must go against wind and tide; the which, I perceive, is against your opinion; you must also own religion in his rags, as well as when in his silver slippers, and stand by him too when bound in irons, as well as when he walketh the streets with applause.

BY-ENDS. You must not impose, nor <u>lord it</u> over my faith; leave me to my liberty, and let me go with you.

CHR. Not a step further, unless you will do in what I propound as we.

Then said By-ends, I shall never desert my

lord it. "Not for that we have dominion over your faith" (2 Corinthians 1:24). People who want to go their own way can appeal to the Bible for support.

117

old principles, since they are harmless and profitable. If I may not go with you, I must do as I did before you overtook me, even go by myself, until some overtake me that will be glad of my company.

Now I saw in my dream that Christian and Hopeful forsook him, and kept their distance before him; but one of them looking back saw three men following Mr. By-ends, and behold, as they came up with him, he made them a very low *congé;* and they also gave him a compliment. The men's names were Mr. Hold-the-world, Mr. Money-love, and Mr. Save-all; men that Mr. By-ends had formerly been acquainted with; for in their minority they were schoolfellows, and were taught by one Mr. Gripe-man, a schoolmaster in Love-gain, which is a market town in the county of Coveting in the north. This schoolmaster taught them the art of getting, either by violence, cozenage, flattery, lying, or by putting on a guise of religion; and these four gentlemen had attained much of the art of their master, so that they could each of them have kept such a school themselves.

Well, when they had, as I said, thus saluted each other, Mr. Money-love said to Mr. By-ends, Who are they upon the road before us? (for Christian and Hopeful were yet within view).

BY-ENDS. They are a couple of far countrymen, that, after their mode, are going on pilgrimage.

MONEY-LOVE. Alas, why did they not stay, that we might have had their good company? for they, and we, and you, sir, I hope, are all going on pilgrimage.

BY-ENDS. We are so indeed; but the men before us are so rigid, and love so much their own notions, and do also so lightly esteem the opinions of others, that let a man be never so godly, yet if he jumps not with them in all things, they thrust him quite out of their company.

congé. French for "unceremonious leave-taking." By-ends was rude to Christian and Hopeful as he welcomed the three new companions.

cozenage. Cheating, fraud.

guise. See 1 Thessalonians 2:1-6.

rigid. The Puritans were criticized for their discipline of life and convictions in matters of faith. The average church member in that day did not take his religious faith seriously.

118

SAVE-ALL. That is bad, but we read of some that are righteous overmuch; and such men's rigidness prevails with them to judge and condemn all but themselves. But I pray, what and how many were the things wherein you differed?

BY-ENDS. Why, they, after their headstrong manner, conclude that it is duty to rush on their journey all weathers, and I am for waiting for wind and tide. They are for hazarding all for God at a clap, and I am for taking all advantages to secure my life and estate. They are for holding their notions, though all other men are against them; but I am for religion in what and so far as the times and my safety will bear it. They are for religion when in rags and contempt, but I am for him when he walks in his golden slippers in the sunshine and with applause.

MR. HOLD-THE-WORLD. Ay, and hold you there still, good Mr. By-ends; for, for my part, I can count him but a fool that, having the liberty to keep what he has, shall be so unwise as to lose it. Let us be wise as serpents; it is best to make hay when the sun shines; you see how the bee lieth still all winter, and bestirs her only when she can have profit with pleasure. God sends sometimes rain and sometimes sunshine; if they be such fools to go through the first, yet let us be content to take fair weather along with us. For my part, I like that religion best that will stand with the security of God's good blessings unto us; for who can imagine, that is ruled by his reason, since God has bestowed upon us the good things of this life, but that he would have us keep them for his sake? Abraham and Solomon grew rich in religion. And Job says, that a good man shall lay up gold as dust. But he must not be such as the men before us, if they be as you have described them.

MR. SAVE-ALL. I think that we are all agreed in

righteous. "Be not righteous over much" (Ecclesiastes 7:16).

hazarding. "Men that have hazarded their lives for the name of our Lord Jesus Christ" (Acts 15:26).

keep what he has. Martyred missionary Jim Elliot said, "He is no fool to give what he cannot keep to gain what he cannot lose." Jesus said, "For whosoever will save his life shall lose it: and whosoever will lose his life for my sake shall find it" (Matthew 16:25).

wise. "Be ye therefore wise as serpents, and harmless as doves" (Matthew 10:16). See Genesis 3:1.

make hay. This familiar proverb was already over a hundred years old when Bunyan quoted it, having been published in England in 1546.

good things. See Acts 14:17 and 1 Timothy 6:17.

Job says. Quoted from Job 22:24.

this matter, and therefore there needs no more words about it.

MR. MONEY-LOVE. No, there needs no more words about this matter indeed; for he that believes neither Scripture nor reason (and you see we have both on our side) neither knows his own liberty, nor seeks his own safety.

MR. BY-ENDS. My brethren, we are, as you see, going all on pilgrimage; and for our better diversion from things that are bad, give me leave to propound unto you this question:

Suppose a man, a minister, or a tradesman, etc., should have an advantage lie before him to get the good blessings of this life, yet so as that he can by no means come by them except, in appearance at least, he becomes extraordinary zealous in some points of religion that he meddled not with before; may he not use this means to attain his end, and yet be a right honest man?

MR. MONEY-LOVE. I see the <u>bottom</u> of your question; and, with these gentlemen's good leave, I will endeavour to shape you an answer. And first, to speak to your question as it concerns a minister himself: Suppose a minister, a worthy man, possessed but of a very small <u>benefice,</u> and has in his eye a greater, more fat and plump by far; he has also now an opportunity of getting of it, yet so as by being more studious, by preaching more frequently and zealously, and, because the temper of the people requires it, by altering of some of his principles; for my part, I see no reason but a man may do this (provided he has a call), ay, and more a great deal besides, and yet be an honest man. For why—

1. His desire of a greater benefice is lawful (this cannot be contradicted), since 'tis set before him by Providence; so then, he may get it, if he can, making <u>no question</u> for conscience' sake.

2. Besides, his desire after that benefice makes him more studious, a more zealous

preacher, etc., and so makes him a better man; yea, makes him better improve his parts, which is according to the mind of God.

3. Now as for his complying with the temper of his people by dissenting, to serve them, some of his principles, this argueth, (1) That his is of a self-denying temper; (2) Of a sweet and winning deportment; (3) And so more fit for the ministerial function.

4. I conclude, then, that a minister that changes a small for a great should not, for so doing, be judged as covetous; but rather, since he has improved in his parts and industry thereby, be counted as one that pursues his call and the opportunity put into his hand to do good.

And now to the second part of the question, which concerns the tradesman you mentioned. Suppose such a one to have but a poor employ in the world, but by becoming religious, he may mend his market, perhaps get a rich wife, or more and far better customers to his shop; for my part, I see no reason but that this may be lawfully done. For why—

1. To become religious is a virtue, by what means soever a man becomes so.

2. Nor is it unlawful to get a rich wife, or more <u>custom</u> to my shop.

custom. We would say customers, people accustomed to use the shop.

3. Besides, the man that gets these by becoming religious, gets that which is good of them that are good, by becoming good himself; so then here is a good wife, and good customers, and good gain, and all these by becoming religious, which is good; therefore to become religious to get all these is a good and profitable design.

This answer, thus made by this Mr. Moneylove to Mr. By-ends' question, was highly applauded by them all; wherefore they concluded, upon the whole, that it was most wholesome and advantageous. And because, as they thought, no man was able to contradict it, and because Christian and Hopeful were yet within call, they jointly agreed to assault them with the question as soon as they overtook them; and the rather because they had opposed Mr. By-ends before. So they called after them, and they stopped and stood still till they came up to them; but they concluded, as they went, that not Mr. By-ends, but old Mr. Hold-the-world, should propound the question to them, because, as they supposed, their answer to him would be without the remainder of that heat that was kindled betwixt Mr. By-ends and them, at their parting a little before.

So they came up to each other, and after a short salutation, Mr. Hold-the-world propounded the question to Christian and his fellow, and bid them to answer it if they could.

CHR. Then said Christian, Even a babe in religion may answer ten thousand such questions. For if it be unlawful to follow Christ for loaves, as it is, how much more abominable is it to make him and religion a stalking-horse to get and enjoy the world. Nor do we find any other than heathens, hypocrites, devils, and witches, that are of this opinion.

1. Heathens; for when Hamor and Shechem had a mind to the daughter and cattle of Jacob, and saw that there was no way for them to come at them, but by becoming circumcised; they say to their companions, If every male of us be circumcised as they are circumcised, shall not their cattle, and their substance, and every beast of theirs, be ours? Their daughter and their cattle were that which they sought to obtain, and their religion the stalking-horse they made use of to come at them. Read the whole story.

2. The hypocritical Pharisees were also of this religion; long prayers were their pretence, but to get widows' houses was their intent; and greater damnation was from God their judgment.

3. Judas the devil was also of this religion; he

---

loaves. "Ye seek me, not because ye saw the miracles, but because ye did eat of the loaves, and were filled" (John 6:26). The crowd followed Jesus to be fed, not to be made holy.

stalking-horse. Something used to hide a real purpose. Hunters used to hide behind horses to go after game. There are people who use religion only to promote themselves or their business.

Hamor and Shechem. The story is in Genesis 34. The sons of Jacob offered to let their sister marry the heathen prince if all the men would be circumcised. The men agreed, and while the men were healing, two of Jacob's sons, Simeon and Levi, killed them all. They used their religion as a cover-up for murder.

Pharisees. Luke 20:46-47.

Judas. He was treasurer of the disciple band and kept the bag of money (John 12:6). He was in the habit of taking money out of the bag for himself. Of course, he also sold Christ for thirty pieces of silver. See John 6:70-71 and 17:12. "Perdition" means "destruction, waste, ruin."

122

was religious for the bag, that he might be possessed of what was therein; but he was lost, cast away, and the very son of perdition.

4. Simon the witch was of this religion too; for he would have had the Holy Ghost, that he might have got money therewith; and his sentence from Peter's mouth was according.

5. Neither will it out of my mind, but that man that takes up religion for the world will throw away religion for the world; for so surely as Judas designed the world in becoming religious, so surely did he also sell religion and his Master for the same. To answer the question therefore affirmatively, as I perceive you have done, and to accept of as authentic such answer, is both heathenish, hypocritical, and devilish; and your reward will be according to your works. Then they stood staring one upon another, but had not wherewith to answer Christian. Hopeful also approved of the soundness of Christian's answer; so there was a great silence among them. Mr. By-ends and his company also staggered and kept behind, that Christian and Hopeful might outgo them. Then said Christian to his fellow, If these men cannot stand before the sentence of men, what will they do with the sentence of God? And if they are mute when dealt with by vessels of clay, what will they do when they shall be rebuked by the flames of a devouring fire?

Then Christian and Hopeful outwent them again, and went till they came at a delicate plain called Ease, where they went with much content; but that plain was but narrow, so they were quickly got over it. Now at the further side of that plain was a little hill called Lucre, and in that hill a silver mine, which some of them that had formerly gone that way, because of the rarity of it, had turned aside to see; but going too near the brink of the pit, the ground being deceitful under them broke, and they were slain; some also had been maimed there, and could

Simon the witch. The reference is to Acts 8:1-24. Originally the term "witch" referred to any person who dabbled in the occult. There were he-witches and she-witches. The term *simony* comes from this event, the offering of money to buy religious power and position.

designed. Some texts read "resigned," which makes good sense.

great silence. The silence of spiritual conviction. "That every mouth may be stopped, and all the world may become guilty before God" (Romans 3:19).

devouring fire. "For our God is a consuming fire" (Hebrews 12:29). See also Exodus 24:17.

Ease. God balances the difficulties with delights. But note that the plain was narrow. The Puritans did not approve of too much ease!

Lucre. From the Latin meaning "wealth, profit." Samuel's sons "turned aside after lucre" (1 Samuel 8:3). Church officers were to avoid "filthy lucre" (1 Timothy 3:3, 8). False teachers go after filthy lucre (Titus 1:11). Pastors should serve the Lord willingly, not for money (1 Peter 5:2). The Puritans believed in honest pay for honest toil, but they did not encourage the love of money, which is "the root of all evil" (1 Timothy 6:10).

deceitful. "The deceitfulness of riches" (Matthew 13:22).

not to their dying day be their own men again.

Then I saw in my dream that a little off the road, over against the silver mine, stood Demas (gentleman-like) to call to passengers to come and see; who said to Christian and his fellow, Ho! turn aside hither, and I will show you a thing.

CHR. What thing so deserving as to turn us out of the way?

DEMAS. Here is a silver mine, and some digging in it for treasure. If you will come, with a little pains you may richly provide for yourselves.

HOPE. Then said Hopeful, Let us go see.

CHR. Not I, said Christian, I have heard of this place before now; and how many have been slain; and besides that, treasure is a snare to those that seek it; for it hindereth them in their pilgrimage. Then Christian called to Demas, saying, Is not the place dangerous? Hath it not hindered many in their pilgrimage?

DEMAS. Not very dangerous, except to those that are careless (but withal, he blushed as he spake).

CHR. Then said Christian to Hopeful, Let us not stir a step, but still keep on our way.

HOPE. I will warrant you, when By-ends comes up, if he hath the same invitation as we, he will turn in thither to see.

CHR. No doubt thereof, for his principles lead him that way, and a hundred to one but he dies there.

DEMAS. Then Demas called again, saying, But will you not come over and see?

CHR. Then Christian roundly answered, saying, Demas, thou art an enemy to the right ways of the Lord of this way, and hast been already condemned for thine own turning aside by one of His Majesty's judges; and why seekest thou to bring us into the like condemnation? Besides, if we at all turn aside, our Lord the King will certainly hear thereof, and will there put us to

---

Demas. At one time, Demas had been Paul's fellow worker (Philemon 24); but he left Paul, "having loved this present world" (2 Timothy 4:10). He stands for all who abandon their faith to get rich.

little pains. The danger of getting rich quick! "He that maketh haste to be rich shall not be innocent" (Proverbs 28:20). "He that hasteth to be rich hath an evil eye" (Proverbs 28:22).

snare. "But they that will be rich fall into temptation and a snare, and into many foolish and hurtful lusts" (1 Timothy 6:9).

hindered. Covetousness is idolatry (Colossians 3:5). Bunyan here refers to Israel's backsliding (Hosea 4:16-19 and 14:8) because of her idolatry.

roundly answered. Reproved, rebuked.

enemy. Paul's rebuke to Elymas, the sorcerer (Acts 13:10).

judges. Paul condemns Demas in 2 Timothy 4:10.

shame, where we would stand with boldness before him.

Demas cried again that he also was one of their fraternity; and that if they would tarry a little, he also himself would walk with them.

CHR. Then said Christian, What is thy name? Is it not the same by the which I have called thee?

DEMAS. Yes, my name is Demas; I am the son of Abraham.

CHR. I know you; Gehazi was your great-grandfather, and Judas your father; and you have trod their steps. It is but a devilish prank that thou usest; thy father was hanged for a traitor, and thou deservest no better reward. Assure thyself that when we come to the King, we will do him word of this thy behaviour. Thus they went their way.

By this time By-ends and his companions were come again within sight, and they at the first beck went over to Demas. Now whether they fell into the pit by looking over the brink thereof, or whether they went down to dig, or whether they were smothered in the bottom by the damps that commonly arise, of these things I am not certain; but this I observed, that they never were seen again in the way. Then sang Christian,

> By-ends and silver Demas both agree;
> One calls, the other runs, that he may be
> A sharer in his lucre; so these do
> Take up in this world, and no further go.

Now I saw that, just on the other side of this plain, the pilgrims came to a place where stood an old monument, hard by the highway side, at the sight of which they were both concerned, because of the strangeness of the form thereof; for it seemed to them as if it had been a woman transformed into the shape of a pillar; here therefore they stood looking and looking upon it, but could not for a time tell what they should

Gehazi. He was the prophet Elisha's servant (2 Kings 4-5). He lied to Naaman, whom Elisha had healed, and took some wealth from him against Elisha's will. He was judged by God for this sin.

Judas. The disciple who turned traitor and sold Christ (Matthew 26:14-15 and 27:3-5).

monument. Lot's wife disobeyed God, turned back toward Sodom, and became a pillar of salt (Genesis 19:26). "Remember Lot's wife" (Luke 17:32).

make thereof. At last Hopeful espied written above upon the head thereof, a writing in an unusual hand; but he being no scholar, called to Christian (for he was learned) to see if he could pick out the meaning; so he came, and after a little laying of letters together, he found the same to be this, "Remember Lot's wife." So he read it to his fellow; after which they both concluded that this was the pillar of salt into which Lot's wife was turned, for her looking back with a covetous heart, when she was going from Sodom for safety. Which sudden and amazing sight gave them occasion of this discourse.

CHR. Ah, my brother! this is a seasonable sight; it came opportunely to us after the invitation which Demas gave us to come over to view the Hill Lucre; and had we gone over as he desired us, and as thou wast inclining to do, my brother, we had, for aught I know, been made ourselves like this woman, a spectacle for those that shall come after to behold.

HOPE. I am sorry that I was so foolish, and am made to wonder that I am not now as Lot's wife; for wherein was the difference betwixt her sin and mine? She only looked back; and I had a desire to go see. Let grace be adored, and let me be ashamed that ever such a thing should be in mine heart.

CHR. Let us take notice of what we see here for our help for time to come. This woman escaped one judgment, for she fell not by the destruction of Sodom; yet she was destroyed by another; as we see, she is turned into a pillar of salt.

HOPE. True; and she may be to us both caution and example; caution, that we should shun her sin; or a sign of what judgment will overtake such as shall not be prevented by this caution; so Korah, Dathan, and Abiram, with the two hundred and fifty men that perished in their sin, did also become a sign or example to others to beware. But above all, I muse at one thing, to

Korah. A Jewish man who led a revolt against Moses (Numbers 16). Dathan and Abiram assisted him and were also

126

wit, how Demas and his fellows can stand so confidently yonder to look for that treasure, which this woman, but for looking behind her after (for we read not that she stepped one foot out of the way), was turned into a pillar of salt; especially since the judgment which overtook her did make her an example within sight of where they are; for they cannot choose but see her, did they but lift up their eyes.

CHR. It is a thing to be wondered at, and it argueth that their hearts are grown desperate in the case; and I cannot tell who to compare them to so fitly, as to them that pick pockets in the presence of the judge, or that will cut purses under the gallows. It is said of the men of Sodom "that they were sinners exceedingly," because they were sinners "before the Lord," that is, in his eyesight, and notwithstanding the kindnesses that he had showed them; for the land of Sodom was now like the garden of Eden heretofore. This therefore provoked him the more to jealousy, and made their plague as hot as the fire of the Lord out of heaven could make it. And it is most rationally to be concluded that such, even such as these are, that shall sin in the sight, yea, and that too in despite of such examples that are set continually before them, to caution them to the contrary, must be partakers of severest judgments.

HOPE. Doubtless thou hast said the truth; but what a mercy is it that neither thou, but especially I, am not made myself this example. This ministereth occasion to us to thank God, to fear before him, and always to remember Lot's wife.

I saw then that they went on their way to a pleasant river; which David the king called "the river of God," but John, "the river of the water of life." Now their way lay just upon the bank of the river; here therefore Christian and his companion walked with great delight; they drank also of the water of the river, which was pleasant and enlivening to their weary spirits:

judged (Numbers 26:9-10). The earth opened and swallowed them up.

cut purses. Many people kept their purses hanging on a belt, and thieves would cut the purses and steal them or empty the contents. It was the usual thing for thieves to pick pockets and steal purses in the huge crowds that attended executions. The fear of being caught themselves and hanged did not stop them.

Sodom. Genesis 13:10, 13. Men may not consider us sinners, but it is before God that we are judged.

river. Another brief period of rest and refreshment. "There is a river, the streams whereof shall make glad the city of God" (Psalm 46:4). "And he shewed me a pure river of water of life, clear as crystal" (Revelation 22:1). Jesus offers the living water to all who will come and drink (John 7:37-39). See also Psalm 65:9 and Ezekiel 47.

leaves. A reference to the tree of life in heaven (Revelation 22:2).

surfeits. Overindulgences, and illness from overindulgence.

meadow. The green pastures of Psalm 23:2. "And the firstborn of the poor shall feed, and the needy shall lie down in safety" (Isaiah 14:30).

besides, on the banks of this river, on either side, were green trees that bore all manner of fruit; and the leaves of the trees were good for medicine; with the fruit of these trees they were also much delighted; and the leaves they ate to prevent surfeits and other diseases that are incident to those that heat their blood by travels. On either side of the river was also a meadow, curiously beautified with lilies, and it was green all the year long. In this meadow they lay down and slept; for here they might lie down safely. When they awoke, they gathered again of the fruit of the trees, and drank again of the water of the river, and then lay down again to sleep. Thus they did several days and nights. Then they sang,

> Behold ye how these crystal streams do glide
> (To comfort pilgrims) by the highway side;
> The meadows green,
>   besides their fragrant smell,
> Yield dainties for them: and he that can tell
> What pleasant fruit, yea, leaves,
>   these trees do yield,
> Will soon sell all, that he may buy this field.

sell all. An allusion to Matthew 13:44.

So when they were disposed to go on (for they were not, as yet, at their journey's end), they ate and drank, and departed.

Now I beheld in my dream that they had not journeyed far, but the river and the way for a time parted; at which they were not a little sorry; yet they durst not go out of the way. Now the way from the river was rough, and their feet tender by reason of their travels; "so the souls of the pilgrims were much discouraged because of the way." Wherefore still as they went on, they wished for better way. Now a little before them, there was on the left hand of the road a meadow, and a stile to go over into it; and that meadow is called By-path Meadow. Then said Christian to his fellow, If this meadow lieth along by our wayside, let's go over into it. Then he went to the stile to see, and, behold, a path lay along by

souls. A description of the feelings of Israelites when they were wandering in the wilderness (Numbers 21:4). Like Israel, the two pilgrims got into trouble because they wanted a better way and did not submit to God's will.

left hand. "Let thine eyes look right on . . . Turn not to the right hand nor to the left" (Proverbs 4:25-27). They had been warned about detours.

the way on the other side of the fence. 'Tis according to my wish, said Christian. Here is the easiest going; come, good Hopeful, and let us go over.

HOPE. But how if this path should lead us out of the way?

CHR. That's not like, said the other. Look, doth it not go along by the wayside? So Hopeful, being persuaded by his fellow, went after him over the stile. When they were gone over and were got into the path, they found it very easy for their feet; and withal, they looking before them, espied a man walking as they did (and his name was Vain-confidence); so they called after him and asked him whither that way led. He said, To the Celestial Gate. Look, said Christian, did not I tell you so? By this you may see we are right. So they followed, and he went before them. But behold, the night came on and it grew very dark; so that they that were behind lost the sight of him that went before.

> The pilgrims now, to gratify the flesh,
> Will seek its ease; but oh! how they afresh
> Do thereby plunge themselves new grief into!
> Who seek to please the flesh, themselves undo.

He therefore that went before (Vain-confidence by name), not seeing the way before him, fell into a deep pit which was on purpose there made by the Prince of those grounds, to catch vain-glorious fools withal, and was dashed in pieces with his fall.

Now Christian and his fellow heard him fall. So they called to know the matter, but there was none to answer, only they heard a groaning. Then said Hopeful, Where are we now? Then was his fellow silent, as mistrusting that he had led him out of the way; and now it began to rain, and thunder, and lighten in a very dreadful manner, and the water rose amain.

Then Hopeful groaned in himself, saying, Oh, that I had kept on my way!

easiest. This had been the philosophy of By-ends! Take the easiest way! The pilgrims were walking by sight, not by faith (Romans 14:23).

That's not like. . . . "That's not likely." Christian is overconfident and leads himself and his brother astray. Bunyan adds a note: "Strong Christians may lead weak ones out of the way." Even Peter went astray and led Barnabas into sin (Galatians 2:11-21).

Vain-confidence. "It is better to trust in the LORD than to put confidence in man" (Psalm 118:8).

pit. "For the leaders of this people cause them to err; and they that are led of them are destroyed" (Isaiah 9:16). See also Proverbs 14:12.

CHR. Who could have thought that this path should have led us out of the way?

HOPE. I was afraid on it at very first, and therefore gave you that gentle caution. I would have spoke plainer, but that you are older than I.

CHR. Good brother, be not offended; I am sorry I have brought thee out of the way, and that I have put thee into such imminent danger; pray, my brother, forgive me; I did not do it of an evil intent.

HOPE. Be comforted, my brother, for I forgive thee; and believe too that this shall be for our good.

good. "And we know that all things work together for good to them that love God, to them who are the called according to his purpose" (Romans 8:28). This is not an excuse for sin, but it is an encouragement in difficulty.

CHR. I am glad I have with me a merciful brother; but we must not stand thus: let's try to go back again.

HOPE. But good brother, let me go before.

CHR. No, if you please, let me go first, that if there be any danger, I may be first therein, because by my means we are both gone out of the way.

HOPE. No, said Hopeful, you shall not go first; for your mind being troubled may lead you out of the way again. Then for their encouragement they heard the voice of one saying, "Let thine heart be towards the highway, even the way that thou wentest, turn again." But by this time the waters were greatly risen, by reason of which the way of going back was very dangerous. (Then I thought that it is easier going out of the way when we are in, than going in when we are out.) Yet they adventured to go back, but it was so dark, and the flood was so high, that in their going back they had like to have been drowned nine or ten times.

Let thine heart . . . . Quoted from Jeremiah 31:21.

Neither could they, with all the skill they had, get again to the stile that night. Wherefore, at last, lighting under a little shelter, they sat down there till the day break; but, being weary, they fell asleep. Now there was, not far from the place where they lay, a castle called Doubting

130

Castle, the owner thereof was Giant Despair; and it was in his grounds they now were sleeping: wherefore he, getting up in the morning early, and walking up and down in his fields, caught Christian and Hopeful asleep in his grounds. Then with a grim and surly voice he bid them awake, and asked them whence they were and what they did in his grounds. They told him they were pilgrims and that they had lost their way. Then said the giant, You have this night trespassed on me by trampling in and lying on my grounds, and therefore you must go along with me. So they were forced to go, because he was stronger than they. They also had but little to say for they knew themselves in a fault. The giant therefore drove them before him and put them into his castle, into a very dark dungeon, nasty and stinking to the spirits of these two men. Here then they lay from Wednesday morning till Saturday night, without one bit of bread, or drop of drink, or light, or any to ask how they did; they were therefore here in evil case, and were far from friends and acquaintance. Now in this place Christian had double sorrow, because 'twas through his unadvised haste that they were brought into this distress.

Now Giant Despair had a wife, and her name was Diffidence. So when he was gone to bed, he told his wife what he had done; to wit, that he had taken a couple of prisoners and cast them into his dungeon for trespassing on his grounds. Then he asked her also what he had best to do further to them. So she asked him what they were, whence they came, and whither they were bound; and he told her. Then she counselled him that when he arose in the morning he should beat them without any mercy. So when he arose, he getteth him a grievous crab-tree cudgel, and goes down into the dungeon to them, and there first falls to rating of them as if they were dogs, although they never gave him a

Doubting Castle. Bunyan often had his doubts and times of despair when he was seeking the Lord and the assurance of salvation. He wrote in *Grace Abounding*: "I found it hard work now to pray to God, because despair was swallowing me up . . . ." Even experienced pilgrims like Christian and Hopeful can have times of doubt and despair. The apostle Paul "despaired even of life" (2 Corinthians 1:8).

morning. This event begins on Wednesday morning and ends on Sunday morning.

acquaintance. "Lover and friend hast thou put far from me, and mine acquaintance into darkness." (Psalm 88:18). Bunyan's own experiences in jail are certainly seen here.

Diffidence. Lack of confidence, mistrust. It is logical that Giant Despair be married to Diffidence, for distrust and despair go together. The wife does nothing to the pilgrims herself, but always tells her husband what to do. On Thursday he beat them, and on Friday he suggested that they commit suicide. Saturday he warned them that, within ten days, they would be dead.

rating. Berating, beating.

131

word of distaste. Then he falls upon them and beats them fearfully, in such sort that they were not able to help themselves, or to turn them upon the floor. This done, he withdraws and leaves them there to condole their misery and to mourn under their distress. So all that day they spent the time in nothing but sighs and bitter lamentations. The next night she, talking with her husband about them further, and understanding they were yet alive, did advise him to counsel them to make away themselves. So when morning was come, he goes to them in a surly manner as before, and perceiving them to be very sore with the stripes that he had given them the day before, he told them that since they were never like to come out of that place, their only way would be forthwith to <u>make an end</u> of themselves, either with knife, halter, or poison. For why, said he, should you choose life, seeing it is attended with so much bitterness? But they desired him to let them go. With that he looked ugly upon them, and rushing to them, had doubtless made an end of them himself, but that he fell into one of his fits (for he sometimes in <u>sunshiny weather</u> fell into fits), and lost for a time the use of his hand; wherefore he withdrew, and left them as before to consider what to do. Then did the prisoners consult between themselves, whether 'twas best to take his counsel or no; and thus they began to discourse:

CHR. Brother, said Christian, what shall we do? The life that we now live is miserable. For my part I know not whether it is best to live thus, or to die out of hand. "<u>My soul</u> chooseth strangling rather than life," and the grave is more easy for me than this dungeon. Shall we be ruled by the giant?

HOPE. Indeed our present condition is dreadful, and death would be far more welcome to me than thus for ever to abide; but yet let us consider, the Lord of the country to which we are

make an end. Job's wife counseled him to commit suicide (Job 2:9-10) just as the giant's wife did the two prisoners. It is worth noting that John Donne's treatise on suicide was published in 1646, and in it he stated that there were times when suicide was the right course to take.

sunshiny weather. Doubt thrives in darkness.

My soul. Quoted from Job 7:15. Christian is giving in to his feelings. It is Hopeful who has the encouragement.

132

going hath said, <u>Thou shalt</u> do no murder: no, not to another man's person; much more then are we forbidden to take his counsel to kill ourselves. Besides, he that kills another can but commit murder upon his body; but for one to kill himself is to kill body and soul at once. And moreover, my brother, thou talkest of ease in the grave; but hast thou forgotten the hell whither for certain the murderers go? For <u>"no murderer</u> hath eternal life," etc. And let us consider again that all the law is not in the hand of Giant Despair. Others, so far as I can understand, have been taken by him, as well as we; and yet have escaped out of his hand. Who knows but that God that made the world may cause that Giant Despair may die? or that at some time or other he may forget to lock us in? or but he may in short time have another of his fits before us, and may lose the use of his limbs? And if ever that should come to pass again, for my part, I am resolved to pluck up the heart of a man, and to try my utmost to get from under his hand. I was a fool that I did not try to do it before; but however, my brother, let's be <u>patient,</u> and endure a while. The time may come that may give us a happy release; but let us not be our own murderers. With these words Hopeful at present did moderate the mind of his brother; so they continued together (in the dark) that day, in their sad and doleful condition.

Well, towards evening the giant goes down into the dungeon again, to see if his prisoners had taken his counsel; but when he came there he found them alive; and truly, alive was all; for now, what for want of bread and water, and by reason of the wounds they received when he beat them, they could do little but breathe. But, I say, he found them alive; at which he fell into a grievous rage, and told them that, seeing they had disobeyed his counsel, it should be worse with them than if they had never been born.

At this they trembled greatly, and I think that

Thou shalt. Exodus 20:13.

no murderer. Quoted from 1 John 3:15.

patient. "And so, after he had patiently endured, he obtained the promise" (Hebrews 6:15). "My son, despise not thou the chastening of the Lord, nor faint when thou art rebuked of him" (Hebrews 12:5). Hopeful realized that they had got themselves into the situation, that the Lord was chastening them, and that all they could do was trust and be patient. He reminds his friend that God had seen him through all the other trials, and that He would see him through this one.

133

Christian fell into a swoon; but coming a little to himself again, they renewed their discourse about the giant's counsel; and whether yet they had best to take it or no. Now Christian again seemed to be for doing it, but Hopeful made his second reply as followeth:

HOPE. My brother, said he, rememberest thou not how valiant thou hast been heretofore? Apollyon could not crush thee, nor could all that thou didst hear, or see, or feel, in the Valley of the Shadow of Death. What hardship, terror, and amazement hast thou already gone through, and art thou now nothing but fear? Thou seest that I am in the dungeon with thee, a far weaker man by nature than thou art; also this giant has wounded me as well as thee, and hath also cut off the bread and water from my mouth; and with thee I mourn without the light. But let us exercise a little more patience; remember how thou playedst the man at Vanity Fair, and wast neither afraid of the chain, nor cage, nor yet of bloody death. Wherefore let us (at least to avoid the shame that becomes not a Christian to be found in) bear up with patience as well as we can.

Now night being come again, and the giant and his wife being in bed, she asked him concerning the prisoners, and if they had taken his counsel. To which he replied, They are sturdy rogues, they choose rather to bear all hardship, than to make away themselves. Then said she, Take them into the castle-yard to-morrow, and show them the bones and skulls of those that thou hast already dispatched, and make them believe, ere a week comes to an end, thou also wilt tear them in pieces, as thou hast done their fellows before them.

So when the morning was come, the giant goes to them again, and takes them into the castle-yard, and shows them, as his wife had bidden him. These, said he, were pilgrims as you are once, and they trespassed in my grounds, as you have done; and when I thought, fit, I tore them in pieces, and so within ten days I will do you. Go, get you down to your den again; and with that he beat them all the way thither. They lay therefore all day on Saturday in a lamentable case, as before. Now when night was come, and when Mrs. Diffidence and her husband the giant were got to bed, they began to renew their discourse of their prisoners; and withal the old giant wondered that he could neither by his blows nor his counsel bring them to an end. And with that his wife replied, I fear, said she, that they live in hope that some will come to relieve them, or that they have picklocks about them, by the means of which they hope to escape. And sayest thou so, my dear? said the giant; I will therefore search them in the morning.

Well, on Saturday about midnight they began to pray, and continued in prayer till almost break of day.

Now a little before it was day, good Christian, as one half amazed, brake out in this passionate speech: What a fool (quoth he) am I, thus to lie in a stinking dungeon, when I may as well walk with liberty! I have a key in my bosom called Promise, that will, I am persuaded, open any lock in Doubting Castle. Then said Hopeful, That is good news, good brother; pluck it out of thy bosom and try.

Then Christian pulled it out of his bosom, and began to try at the dungeon door, whose bolt (as he turned the key) gave back, and the door flew open with ease, and Christian and Hopeful both came out. Then he went to the outward door that leads into the castle-yard, and with his key opened that door also. After, he went to the iron gate, for that must be opened too; but that lock went damnable hard, yet the key did open it. Then they thrust open the gate to make their escape with speed, but that gate, as it opened, made such a creaking that it waked

ten days. "Behold the devil shall cast some of you into prison, that ye may be tried; and ye shall have tribulation ten days: be thou faithful unto death, and I will give thee a crown of life" (Revelation 2:10).

midnight. "And at midnight Paul and Silas prayed" (Acts 16:25). This dungeon experience is based on Peter's experience in Acts 12, and that of Paul and Silas in Acts 16.

day. It is now Sunday, the Lord's Day, when Jesus Christ broke the chains of death and came forth from the tomb in power and glory. The promises of God, when believed, open the prison doors. "I am he that liveth, and was dead; and, behold, I am alive for evermore, Amen; and have the keys of hell and of death" (Revelation 1:18).

iron gate. See Peter's prison deliverance, Acts 12:10.

Giant Despair, who, hastily rising to pursue his prisoners, felt his limbs to fail, for his fits took him again, so that he could by no means go after them. Then they went on and came to the King's highway, and so were safe because they were out of his jurisdiction.

Now when they were gone over the stile, they began to contrive with themselves what they should do at that stile to prevent those that should come after from falling into the hands of Giant Despair. So they consented to erect there a pillar, and to engrave upon the side thereof this sentence: "Over this stile is the way to Doubting Castle, which is kept by Giant Despair, who despiseth the King of the Celestial Country, and seeks to destroy his holy pilgrims." Many therefore that followed after, read what was written and escaped the danger. This done, they sang as follows:

> Out of the way we went, and then we found
> What 'twas to tread upon forbidden ground;
> And let them that come after have a care,
> Lest heedlessness makes them, as we, to fare.
> Lest they for trespassing his prisoners are,
>   Whose castle's Doubting and whose name's Despair.

Delectable Mountains. Again, suffering is balanced by rest and joy. Christian had seen these mountains from afar (page 71), and now he had actually arrived. The description is based on Ecclesiastes 2:4-6.

They went then till they came to the Delectable Mountains, which mountains belong to the Lord of that hill of which we have spoken before; so they went up to the mountains, to behold the gardens and orchards, the vineyards and fountains of water; where also they drank and washed themselves, and did freely eat of the vineyards. Now there were on the tops of these mountains shepherds feeding their flocks, and they stood by the highway side. The pilgrims therefore went to them, and leaning upon their staves (as is common with weary pilgrims, when they stand to talk with any by the way), they asked, Whose Delectable Mountains are these And whose be the sheep that feed upon them?

Mountains delectable they now ascend,
Where Shepherds be,
    which to them do commend
Alluring things, and things that cautious are,
Pilgrims are steady kept by faith and fear.

SHEP. These mountains are <u>Immanuel's Land,</u> and they are within sight of his city; and the <u>sheep</u> also are his, and he laid down his life for them.

CHR. Is this the way to the Celestial City?

SHEP. You are just in your way.

CHR. How far is it thither?

SHEP. Too far for any but those that shall get thither indeed.

CHR. Is the way safe or dangerous?

SHEP. Safe for those for whom it is to be safe; "but <u>transgressors</u> shall fall therein."

CHR. Is there in this place any relief for pilgrims that are weary and faint in the way?

SHEP. The Lord of these mountains hath given us a <u>charge,</u> "not to be forgetful to entertain strangers," therefore the good of the place is before you.

I saw also in my dream that when the Shepherds perceived that they were wayfaring men, they also put <u>questions</u> to them (to which they made answer as in other places), as, Whence came you? and, How got you into the way? and, By what means have you so persevered therein? For but <u>few</u> of them that begin to come hither do show their face on these mountains. But when the Shepherds heard their answers, being pleased therewith, they looked very <u>lovingly</u> upon them and said, Welcome to the Delectable Mountains.

The Shepherds, I say, whose <u>names</u> were Knowledge, Experience, Watchful, and Sincere, took them by the hand, and had them to their tents, and made them partake of that which was ready at present. They said, moreover, We would that ye should stay here awhile, to be ac-

Immanuel's Land. A name for Palestine (Isaiah 8:8). "Immanuel" means "God with us" (Matthew 1:23).

sheep. "I am the good shepherd: the good shepherd giveth his life for the sheep. . . . I lay down my life for the sheep" (John 10:11, 15).

transgressors. Hosea 14:9.

charge. Hebrews 13:2.

questions. Again, a time of examination and testimony. "Be ready always to give an answer to every man that asketh you a reason of the hope that is in you" (1 Peter 3:15).

few. "Many be called, but few chosen" (Matthew 20:16). Christian and Hopeful will reach the heavenly city, but many whom they meet on the way will not arrive. "Then said one unto him, Lord, are there few that be saved? And he said unto them, Strive to enter in at the strait gate: for many, I say unto you, will seek to enter in, and shall not be able" (Luke 13:23-24).

lovingly. "Then Jesus beholding him loved him" (Mark 10:21).

names. These men represent pastors (the word "pastor" means "shepherd"); their names describe the characteristics of a spiritual pastor. Bunyan himself served as a pastor.

quainted with us; and yet more to solace yourselves with the good of these Delectable Mountains. They then told them that they were content to stay; so they went to rest that night, because it was very late.

Then I saw in my dream that in the morning
the Shepherd called up Christian and Hopeful
to walk with them upon the mountains; so they
went forth with them and walked a while, having a pleasant prospect on every side. Then said
the Shepherds one to another, Shall we show
these pilgrims some wonders? So when they had
concluded to do it, they had them first to the top

hill. Another hill! "Error" refers to doctrinal error.

of a <u>hill</u> called Error, which was very steep on
the furthest side, and bid them look down to the
bottom. So Christian and Hopeful looked down,
and saw at the bottom several men dashed all to
pieces by a fall that they had from the top. Then
said Christian, What meaneth this? The
Shepherds answered, Have you not heard of
them that were made to err, by hearkening to

Hymenaeus and Philetus. Two
heretics in Paul's day who erred
from the truth (2 Timothy
2:17-18).

<u>Hymeneus and Philetus,</u> as concerning the faith
of the resurrection of the body? They answered,
Yes. Then said the Shepherds, Those that you
see lie dashed in pieces at the bottom of this
mountain are they; and they have continued to
this day unburied, as you see, for an example to
others to take heed how they clamber too high,
or how they come too near the brink of this
mountain.

Then I saw that they had them to the top of

Caution. A vantage point to see
where they had been and what
could have happened to them
had they not escaped Doubting
Castle. It is good to look back
and learn, and be warned for
the future.

another mountain, and the name of that is <u>Cau-
tion,</u> and bid them look afar off; which when
they did, they perceived, as they thought, several men walking up and down among the
tombs that were there; and they perceived that
the men were blind, because they stumbled
sometimes upon the tombs, and because they
could not get out from among them. Then said
Christian, What means this?

The Shepherds then answered, Did you not
see a little below these mountains a stile, that led

into a meadow, on the left hand of this way? They answered, Yes. Then said the Shepherds, From that stile there goes a path that leads directly to Doubting Castle, which is kept by Giant Despair, and these men (pointing to them among the tombs) came once on pilgrimage, as you do now, even till they came to that same stile; and because the right way was rough in that place, they chose to go out of it into that meadow, and there were taken by Giant Despair, and cast into Doubting Castle; where, after they had been a while kept in the dungeon, he at last did put out their eyes, and led them among those tombs, where he has left them to wander to this very day, that the saying of the wise man might be <u>fulfilled,</u> "He that wandereth out of the way of understanding shall remain in the congregation of the dead." Then Christian and Hopeful looked upon one another with tears gushing out, but yet said nothing to the Shepherds.

Then I saw in my dream that the Shepherds had them to another place, in a bottom, where was a door in the side of a hill, and they opened the door and bid them look in. They looked in therefore and saw that within, it was very dark and smoky; they also thought that they heard there a rumbling noise as of fire, and a cry of some tormented, and that they smelt the scent of brimstone. Then said Christian, What means this? The Shepherds told them, This is a <u>byway</u> to hell, a way that hypocrites go in at; namely, such as sell their birthright, with <u>Esau;</u> such as sell their master, with Judas; such as blaspheme the gospel, with <u>Alexander;</u> and that lie and dissemble, with <u>Ananias</u> and Sapphira his wife. Then said Hopeful to the Shepherds, I perceive that these had on them even every one, a show of pilgrimage, as we have now; had they not?

SHEP. Yes, and held it a long time too.

HOPE. How far might they go on pilgrimage in their day, since they notwithstanding were

fulfilled. Proverbs 21:16.

byway. And this is not the first one! Christian saw "the mouth of hell" by the wayside when he went through the Valley of the Shadow of Death (page 79). He will discover a way to hell even at the gate of heaven!

Esau. He sold his birthright for a single meal of pottage (Genesis 25:29-34 and Hebrews 12:16). In Bunyan's day, Christians who opposed the state church called the prayer book "pottage." People who compromised with the state religion were compared with Esau, who sold the spiritual that he might gain the material.

Alexander. "Of whom is Hymenaeus and Alexander; whom I have delivered unto Satan, that they may learn not to blaspheme" (1 Timothy 1:20).

Ananias. He and his wife, Sapphira, lied about their gift to God and were slain for their hypocrisy (Acts 5:1-11).

thus miserably cast away?

SHEP. Some further, and some not so far as these mountains.

Then said the pilgrims one to another, We had need cry to the Strong for strength.

SHEP. Ay, and you will have need to use it when you have it too.

By this time the pilgrims had a desire to go forward, and the Shepherds a desire they should; so they walked together towards the end of the mountains. Then said the Shepherds one to another, Let us here show to the pilgrims the gates of the Celestial City, if they have skill to look through our perspective glass. The pilgrims then lovingly accepted the motion; so they had them to the top of a high hill called Clear, and gave them their glass to look.

Then they essayed to look, but the remembrance of that last thing that the Shepherds had shown them made their hands shake; by means of which impediment they could not look steadily through the glass; yet they thought they saw something like the gate, and also some of the glory of the place. Then they went away and sang this song:

> Thus by the Shepherds secrets are revealed,
> Which from all other men are kept concealed.
> Come to the Shepherds then, if you would see
> Things deep, things hid,
>   and that mysterious be.

When they were about to depart, one of the Shepherds gave them a note of the way. Another of them bid them beware of the Flatterer. The third bid them take heed that they sleep not upon the Enchanted Ground. And the fourth bid them God-speed. So I awoke from my dream.

And I slept, and dreamed again, and saw the same two pilgrims going down the mountains along the highway towards the city. Now a little below these mountains, on the left hand, lieth the country of Conceit; from which country

perspective glass. Telescope.

hill. Still another hill. From this one Christian and Hopeful could see something of the heavenly city. It is the infirmity of our own nature that keeps us from seeing as we should see.

note. Map.

So I awoke. . . . And I slept. . . . These sentences really add nothing to the story. Bunyan scholars think that they represent the author's release from jail, and then his subsequent completing of the book begun in jail. Or perhaps Bunyan does not want his readers to think that he sleeps too long! The Puritans opposed laziness.

Conceit. As we make spiritual progress, we are in danger of getting conceited. Paul joins "ignorance" and "conceit" in Romans 11:25. See also Proverbs 26:12 and Romans 12:16.

140

there comes into the way in which the pilgrims walked, a little crooked lane. Here therefore they met with a very brisk lad that came out of that country; and his name was Ignorance. So Christian asked him from what parts he came and whither he was going.

IGNOR. Sir, I was born in the country that lieth off there a little on the left hand, and I am going to the Celestial City.

CHR. But how do you think to get in at the gate? for you may find some difficulty there.

IGNOR. As other good people do, said he.

CHR. But what have you to show the gate, that may cause that the gate should be opened to you?

IGNOR. I know my Lord's will, and I have been a good liver; I pay every man his own; I pray, fast, pay tithes, and give alms, and have left my country for whither I am going.

I pray. See Luke 18:9-14.

CHR. But thou camest not in at the wicket-gate that is at the head of this way; thou camest in hither through that same crooked lane, and therefore I fear, however thou mayest think of thyself, when the reckoning day shall come, thou wilt have laid to thy charge that thou art a thief and a robber, instead of getting admittance into the city.

thief. "He that entereth not by the door into the sheepfold, but climbeth up some other way, the same is a thief and a robber" (John 10:1).

IGNOR. Gentlemen, ye be utter strangers to me, I know you not; be content to follow the religion of your country, and I will follow the religion of mine. I hope all will be well. And as for the gate that you talk of, all the world knows that that is a great way off of our country. I cannot think of any man in all our parts doth so much as know the way to it, nor need they matter whether they do or no, since we have, as you see, a fine pleasant green lane that comes down from our country, the next way into the way.

When Christian saw that the man was "wise in his own conceit," he said to Hopeful whisperingly, "There is more hope of a fool than of him." And said, moreover, "When he that is a

wise. Proverbs 26:5.
There is . . . . Proverbs 26:12.
When he . . . . Ecclesiastes 10:3.

141

fool walketh by the way, his wisdom faileth him, and he said to every one that he is a fool."

What, shall we talk further with him, or out-go him at present, and so leave him to think of what he hath heard already, and then stop again for him afterwards, and see if by degrees we can do any good to him? Then said Hopeful,

Let Ignorance a little while now muse
On what is said, and let him not refuse
Good counsel to embrace, lest he remain
Still ignorant of what's the chiefest gain.
God saith, those that no understanding have
Although he made them, them he will not save.

HOPE. He further added, It is not good, I think, to say all to him at once; let us pass him by, if you will, and talk to him anon, even as he is able to bear it.

So they both went on, and Ignorance he came after. Now when they had passed him a little way, they entered into a very dark lane, where they met a man whom seven devils had bound with seven strong cords, and were carrying of him back to the door that they saw on the side of the hill. Now good Christian began to tremble, and so did Hopeful his companion; yet as the devils led away the man, Christian looked to see if he knew him; and he thought it might be one Turn-away, that dwelt in the town of Apostasy. But he did not perfectly see his face, for he did hang his head like a thief that is found. But once past, Hopeful looked after him, and espied on his back a paper with this inscription, "Wanton professor and damnable apostate." Then said Christian to his fellow, Now I call to remembrance that which was told me of a thing that happened to a good man hereabout. The name of the man was Little-faith, but a good man, and he dwelt in the town of Sincere. The thing was this: At the entering in at this passage, there comes down from Broad-way Gate a lane called Dead Man's Lane; so called because of

able to bear it. "I have yet many things to say unto you, but ye cannot bear them now" (John 16:12). See also 1 Corinthians 3:2.

seven devils. An allusion to Matthew 12:45, and to Proverbs 5:22 — "His own iniquities shall take the wicked himself, and he shall be holden with the cords of his sins."

Apostasy. This is the sin of openly turning away from the faith once professed. "See that ye refuse not him that speaketh. For if they escaped not who refused him that spake on earth, much more shall not we escape, if we turn away from him that speaketh from heaven" (Hebrews 12:25). This is the origin of the name "Turn-away." Bunyan does not think that Turn-away is a true Christian, for he calls him "Wanton professor"—that is, one who professes faith but does not possess it.

Little-faith. This was one of our Lord's favorite names for His disciples. See Matthew 8:26; 14:31; 16:8. Bunyan seems to contrast Little-faith with Turn-away. Even though Little-faith suffered and was robbed, he did not lose his certificate that gave him entrance into heaven. God honors even a little faith. Not all Christians are great victors!

the murders that are commonly done there; and this Little-faith going on pilgrimage, as we do now, chanced to sit down there, and slept. Now there happened at that time to come down the lane from Broad-way Gate, three sturdy rogues, and their names were Faint-heart, Mistrust, and Guilt (three brothers), and they espying Little-faith where he was, came galloping up with speed. Now the good man was just awake from his sleep, and was getting up to go on his journey. So they came up all to him, and with threatening language bid him stand. At this Little-faith looked as white as a <u>clout</u>, and had neither power to fight nor fly. Then said Faint-heart, Deliver thy purse. But he making no haste to do it (for he was loath to lose his money), Mistrust ran up to him, and thrusting his hand into his pocket, pulled out thence a bag of silver. Then he cried out, Thieves! Thieves! With that, Guilt with a great club that was in his hand struck Little-faith on the head, and with that blow felled him flat to the ground, where he lay bleeding as one that would bleed to death. All this while the thieves stood by. But at last, they hearing that some were upon the road, and fearing lest it should be one Great-grace that dwells in the city of Good-confidence, they betook themselves to their heels, and left this good man to shift for himself. Now after a while, Little-faith came to himself, and getting up, made shift to <u>scrabble</u> on his way. This was the story.

clout. "White as a sheet." A "clout" is a white cloth used in an archery frame.

scrabble. To stumble along, to struggle.

HOPE. But did they take from him all that ever he had?

CHR. No; the place where his jewels were they never ransacked, so those he kept still. But as I was told, the good man was much afflicted for his loss, for the thieves got most of his spending-money. That which they got not (as I said) were jewels, also he had a little odd money left, but <u>scarce enough</u> to bring him to his journey's end; nay, if I was not misinformed, he was

scarce enough. "And if the righteous scarcely be saved, where shall the ungodly and the sinner appear?" (1 Peter 4:18).

forced to beg as he went, to keep himself alive; for his jewels he might not sell. But, beg and do what he could, he went (as we say) with many a hungry belly the most part of the rest of the way.

HOPE. But is it not a wonder they got not from him his certificate, by which he was to receive his admittance at the Celestial Gate?

CHR. 'Tis a wonder, but they got not that; though they missed it not through any good cunning of his; for he, being dismayed with their coming upon him, had neither power nor skill to hide anything; so 'twas more by good Providence than by his endeavour, that they missed of that <u>good thing</u>.

good thing. "That good thing which was committed unto thee keep by the Holy Ghost which dwelleth in us" (2 Timothy 1:14). "The Lord knoweth how to deliver the godly out of temptations, and to reserve the unjust unto the day of judgment to be punished" (2 Peter 2:9).

HOPE. But it must needs be a comfort to him that they got not his jewels from him.

CHR. It might have been great comfort to him, had he used it as he should; but they that told me the story said that he made but little use of it all the rest of the way, and that because of the dismay that he had in their taking away his money; indeed he forgot it a great part of the rest of his journey; and besides, when at any time it came into his mind, and he began to be comforted therewith, then would fresh thoughts of his loss come again upon him, and those thoughts would swallow up all.

HOPE. Alas, poor man! This could not but be a great grief to him.

CHR. Grief! ay, a grief indeed! Would it not have been so to any of us, had we been used as he, to be robbed, and wounded too, and that in a strange place, as he was? It is a wonder he did not die with grief, poor heart! I was told that he scattered almost all the rest of the way with nothing but doleful and bitter complaints; telling also to all that overtook him, or that he overtook in the way as he went, where he was robbed, and how; who they were that did it, and what he lost; how he was wounded, and that he hardly escaped with his life.

144

HOPE. But 'tis a wonder that his necessity did not put him upon selling or pawning some of his jewels, that he might have wherewith to relieve himself in his journey.

CHR. Thou talkest like one upon whose <u>head is the shell</u> to this very day; for what should he pawn them, or to whom should he sell them? In all that country where he was robbed his jewels were not accounted of; nor did he want that relief which could from thence be administered to him. Besides, had his jewels been missing at the gate of the Celestial City, he had (and that he knew well enough) been excluded from an inheritance there; and that would have been worse to him than the appearance and villainy of ten thousand thieves.

HOPE. Why art thou so tart, my brother? Esau sold his birthright, and that for a mess of <u>pottage,</u> and that birthright was his greatest jewel; and if he, why might not Little-faith do so too?

CHR. Esau did sell his birthright indeed, and so do many besides, and by so doing exclude themselves from the chief blessing, as also that <u>caitiff</u> did; but you must put a difference betwixt Esau and Little-faith, and also betwixt their estates. Esau's birthright was typical, but Little-faith's jewels were not so; Esau's belly was his god, but Little-faith's belly was not so; Esau's want lay in his fleshly appetite, Little-faith's did not so. Besides, Esau could see no further than to the fulfilling of his lusts; "<u>For I am</u> at the point to die (said he), and what good will this birthright do me?" But Little-faith, though it was his lot to have but a little faith, was by his little faith kept from such extravagancies, and made to see and prize his jewels more than to sell them, as Esau did his birthright. You read not anywhere that Esau had faith, no, not so much as a little; therefore no marvel if, where the flesh only bears sway (as it will in that man where no faith is to resist), if he sells his birth-

head is the shell. Like a baby bird just out of the shell. This was certainly an unkind statement on the part of Christian and it almost made Hopeful angry. Can you blame him?

pottage. Hebrews 12:16.

caitiff. A base, vile coward. Christian explains the difference between an unbeliever, like Esau, and Little-faith, who stayed true to the Lord.

For I am . . . . Quoted from Genesis 25:32.

145

her occasions. The reference is to Jeremiah 2:24, describing the wild ass in her time of heat. Esau acted like an animal, not a man.

right, and his soul and all, that to the devil of hell; for it is with such, as it is with the ass, who in <u>her occasions</u> cannot be turned away. When their minds are set upon their lusts, they will have them whatever they cost. But Little-faith was of another temper, his mind was on things divine; his livelihood was upon things that were spiritual, and from above; therefore to what end should he that is of such a temper sell his jewels (had there been any that would have bought them) to fill his mind with empty things? Will a man give a penny to fill his belly with hay; or can you persuade the turtle-dove to live upon the carrion like the crow? Though faithless ones can, for carnal lusts, pawn, or mortgage, or sell what they have, and themselves outright to boot; yet they that have faith, saving faith, though but a little of it, cannot do so. Here therefore, my brother, is thy mistake.

HOPE. I acknowledge it; but yet your severe reflection had almost made me angry.

CHR. Why, I did but compare thee to some of the birds that are of the brisker sort, who will run to and fro in untrodden paths with the shell upon their heads; but pass by that, and consider the matter under debate, and all shall be well bewixt thee and me.

HOPE. But Christian, these three fellows, I am persuaded in my heart, are but a company of cowards; would they have run else, think you, as they did, at the noise of one that was coming on the road? Why did not Little-faith pluck up a greater heart? He might, methinks, have stood one brush with them, and have yielded when there had been no remedy.

CHR. That they are cowards, many have said, but few have found it so in the time of trial. As for a great heart, Little-faith had none; and I perceive by thee, my brother, hadst thou been the man concerned, thou art but for a brush and then to yield. And verily, since this is the height of thy stomach, now they are at a distance

146

from us, should they appear to thee as they did to him, they might put thee to second thoughts.

But consider again, they are but journeymen thieves, they serve under the <u>king</u> of the bottomless pit, who, if need be, will come to their aid himself, and his voice is as the roaring of a <u>lion</u>. I myself have been engaged as this Little-faith was, and I found it a terrible thing. These three villains set upon me, and I beginning like a Christian to resist, they gave but a call, and in came their master. I would, as the saying is, have given my life for a penny; but that, as God would have it, I was clothed with armour of proof. Ay, and yet, though I was so harnessed, I found it hard work to quit myself like a man. No man can tell what in that combat attends us, but he that hath been in the battle himself.

HOPE. Well, but they ran, you see, when they did but suppose that one <u>Great-grace</u> was in the way.

CHR. True, they have often fled, both they and their master, when Great-grace hath but appeared; and no marvel, for he is the King's <u>champion</u>. But I trow, you will put some difference between Little-faith and the King's champion. All the King's subjects are not his champions, nor can they, when tried, do such feats of war as he. Is it meet to think that a little child should handle Goliath as David did? Or that there should be the strength of an ox in a wren? Some are strong, some are weak; some have great faith, some have little. This man was one of the weak, and therefore he went to the wall.

HOPE. I would it had been Great-grace for their sakes.

CHR. If it had been he, he might have had his hands full; for I must tell you that though Great-grace is excellent good at his weapons, and has, and can, so long as he keeps them at sword's point, do well enough with them; yet if they get within him, even Faint-heart, Mistrust, or the other, it shall go hard but they will throw

king. Satan (Revelation 9:1-2, 11).

lion. 1 Peter 5:8. Another picture of Satan.

Great-grace. "And great grace was upon them all" (Acts 4:33).

champion. See 1 Samuel 17:4, 51. Instead of both armies fighting, each king would select a champion, and they would battle.

up his heels. And when a man is down, you know, what can he do?

Whoso looks well upon Great-grace's face shall see those scars and cuts there that shall easily give demonstration of what I say. Yea, once I heard that he should say (and that when he was in the combat), "We despaired even of life." How did these sturdy rogues and their fellows make David groan, mourn, and roar? Yea, Heman and Hezekiah too, though champions in their day, were forced to bestir them, when by these assaulted; and yet, notwithstanding, they had their coats soundly brushed by them. Peter upon a time would go try what he could do; but though some do say of him that he is the prince of the apostles, they handled him so that they made him at last afraid of a sorry girl.

Besides, their king is at their whistle. He is never out of hearing; and if at any time they be put to the worst, he, if possible, comes in to help them; and of him it is said, "The sword of him that layeth at him cannot hold the spear, the dart, nor the habergeon; he esteemeth iron as straw, and brass as rotten wood. The arrow cannot make him fly; slingstones are turned with him into stubble, darts are counted as stubble: he laugheth at the shaking of a spear." What can a man do in this case? 'Tis true, if a man could at every turn have Job's horse, and had skill and courage to ride him, he might do notable things. "For his neck is clothed with thunder, he will not be afraid of the grasshopper, the glory of his nostrils is terrible, he paweth in the valley, rejoiceth in his strength, and goeth out to meet the armed men. He mocketh at fear, and is not affrighted, neither turneth back from the sword. The quiver rattleth against him, the glittering spear, and the shield. He swalloweth the ground with fierceness and rage, neither believeth he that it is the sound of the trumpet. He saith among the trumpets, Ha, ha! and he smelleth the battle afar off, the thundering of the

We despaired . . . . Paul's statement in 2 Corinthians 1:8.

Heman. The author of Psalm 88, certainly a song of despair and trouble.

Hezekiah. A godly king of Judah, See Isaiah 36-38.

Peter. Luke 22:54-62 records this apostle's temptation and defeat.

sorry girl. A weak girl. The servant girl who questioned Peter.

The sword. Quoted from Job 41:26-29. "Habergeon" means "breastplate."

For his neck . . . . Quoted from Job 39:19-25.

148

captains, and the shoutings."

But for such footmen as thee and I are, let us never desire to meet with an enemy, nor vaunt as if we could do better, when we hear of others that they have been foiled, nor be tickled at the thoughts of our own manhood; for such commonly come by the worst when tried. Witness Peter, of whom I made mention before. He would swagger, ay, he would; he would, as his vain mind prompted him to say, do better, and stand more for his Master than all men; but who so foiled and run down by these villains as he?

When therefore we hear that such robberies are done on the King's highway, two things become us to do: 1. To go out harnessed, and to be sure to take a shield with us; for it was for want of that, that he that laid so lustily at Leviathan could not make him yield: for indeed, if that be wanting, he fears us not at all. Therefore he that had skill hath said, "Above all take the shield of faith, wherewith ye shall be able to quench all the fiery darts of the wicked."

2. 'Tis good, also, that we desire of the King a convoy, yea, that he will go with us himself. This made David rejoice when in the Valley of the Shadow of Death; and Moses was rather for dying where he stood, than to go one step without his God. Oh, my brother, if he will but go along with us, what need we be afraid of ten thousands that shall set themselves against us? But without him, the proud helpers "fall under the slain."

I for my part have been in the fray before now, and though, through the goodness of him that is best, I am, as you see, alive; yet I cannot boast of my manhood. Glad shall I be, if I meet with no more such brunts; though I fear we are not got beyond all danger. However, since the lion and the bear have not as yet devoured me, I hope God will also deliver us from the next uncircumcised Philistine. Then sang Christian,

harnessed. Clad in armor.

Leviathan. See Job 41:26-29. This is probably a poetic description of a crocodile. It symbolizes Satan.

Above all . . . . Quoted from Ephesians 6:16. It means "in addition to all the other parts."

David. "Yea, though I walk through the valley of the shadow of death, I will fear no evil: for thou art with me" (Psalm 23:4).

Moses. "If thy presence go not with me, carry us not up hence" (Exodus 33:15).

ten thousands. An allusion to Psalm 3:6 and Psalm 27:1-3.

fall . . . . Quoted from Isaiah 10:4.

lion and the bear. Referring to David's victories (1 Samuel 17:34-36).

Philistine. A reference to David's victory over the Philistine giant, Goliath (1 Samuel 17:26-36).

149

Poor Little-faith! Hast been among the thieves?
Wast robbed? Remember this, whoso believes
And gets more faith; shall then a victor be
Over ten thousand, else scarce over three.

victor. "And this is the victory that overcometh the world, even our faith" (1 John 5:4).

a way. Another dangerous detour. "There is a way which seemeth right unto a man, but the end thereof are the ways of death" (Proverbs 14:12). Note that this new road seems as straight as the one they were on. As we progress in the Christian life, temptations become more and more subtle. Previous detours were rather obvious.

a man. This turns out to be the Flatterer they were warned about by the Shepherds.

by degrees. The enemy leads us astray gradually.

So they went on, and Ignorance followed. They went then till they came at a place where they saw a way put itself into their way, and seemed withal to lie as straight as the way which they should go: and here they knew not which of the two to take, for both seemed straight before them; therefore here they stood still to consider. And as they were thinking about the way, behold a man, black of flesh, but covered with a very light robe, came to them, and asked them why they stood there. They answered they were going to the Celestial City, but knew not which of these ways to take. Follow me, said the man, it is thither that I am going. So they followed him in the way that but now came into the road, which by degrees turned, and turned them so from the city that they desired to go to, that in little time their faces were turned away from it; yet they followed him. But by and by, before they were aware, he led them both within the compass of a net, in which they were both so entangled that they knew not what to do; and with that the white robe fell off the black man's back. Then they saw where they were. Wherefore there they lay crying some time, for they could not get themselves out.

CHR. Then said Christian to his fellow, Now do I see myself in error. Did not the Shepherds bid us beware of the flatterers? As is the saying of the wise man, so we have found it this day, "A man that flattereth his neighbour spreadeth a net for his feet."

HOPE. They also gave us a note of directions about the way, for our more sure finding thereof; but therein we have also forgotten to read, and have not kept ourselves from the paths of the destroyer. Here David was wiser than we;

A man. . . . Quoted from Proverbs 29:5.

David. Psalm 17:4.

for saith he, "Concerning the works of men, by the word of thy lips, I have kept me from the paths of the destroyer." Thus they lay bewailing themselves in the net. At last they espied a Shining One coming towards them with a whip of small cord in his hand. When he was come to the place where they were, he asked them whence they came, and what they did there. They told him that they were poor pilgrims going to Zion, but were led out of their way by a black man, clothed in white; who bid us, said they, follow him, for he was going thither too. Then said he with the whip, It is Flatterer, a false apostle, that hath transformed himself into an angel of light. So he rent the net, and let the men out. Then said he to them, Follow me, that I may set you in your way again. So he led them back to the way which they had left to follow the Flatterer. Then he asked them, saying, Where did you lie the last night? They said, With the Shepherds, upon the Delectable Mountains. He asked them then, if they had not of those Shepherds a note of direction for the way. They answered, Yes. But did you, said he, when you were at a stand, pluck out and read your note? They answered, No. He asked them, Why? They said, they forgot. He asked, moreover, if the Shepherds did not bid them beware of the Flatterer. They answered, Yes, but we did not imagine, said they, that this fine-spoken man had been he.

Then I saw in my dream that he commanded them to lie down; which when they did, he chastised them sore, to teach them the good way wherein they should walk; and as he chastised them he said, "As many as I love, I rebuke and chasten; be zealous, therefore, and repent." This done, he bid them go on their way, and take good heed to the other directions of the Shepherds. So they thanked him for all his kindness, and went softly along the right way, singing,

whip. Such as Jesus used in the temple (John 2:15).

false apostle. "For such are false apostles, deceitful workers, transforming themselves into the apostles of Christ. And no marvel; for Satan himself is transformed into an angel of light" (2 Corinthians 11:13-14). See also Daniel 11:32.

fine-spoken man. An allusion to Romans 16:17-18.

chastised. "For whom the Lord loveth he chasteneth" (Hebrews 12:6). See also Deuteronomy 25:2; 2 Chronicles 6:27; and Revelation 3:19.

softly. Carefully. See 1 Kings 21:27 and Isaiah 38:15.

151

Come hither, you that walk along the way;
See how the pilgrims fare that go astray!
They catched are in an entangling net,
'Cause they good counsel lightly did forget:
'Tis true they rescued were, but yet you see,
They're scourged to boot.
Let this your caution be.

Now after a while they perceived, afar off, one coming softly and alone all along the highway to meet them. Then said Christian to his fellow, Yonder is a man with his back towards Zion, and he is coming to meet us.

HOPE. I see him; let us take heed to ourselves now, lest he should prove a flatterer also. So he drew nearer and nearer, and at last came up unto them. His name was Atheist, and he asked them whither they were going.

CHR. We are going to Mount Zion.

Then Atheist fell into a very great laughter.

CHR. What is the meaning of your laughter?

ATHEIST. I laugh to see what ignorant persons you are, to take upon you so tedious a journey, and you are like to have nothing but your travel for your pains.

CHR. Why, man, do you think we shall not be received?

ATHEIST. Received! There is no such place as you dream of in all this world.

CHR. But there is in the world to come.

ATHEIST. When I was at home in mine own country, I heard as you now affirm, and from that hearing went out to see, and have been seeking this city this twenty years; but find no more of it than I did the first day I set out.

CHR. We have both heard and believe that there is such a place to be found.

ATHEIST. Had not I, when at home, believed, I had not come thus far to seek; but finding none (and yet I should, had there been such a place to be found, for I have gone to seek it further than you), I am going back again, and will seek to refresh myself with the things that I then cast

set out. "The labour of the foolish wearieth every one of them, because he knoweth not how to go to the city" (Ecclesiastes 10:15). "Behold, they say unto me, Where is the word of the LORD. Let it come now" (Jeremiah 17:15).

152

away for hopes of that which I now see is not.

CHR. Then said Christian to Hopeful his fellow, Is it true which this man hath said?

HOPE. Take heed, he is one of the flatterers; remember what it hath cost us once already for our hearkening to such kind of fellows. What! no Mount Zion? Did we not see from the Delectable Mountains the gate of the city? Also, are we not now to walk by faith? Let us go on, said Hopeful, lest the man with the whip overtake us again. You should have taught me that lesson, which I will round you in the ears withal: "Cease, my son, to hear the instruction that causeth to err from the words of knowledge." I say, my brother, cease to hear him, and let us "believe to the saving of the soul."

walk. "For we walk by faith, not by sight" (2 Corinthians 5:7).

round you in the ears. Speak privately, whisper.

Cease . . . . Quoted from Proverbs 19:27; and see Hebrews 10:39.

CHR. My brother, I did not put the question to thee for that I doubted of the truth of our belief myself, but to prove thee, and to fetch from thee a fruit of the honesty of thy heart. As for this man, I know that he is blinded by the god of this world. Let thee and I go on, knowing that we have belief of the truth, and "no lie is of the truth."

blinded. "The god of this world hath blinded the minds of them which believe not" (2 Corinthians 4:4).

no lie. Quoted from 1 John 2:21.

HOPE. Now do I rejoice in hope of the glory of God. So they turned away from the man; and he, laughing at them, went his way.

rejoice. Quoted from Romans 5:2.

I saw then in my dream that they went till they came into a certain country whose air naturally tended to make one drowsy, if he came a stranger into it. And here Hopeful began to be very dull and heavy of sleep; wherefore he said unto Christian, I do now begin to grow so drowsy that I can scarcely hold up mine eyes; let us lie down here and take one nap.

one nap. Hopeful has forgotten the warning of the Shepherds.

CHR. By no means, said the other, lest sleeping, we never awake more.

HOPE. Why, my brother? Sleep is sweet to the labouring man; we may be refreshed if we take a nap.

sweet. "The sleep of a labouring man is sweet" (Ecclesiastes 5:12).

CHR. Do you not remember that one of the Shepherds bid us beware of the Enchanted

watch. 1 Thessalonians 5:6.

Two are better. . . . Ecclesiastes 4:9.

discourse. Christian and Hopeful here enter into a rather lengthly theological discussion for the purpose of staying awake. If you find it is putting you to sleep, keep in mind that such conversation was common to the Puritans. Talking about personal experiences, and scriptural truths, is an encouragement to believers. See Deuteronomy 6:6-9.

drowned me. Quoted from 1 Timothy 6:9.

Ground? He meant by that, that we should beware of sleeping; wherefore let us not sleep, as do others, but let us watch and be sober.

HOPE. I acknowledge myself in a fault; and had I been here alone, I had by sleeping run the danger of death. I see it is true that the wise man saith, "Two are better than one." Hitherto hath thy company been my mercy, "and thou shalt have a good reward for thy labour."

CHR. Now then, said Christian, to prevent drowsiness in this place, let us fall into good discourse.

HOPE. With all my heart, said the other.

CHR. Where shall we begin?

HOPE. Where God began with us. But do you begin, if you please.

CHR. I will sing you first this song:

> When saints do sleepy grow,
>   let them come hither,
> And hear how these two pilgrims talk together:
> Yea, let them learn of them, in any wise,
> Thus to keep ope their drowsy slumbering
>   eyes.
> Saints' fellowship, if it be managed well,
> Keeps them awake, and that in spite of hell.

Then Christian began and said, I will ask you a question. How come you to think at first of so doing as you do now?

HOPE. Do you mean, how came I at first to look after the good of my soul?

CHR. Yes, that is my meaning.

HOPE. I continued a great while in the delight of those things which were seen and sold at our fair; things which, I believe now, would have (had I continued in them still) drowned me in perdition and destruction.

CHR. What things are they?

HOPE. All the treasures and riches of the world. Also I delighted much in rioting, revelling, drinking, swearing, lying, uncleanness, Sabbath-breaking, and what not, that tended to

154

destroy the soul. But I found at last, by hearing and considering of things that are divine, which indeed I heard of you, as also of beloved Faithful, that was put to death for his faith and good living in Vanity Fair, that "the <u>end</u> of these things is death." And that for these things' sake "the <u>wrath</u> of God cometh upon the children of disobedience."

end. Quoted from Romans 6:21.

the wrath. . . . Quoted from Ephesians 5:6.

CHR. And did you presently fall under the power of this conviction?

HOPE. No, I was not willing presently to know the evil of sin, nor the damnation that follows upon the commission of it; but endeavoured, when my mind at first began to be shaken with the Word, to shut mine eyes against the light thereof.

CHR. But what was the cause of your carrying of it thus to the first workings of God's blessed Spirit upon you?

HOPE. The causes were: 1. I was ignorant that this was the work of God upon me. I never thought that by awakenings for sin God at first begins the conversion of a sinner. 2. Sin was yet very sweet to my flesh, and I was loath to leave it. 3. I could not tell how to part with mine old companions, their presence and actions were so desirable unto me. 4. The hours in which convictions were upon me were such troublesome and such heart-affrighting hours, that I could not bear, no not so much as the remembrance of them upon my heart.

CHR. Then, as it seems, sometimes you got rid of your trouble.

HOPE. Yes, verily, but it would come into my mind again, and then I should be as bad, nay, worse, than I was before.

CHR. Why, what was it that brought your sins to mind again?

HOPE. Many things, as,

1. If I did but meet a good man in the streets; or,

2. If I have heard any read in the Bible; or,

3. If mine head did begin to ache; or,

4. If I were told that some of my neighbours were sick; or,

5. If I heard the <u>bell toll</u> for some that were dead; or,

6. If I thought of dying myself; or,

7. If I heard that sudden death happened to others;

8. But especially, when I thought of myself, that I must quickly come to judgment.

CHR. And could you at any time with ease get off the guilt of sin, when by any of these ways it came upon you?

HOPE. No, not I, for then they got faster hold of my conscience; and then, if I did but think of going back to sin (though my mind was turned against it), it would be double torment to me.

CHR. And how did you do then?

HOPE. I thought I must endeavour to mend my life; for else, thought I, I am sure to be damned.

CHR. And did you endeavour to mend?

HOPE. Yes; and fled from not only my sins, but sinful company too; and betook me to religious duties, as prayer, reading, weeping for sin, speaking truth to my neighbours, etc. These things did I, with many others, too much here to relate.

CHR. And did you think yourself well then?

HOPE. Yes, for a while; but at the last my trouble came tumbling upon me again, and that over the neck of all my reformations.

CHR. How came that about, since you were now reformed?

HOPE. There were several things brought it upon me, especially such <u>sayings</u> as these: "All our righteousnesses are as filthy rags." "By the works of the law no man shall be justified." "When you have done all things, say, We are unprofitable"; with many more such like. From whence I began to reason with myself thus: If *all* my righteousnesses are filthy rags; if by the

bell toll. This reminds us of John Donne's famous statement: "Any man's death diminishes me, because I am involved in Mankinde; And therefore never send to know for whom the bell tolls; It tolls for thee." Donne died in 1631. Bunyan himself was an accomplished bell-ringer.

sayings. Quotations from Isaiah 64:6; Galatians 2:16; Luke 17:10.

deeds of the law *no* man can be justified; and it, when we have done *all*, we are yet unprofitable, then 'tis but a folly to think of heaven by the law. I further thought thus: If a man runs a hundred pounds into the shopkeeper's debt, and after that shall pay for all that he shall fetch, yet his old debt stands still in the book <u>uncrossed</u>; for the which the shopkeeper may sue him, and cast him into prison till he shall pay the debt.

uncrossed. Not paid, uncancelled.

CHR. Well, and how did you apply this to yourself?

HOPE. Why, I thought thus with myself: I have by my sins run a great way into God's book, and that my now reforming will not pay off that score; therefore I should think still under all my present amendments, But how shall I be freed from that damnation that I have brought myself in danger of by my former transgressions?

CHR. A very good applicaton: but pray, go on.

HOPE. Another thing that hath troubled me, even since my late amendments, is, that if I look narrowly into the best of what I do now, I still see sin, new sin, <u>mixing itself</u> with the best of that I do; so that now I am forced to conclude that, notwithstanding my former fond conceits of myself and duties, I have committed sin enough in one duty to send me to hell, though my former life had been faultless.

mixing itself. "I find then a law, that, when I would do good, evil is present with me" (Romans 7:21).

CHR. And what did you do then?

HOPE. Do! I could not tell what to do, till I brake my mind to Faithful, for he and I were well acquainted. And he told me that unless I could obtain the righteousness of a man that never had sinned, neither mine own, nor all the righteousness of the world could save me.

CHR. And did you think he spake true?

HOPE. Had he told me so when I was pleased and satisfied with mine own amendment, I had called him fool for his pains; but now, since I see mine own infirmity, and the sin that cleaves to

157

justified by him. Bunyan cites Romans 4:5; Colossians 1:14; Hebrews 10:12-21; and 2 Peter 1:19.

days. "Who in the days of his flesh" (Hebrews 5:7), referring to our Lord's life on earth.

hang on the tree. Die on the cross. "Who his own self bare our sins in his own body on the tree" (1 Peter 2:24).

imputed. Put to one's account. Christ was not guilty, yet God put our sins on His account when Christ died for us. When the sinner trusts Christ, God's righteousness is put to his account. The concept is developed in Romans 4.

invited. "Come unto me, all ye that labour and are heavy laden, and I will give you rest" (Matthew 11:28).

indicting. His authoritative announcing.

heaven and earth. "Heaven and earth shall pass away, but my words shall not pass away" (Matthew 24:35). See also Matthew 5:18. A "jot" is a tiny Hebrew letter. A "tittle" is a small projection on a Hebrew letter.

knees. "O come, let us worship and bow down: let us kneel before the LORD our maker" (Psalm 95:6). "Then shall ye call upon me, and ye shall go and pray unto me, and I will hearken unto you. And ye shall seek me, and find me, when ye shall search for me with all your heart" (Jeremiah 29:12-13). See also Daniel 6:10.

my best performance, I have been forced to be of his opinion.

CHR. But did you think, when at first he suggested it to you, that there was such a man to be found, of whom it might justly be said, that he never committed sin?

HOPE. I must confess the words at first sounded strangely, but after a little more talk and company with him, I had full conviction about it.

CHR. And did you ask him what man this was, and how you must be justified by him?

HOPE. Yes, and he told me it was the Lord Jesus, that dwelleth on the right hand of the Most High. And thus, said he, you must be justified by him, even by trusting to what he hath done by himself in the days of his flesh, and suffered when he did hang on the tree. I asked him further, how that man's righteousness could be of that efficacy to justify another before God? And he told me he was the mighty God, and did what he did, and died the death also, not for himself, but for me; to whom his doings and the worthiness of them should be imputed, if I believed on him.

CHR. And what did you do then?

HOPE. I made my objections against my believing, for that I thought he was not willing to save me.

CHR. And what said Faithful to you then?

HOPE. He bid me go to him and see. Then I said it was presumption; but he said, No, for I was invited to come. Then he gave me a book of Jesus, his indicting, to encourage me the more freely to come; and he said concerning that book, that every jot and tittle thereof stood firmer than heaven and earth. Then I asked him, What I must do when I came; and he told me, I must entreat upon my knees with all my heart and soul, the Father to reveal him to me. Then I asked him further, How I must make my supplication to him. And he said, Go, and thou shalt find him upon a <u>mercy-seat</u>, where he sits all the year long, to give pardon and forgiveness to them that come. I told him that I knew not what to say when I came. And he bid me say to this effect: <u>God be merciful</u> to me a sinner, and make me to know and believe in Jesus Christ; for I see that if his righteousness had not been, or I have not faith in that righteousness, I am utterly cast away. Lord, I have heard that thou art a merciful God, and hast ordained that thy Son Jesus Christ should be the <u>Saviour</u> of the world; and moreover, that thou art willing to bestow him upon such a poor sinner as I am (and I am a sinner indeed); Lord, take therefore this opportunity, and magnify thy grace in the salvation of my soul, through thy Son Jesus Christ. Amen.

CHR. And did you do as you were bidden?

HOPE. Yes, over and over, and over.

CHR. And did the Father reveal his Son to you?

HOPE. Not at the first, nor second, nor third, nor fourth, nor fifth; no, nor at the sixth time neither.

CHR. What did you do then?

HOPE. What! why I could not tell what to do.

CHR. Had you not thoughts of leaving off praying?

HOPE. Yes; an hundred times twice told.

CHR. And what was the reason you did not?

HOPE. I believed that that was true which had been told me, to wit, that without the righteousness of this Christ, all the world could not save me; and therefore, thought I with myself, if I leave off I die, and I can but die at the throne of grace. And withal, this came into my mind, "If it <u>tarry</u>, wait for it; because it will surely come, it will not tarry." So I continued praying until <u>the Father</u> showed me his Son.

CHR. And how was he revealed unto you?

HOPE. I did not see him with my bodily <u>eyes</u>, but with the eyes of my understanding; and thus

---

mercy-seat. The Jewish tabernacle was divided into three parts: an outer court, where the animals were sacrificed; the holy place, where there stood a table, a lampstand, and a golden altar for burning incense; and a holy of holies. In the holy of holies was a wooden chest called "the ark of the covenant." Upon the top of this chest was a golden covering with an image of an angel at each end. This covering was called "the mercy seat." It was the throne of God in the camp of Israel. Once a year, the high priest sprinkled blood on this mercy seat to cover the sins of the people. See Exodus 25:10-22; Leviticus 16; Numbers 7:89; and Hebrews 4:16. Because of Jesus' death for sinners, God's throne is a throne of grace and mercy, not a throne of judgment.

God be merciful. . . . Quoted from Luke 18:13.

Saviour. "And we have seen and do testify that the Father sent the Son to be the Saviour of the world" (1 John 4:14). See also John 4:42.

tarry. Quoted from Habakkuk 2:3. Often verses of Scripture came to Bunyan's mind when he was under conviction, assuring him that God would indeed save him.

the Father. See Matthew 11:27.

eyes. "The eyes of your understanding being enlightened" (see Ephesians 1:18-19).

it was: One day I was very sad, I think sadder than at any one time in my life, and this sadness was through a fresh sight of the greatness and vileness of my sins. And as I was then looking for nothing but hell, and the everlasting damnation of my soul, suddenly, as I thought, I saw the Lord Jesus Christ look down from heaven upon me, and saying, "Believe on the Lord Jesus Christ, and thou shalt be saved."

But I replied, Lord, I am a great, a very great sinner. And he answered, "My grace is sufficient for thee." Then I said, But, Lord, what is believing? And then I saw from that saying, "He that cometh to me shall never hunger, and he that believeth on me shall never thirst," that believing and coming was all one; and that he that came, that is, ran out in his heart and affections after salvation by Christ, he indeed believed in Christ. Then the water stood in mine eyes, and I asked further, But, Lord, may such a great sinner as I am be indeed accepted of thee, and be saved by thee? And I heard him say, "And him that cometh to me, I will in no wise cast out." Then I said, But how, Lord, must I consider of thee in my coming to thee, that my faith may be placed aright upon thee? Then he said, "Christ Jesus came into the world to save sinners." "He is the end of the law for righteousness to every one that believes." "He died for our sins, and rose again for our justification: He loved us, and washed us from our sins in his own blood." "He is mediator between God and us." "He ever liveth to make intercession for us." From all which I gathered, that I must look for righteousness in his person, and for satisfaction for my sins by his blood; that what he did in obedience to his Father's law, and in submitting to the penalty thereof, was not for himself, but for him that will accept it for his salvation, and be thankful. And now was my heart full of joy, mine eyes full of tears, and mine affections running over with love to

160

the name, people, and ways of Jesus Christ.

CHR. This was a revelation of Christ to your soul indeed; but tell me particularly what effect this had upon your spirit.

HOPE. It made me see that all the world, notwithstanding all the righteousness thereof, is in a state of condemnation. It made me see that God the Father, though he be <u>just</u>, can justly justify the coming sinner. It made me greatly ashamed of the vileness of my former life, and confounded me with the sense of mine own ignorance; for there never came thought into my heart before now that showed me so the <u>beauty</u> of Jesus Christ. It made me love a holy life, and long to do something for the honour and glory of the name of the Lord Jesus; yea, I thought that had I now a thousand gallons of blood in my body, I could spill it all for the sake of the Lord Jesus.

I saw then in my dream that Hopeful looked back and saw Ignorance, whom they had left behind, coming after. Look, said he to Christian, how far yonder youngster loitereth behind.

CHR. Ay, ay, I see him; he careth not for our company.

HOPE. But, I trow, it would not have hurt him had he kept pace with us hitherto.

CHR. That's true, but I warrant you he thinketh otherwise.

HOPE. That, I think, he doth; but however, let us tarry for him. So they did.

Then Christian said to him, Come away, man, why do you stay so behind?

IGNOR. I take my pleasure in walking alone, even more a great deal than in company, unless I like it the better.

Then said Christian to Hopeful (but softly), Did I not tell you he cared not for our company? But however, said he, come up, and let us talk away the time in this solitary place. Then directing his speech to Ignorance, he said,

just. A reference to Romans 3:26. How can God declare sinners righteous and still be righteous himself? By having Christ pay the penalty for their sins. Thus, God is just (because sin is paid for) and the justifier of those who trust Christ.

beauty. "Thine eyes shall see the king in his beauty" (Isaiah 33:17). See also Psalm 45.

161

How stands it. This introduces another section of introspection and doctrinal discussion. Generally speaking, in this conversation Christian represents the orthodox Puritan point of view, while Ignorance defends a theology the Puritans would consider unbiblical. Ignorance bases his confidence on feelings and man-made ideas, while Hopeful seeks to defend his position from Scripture. Ignorance lives up to his name: he is ignorant of himself and of God's truth.

devils. "Thou believest that there is one God; thou doest well: the devils also believe, and tremble" (James 2:19). The devils (demons) were more honest than Ignorance, for they at least trembled when they thought of God!

The soul. . . . Quoted from Proverbs 13:4.

He that trusts. . . . Quoted from Proverbs 28:26. Christian does not deny the witness of one's innermost feelings. What he says is that we dare not trust our feelings alone, for they may deceive us. The fact that Ignorance claims to have a "good heart" indicates that he has never seen himself a sinner before the eyes of God.

a good one. This is why he is called Ignorance. He is ignorant of his own sinfulness and of God's righteousness (Romans 10:1-13).

Ask my fellow. Obviously thieves will not tell on each other! Ignorance is reasoning in circles: his heart tells him he

Come, how do you? <u>How stands it</u> between God and your soul now?

IGNOR. I hope well; for I am always full of good motions, that come into my mind to comfort me as I walk.

CHR. What good motions? pray, tell us.

IGNOR. Why, I think of God and heaven.

CHR. So do the <u>devils</u> and damned souls.

IGNOR. But I think of them and desire them.

CHR. So do many that are never like to come there. "<u>The soul</u> of the sluggard desireth, and hath nothing."

IGNOR. But I think of them, and leave all for them.

CHR. That I doubt; for leaving all is a hard matter: yea, a harder matter than many are aware of. But why, or by what, art thou persuaded that thou hast left all for God and heaven?

IGNOR. My heart tells me so.

CHR. The wise man says, "<u>He that trusts</u> his own heart is a fool."

IGNOR. This is spoken of an evil heart, but mine is <u>a good one.</u>

CHR. But how dost thou prove that?

IGNOR. It comforts me in hopes of heaven.

CHR. That may be through its deceitfulness; for a man's heart may minister comfort to him in the hopes of that thing for which he yet has no ground to hope.

IGNOR. But my heart and life agree together, and therefore my hope is well grounded.

CHR. Who told thee that thy heart and life agree together?

IGNOR. My heart tells me so.

CHR. <u>Ask my fellow</u> if I be a thief! Thy heart tells thee so! Except the Word of God beareth witness in this matter, other testimony is of no value.

IGNOR. But is it not a good heart that hath good thoughts? and is not that a good life that is according to God's commandments?

CHR. Yes, that is a good heart that hath good thoughts, and that is a good life that is according to God's commandments; but it is one thing indeed to have these, and another thing only to think so.

IGNOR. Pray, what count you good thoughts, and life according to God's commandments?

CHR. There are good thoughts of divers kinds; some respecting ourselves, some God, some Christ, and some other things.

IGNOR. What be good thoughts respecting ourselves?

CHR. Such as agree with the Word of God.

IGNOR. When do our thoughts of ourselves agree with the Word of God?

CHR. When we pass the same judgment upon ourselves which the Word passes. To explain myself: The Word of God saith of persons in a natural condition, "There is none righteous, there in none that doth good." It saith also, that "every imagination of the heart of man is only evil, and that continually." And again, "The imagination of man's heart is evil from his youth." Now then, when we think thus of ourselves, having sense thereof, then are our thoughts good ones, because according to the Word of God.

IGNOR. I will never believe that my heart is thus bad.

CHR. Therefore thou never hadst one good thought concerning thyself in thy life. But let me go on. As the Word passeth a judgment upon our *heart*, so it passeth a judgment upon our *ways;* and when OUR thoughts of our *hearts* and *ways* agree with the judgment which the Word giveth of both, then are both good, because agreeing thereto.

IGNOR. Make out your meaning.

CHR. Why, the Word of God saith that man's ways are crooked ways, not good, but perverse. It saith they are naturally out of the good way, that they have not known it. Now when a man lives a good life, and his good life agrees with his heart! Only the Word of God can tell us what we are.

There is none. . . . Quoted from Romans 3:10.

every imagination. . . . Quoted from Genesis 6:5.

The imagination. . . . Quoted from Genesis 8:21.

crooked. A reference to Psalm 125:5 and Proverbs 2:15.

known it. "And the way of peace have they not known" (Romans 3:17).

163

judgment. Assurance of salvation comes when we believe God's Word and receive its witness. Bunyan wrote in *Grace Abounding*: "I saw that it was not my good frame of heart that made my righteousness better, nor yet my bad frame that made my righteousness worse; for my righteousness was Jesus Christ, the same yesterday, today, and for ever. Hebrews 13:8."

thus thinketh of his ways, I say when he doth sensibly and with heart-humiliation, thus think, then hath he good thoughts of his own ways, because his thoughts now agree with the judgment of the Word of God.

IGNOR. What are good thoughts concerning God?

CHR. Even as I have said concerning ourselves, when our thoughts of God do agree with what the Word saith of him; and that is, when we think of his being and attributes as the Word hath taught; of which I cannot now discourse at large. But to speak of him with reference to us: Then we have right thoughts of God, when we think that he knows us better than we know ourselves, and can see sin in us when and where we see none in ourselves; when we think he knows our inmost thoughts, and that our heart, with all its depths, is always open unto his eyes; also when we think that all our righteousness stinks in his nostrils, and that therefore he cannot abide to see us stand before him in any confidence, even in all our best performances.

IGNOR. Do you think that I am such a fool as to think God can see no further than I? or that I would come to God in the best of my performances?

CHR. Why, how dost thou think in this matter?

IGNOR. Why, to be short, I think I must believe in Christ for justification.

CHR. How! think thou must believe in Christ, when thou seest not thy need of him! Thou neither seest thy original nor actual infirmities; but hast such an opinion of thyself, and of what thou dost, as plainly renders thee to be one that did never see a necessity of Christ's personal righteousness to justify thee before God. How then dost thou say, I believe in Christ?

IGNOR. I believe well enough for all that.

CHR. How dost thou believe?

IGNOR. I believe that Christ died for sinners

164

and that I shall be justified before God from the curse, through his gracious acceptance of my obedience to his law. Or thus, Christ makes my duties that are religious acceptable to his Father by virtue of his merits; and so shall I be justified.

CHR. Let me give an answer to this confession of thy faith.

1. Thou believest with a fantastical faith, for this faith is nowhere described in the Word.

2. Thou believest with a false faith, because it taketh justification from the personal righteousness of Christ, and applies it to thy own.

3. This faith maketh not Christ a justifier of thy person, but of thy actions; and of thy actions' sake, which is false.

4. Therefore this faith is deceitful, even such as will leave thee under wrath in the day of God Almighty; for true justifying faith puts the soul (as sensible of its lost condition by the law) upon flying for refuge unto Christ's righteousness; which righteousness of his is, not an act of grace by which he maketh for justification thy obedience accepted with God, but his personal obedience to the law, in doing and suffering for us what that required at our hands. This righteousness, I say, true faith accepteth; under the skirt of which the soul being shrouded, and by it presented as spotless before God, it is accepted, and acquit from condemnation.

IGNOR. What! would you have us trust to what Christ in his own person has done without us? This conceit would loosen the reins of our lust, and tolerate us to live as we list. For what matter how we live, if we may be justified by Christ's personal righteousness from all, when we believe it?

CHR. Ignorance is thy name, and as thy name is, so art thou; even this thy answer demonstrateth what I say. Ignorant thou art of what justifying righteousness is, and as ignorant how to secure thy soul through the faith of it from

my obedience. Ignorance thinks that salvation is by works. All that Christ does is make the sinner's works acceptable to God! "Knowing that a man is not justified by the works of the law, but by the faith of Jesus Christ" (Galatians 2:16).

fantastical. Imaginary. Faith is only as good as the object. To trust in good works is to have imaginary faith, because good works cannot save. Faith in Christ is true saving faith, because the Word of God assures us that this is God's way of salvation.

refuge. A reference to the cities of refuge (Joshua 20), a picture of Jesus Christ, our refuge from the judgment of sin (Hebrews 6:18).

loosen the reins. Ignorance uses the old argument, "If we are saved only by faith, without good works, then we shall continue to sin." Paul answers this argument in Romans 6. The true believer is dead to sin and has a new nature within that makes him want to obey God. Hopeful and Christian try to teach Ignorance that there are "true effects" from saving faith, and these change the life.

the heavy wrath of God. Yea, thou also art ignorant of the true effects of saving faith in this righteousness of Christ, which is to bow and win over the heart to God in Christ, to love his name, his word, ways, and people, and not as thou ignorantly imaginest.

HOPE. Ask him if ever he had Christ <u>revealed</u> to him from heaven.

IGNOR. What! you are a man for revelations! I believe that what both you, and all the rest of you, say about that matter is but the fruit of distracted brains.

HOPE. Why, man! Christ is so hid in God from the natural apprehensions of the flesh, that he cannot by any man be savingly known, unless God the Father reveals him to them.

IGNOR. That is your faith, but not mine; yet mine, I doubt not, is as good as yours, though I have not in my head so many whimsies as you.

CHR. Give me leave to put in a word. You ought not so slightly to speak of this matter; for this I will boldly affirm (even as my good companion hath done), that <u>no man</u> can know Jesus Christ but by the revelation of the Father: yea, and faith too, by which the soul layeth hold upon Christ (if it be right), must be wrought by the exceeding greatness of his mighty power; the working of which faith, I perceive, poor Ignorance, thou art ignorant of. Be awakened then, see thine own <u>wretchedness</u>, and fly to the Lord Jesus; and by his righteousness, which is the righteousness of God (for he himself is God), thou shalt be delivered from condemnation.

IGNOR. You go so fast, I cannot keep pace with you. Do you go on before; I must stay a while behind.

Then they said,

> Well, Ignorance, wilt thou yet foolish be,
> To slight good counsel, ten times given thee?
> And if thou yet refuse it, thou shalt know
> Ere long the evil of thy doing so.
> Remember, man, in time; stoop, do not fear,

revealed. God the Father reveals His Son to us in our hearts. See Matthew 11:25-27 and 16:17; also Galatians 1:15-16.

no man. Again, a reference to Matthew 11:27. See also 1 Corinthians 12:3 and Ephesians 1:18-19.

wretchedness. "Because thou sayest, I am rich, and increased with goods, and have need of nothing; and knowest not that thou art wretched, and miserable, and poor, and blind, and naked" (Revelation 3:17). Ignorance was well named!

Good counsel taken well, saves: therefore hear.
But if thou yet shalt slight it, thou wilt be
The loser, Ignorance, I'll warrant thee.

Then Christian addressed thus himself to his fellow:

CHR. Well, come, my good Hopeful, I perceive that thou and I must walk by ourselves again.

So I saw in my dream that they went on apace before, and Ignorance he came hobbling after. Then said Christian to his companion, It pities me much for this poor man, it will certainly go ill with him at last.

at last. At the end of the journey, Ignorance is bound hand and foot and cast into hell—at the very gate of heaven.

HOPE. Alas! there are abundance in our town in his condition, whole families, yea, whole streets, and that of pilgrims too; and if there be so many in our parts, how many, think you, must there be in the place where he was born?

CHR. Indeed the Word saith, "He hath blinded their eyes lest they should see," etc. But now we are by ourselves, what do you think of such men? Have they at no time, think you, convictions of sin, and so consequently fears that their state is dangerous?

the Word. Quoted from John 12:40. God gives men the light of salvation, but if they persistently refuse that light, they become spiritually blinded.

HOPE. Nay, do you answer that question yourself, for you are the elder man.

CHR. Then I say, sometimes (as I think) they may; but they being naturally ignorant, understand not that such convictions tend to their good; and therefore they do desperately seek to stifle them, and presumptuously continue to flatter themselves in the way of their own hearts.

HOPE. I do believe, as you say, that fear tends much to men's good, and to make them right, at their beginning to go on pilgrimage.

CHR. Without all doubt it doth, if it be right; for so says the Word, "The fear of the Lord is the beginning of wisdom."

HOPE. How will you describe right fear?

CHR. True or right fear is discovered by three things:

The fear. . . . Quoted from Proverbs 9:10; see also Job 28:28 and Psalm 111:10. "Fear" means reverence and respect, a proper attitude toward God. It is not the cringing fear of a slave, but the respecful fear of a son to a father.

1. By its rise; it is caused by saving convictions for sin.

2. It driveth the soul to lay fast hold of Christ for salvation.

3. It begetteth and continueth in the soul a great reverence of God, his Word, and ways, keeping it tender, and making it afraid to turn from them, to the right hand or to the left, to anything that may dishonour God, break its peace, grieve the Spirit, or cause the enemy to speak reproachfully.

HOPE. Well said; I believe you have said the truth. Are we now almost got past the Enchanted Ground?

CHR. Why, art thou <u>weary</u> of this discourse?

HOPE. No, verily, but that I would know where we are.

CHR. We have not now above two miles further to go thereon. But let us return to our matter. Now the ignorant know not that such convictions as tend to put them in fear are for their good, and therefore they seek to stifle them.

HOPE. How do they seek to stifle them?

CHR. 1. They think that those fears are wrought by the devil (though indeed they are wrought of God), and thinking so, they resist them as things that directly tend to their overthrow. 2. They also think that these fears tend to the spoiling of their faith, when, alas for them, poor men that they are, they have none at all! and therefore they harden their hearts against them. 3. They presume they ought not to fear, and therefore, in despite of them, wax presumptuously confident. 4. They see that those fears tend to take away from them their pitiful old self-holiness, and therefore they resist them with all their might.

HOPE. I know something of this myself; for before I knew myself it was so with me.

CHR. Well, we will leave at this time our

weary. Christian never tires of discussing spiritual truths! He wants to keep Hopeful awake and alert as they cross the Enchanted Ground. "Lest ye be wearied and faint in your minds" (Hebrews 12:3).

neighbour Ignorance by himself, and fall upon another profitable question.

HOPE. With all my heart, but you shall still begin.

CHR. Well then, did you not know, about ten years ago, one Temporary in your parts, who was a forward man in religion then?

HOPE. Know him! yes, he dwelt in Graceless, a town about two miles off of Honesty, and he dwelt next door to one Turnback.

CHR. Right, he dwelt under the same roof with him. Well, that man was much awakened once; I believe that then he had some sight of his sins, and of the wages that was due thereto.

HOPE. I am of your mind, for, my house not being above three miles from him, he would ofttimes come to me, and that with many tears. Truly I pitied the man, and was not altogether without hope of him; but one may see, it is not every one that cries, Lord, Lord.

CHR. He told me once that he was resolved to go on pilgrimage, as we do now; but all of a sudden he grew acquainted with one Save-self, and then he became a stranger to me.

HOPE. Now since we are talking about him, let us a little inquire into the reason of the sudden backsliding of him and such others.

CHR. It may be very profitable, but do you begin.

HOPE. Well then, there are in my judgment four reasons for it:

1. Though the consciences of such men are awakened, yet their minds are not changed; therefore when the power of guilt weareth away, that which provoked them to be religious ceaseth. Wherefore they naturally turn to their own course again, even as we see the dog that is sick of what he has eaten, so long as his sickness prevails, he vomits and casts up all; not that he doth this of a free mind (if we may say a dog has a mind), but because it troubleth his stomach; but now when his sickness is over, and so his

Lord, Lord. Quoted from Matthew 7:21-22.

Save-self. He represents those who think they can save themselves by good works and character.

backsliding. This is an Old Testament term that describes the believer who is not growing and going forward in his faith. Jeremiah uses it thirteen times, and Hosea four times, to describe the sad spiritual condition of the Jewish nation. Hopeful explains why professed Christians backslide: their repentance was emotional but not sincere; they fear what people say; they want to avoid shame; and they do not honestly face their sins and God's judgment. Bunyan seems to suggest that the backslider is, by his backsliding, proving that he was never genuinely converted at all.

dog. Quoted from 2 Peter 2:22. A sinner can reform outwardly, but this does not change his heart. Eventually he will go where his heart is.

stomach eased, his desires being not at all alienate from his vomit, he turns him about and licks up all; and so it is true which is written, "The dog is turned to his own vomit again." Thus I say, being hot for heaven, by virtue only of the sense and fear of the torments of hell, as their sense of hell and the fears of damnation chills and cools, so their desires for heaven and salvation cool also. So then it comes to pass that when their guilt and fear is gone, their desires for heaven and happiness die, and they return to their course again.

2. Another reason is, they have slavish fears that do overmaster them; I speak now of the **fear of men.** Proverbs 29:25. fears that they have of men, for "the fear of men bringeth a snare." So then, though they seem to be hot for heaven, so long as the flames of hell are about their ears, yet when that terror is a little over, they betake themselves to second thoughts; namely, that 'tis good to be wise, and not to run (for they know not what) the hazard of losing all, or at least, of bringing themselves into unavoidable and unnecessary troubles; and so they fall in with the world again.

3. The shame that attends religion lies also as a block in their way; they are proud and haughty, and religion in their eye is low and comtemptible; therefore, when they have lost their sense of hell and wrath to come, they return again to their former course.

4. Guilt, and to meditate terror, are grievous to them. They like not to see their misery before they come into it; though perhaps the sight of it first, if they loved that sight, might make them fly whither the righteous fly and are safe. But because they do, as I hinted before, even shun the thoughts of guilt and terror, therefore when once they are rid of their awakenings about the terrors and wrath of God, they harden their hearts gladly, and choose such ways as will harden them more and more.

CHR. You are pretty near the business, for the

bottom of all is for want of a change in their mind and will. And therefore they are but like the felon that standeth before the judge; he quakes and trembles, and seems to repent most heartily; but the bottom of all is the fear of the halter, not that he hath any detestation of the offence, as is evident because, let but this man have his liberty, and he will be a thief, and so a rogue still, whereas if his mind was changed, he would be otherwise.

HOPE. Now I have showed you the reasons of their going back, do you show me the manner thereof.

CHR. So I will willingly.

1. They draw off their thoughts, all that they may, from the remembrance of God, death, and judgment to come.

2. Then they cast off by degrees private duties, as closet-prayer, curbing their lusts, watching, sorrow for sin, and the like.

3. Then they shun the company of lively and warm Christians.

4. After that they grow cold to public duty, as hearing, reading, godly conference, and the like.

5. Then they begin to pick holes, as we say, in the coats of some of the godly; and that devilishly, that they may have a seeming colour to throw religion (for the sake of some infirmity they have spied in them) behind their backs.

6. Then they begin to adhere to and associate themselves with carnal, loose, and wanton men.

7. Then they give way to carnal and wanton discourses in secret; and glad are they if they can see such things in any that are counted honest, that they may the more boldly do it through their example.

8. After this they begin to play with little sins openly.

9. And then, being hardened, they show themselves as they are. Thus, being launched again into the gulf of misery, unless a miracle of

bottom . . . want. The fundamental cause is lack of true repentance.

manner. This is one of the best analyses of spiritual decline you will ever read. Bunyan, like most Puritan ministers, was a master at examining his own heart and the hearts of others. Note that secret failures always precede public sins.

grace prevent it, they everlastingly perish in their own deceivings.

Now I saw in my dream that by this time the pilgrims were got over the Enchanted Ground, and entering into the country of Beulah, whose air was very sweet and pleasant; the way lying directly through it, they solaced themselves there for a season. Yea, here they heard continually the singing of birds, and saw every day the flowers appear in the earth, and heard the voice of the turtle in the land. In this country the sun shineth night and day; wherefore this was beyond the Valley of the Shadow of Death, and also out of the reach of Giant Despair, neither could they from this place so much as see Doubting Castle. Here they were within sight of the city they were going to; also here met them some of the inhabitants thereof; for in this land the Shining Ones commonly walked, because it was upon the borders of heaven. In this land also the contract between the bride and the bridegroom was renewed; yea, here, "As the bridegroom rejoiceth over the bride, so did their God rejoice over them." Here they had no want of corn and wine; for in this place they met with abundance of what they had sought for in all their pilgrimage. Here they heard voices from out of the city, loud voices, saying, "Say ye to the daughter of Zion, Behold, thy salvation cometh! Behold, his reward is with him." Here all the inhabitants of the country called them "the holy people, the redeemed of the Lord, sought out," etc.

Now, as they walked in this land, they had more rejoicing than in parts more remote from the kingdom to which they were bound; and drawing near to the city, they had yet a more perfect view thereof. It was builded of pearls and precious stones, also the street thereof was paved with gold; so that by reason of the natural glory of the city, and the reflection of the sunbeams upon it, Christian with desire fell sick;

Beulah. This means "married" in Hebrew. When God restores Israel to her land, she will no longer be called "Forsaken," nor the land "Desolate." Israel will be called "Hephzibah," which means "My delight is in her." The land will be called "Beulah" because Israel and her God shall be "married" again. See Song of Solomon 2:10-12 and Isaiah 62:4-12 for the imagery in this section.

turtle. The turtledove, an allusion to Song of Solomon 2:10-12.

As the. . . . Quoted from Isaiah 62:5.

corn and wine. The two chief crops of Israel, mentioned together some twenty-six times in the Old Testament. See Genesis 27:28, 37. "Plenty of corn and wine" was a mark of God's favor on the land.

Say ye. . . . Quoted from Isaiah 62:11-12.

the city. The description comes from Revelation 21-22. Because there is no need for the sun in heaven (Revelation 21:23 and 22:5), the reflections the pilgrims see may be caused by the sun in their world shining on the heavenly city. Bunyan is suggesting that saints on earth can have a foretaste of the glory of heaven.

desire. "Hope deferred maketh the heart sick: but when the desire cometh, it is a tree of life" (Proverbs 13:12).

172

Hopeful also had a fit or two of the same disease. Wherefore here they lay by it a while, crying out because of their pangs, "If you see my beloved, tell him that I am sick of love."

But being a little strengthened, and better able to bear their sickness, they walked on their way, and came yet nearer and nearer, where were orchards, vineyards, and gardens, and their gates opened into the highway. Now, as they came up to these places, behold the gardener stood in the way, to whom the pilgrims said, Whose goodly vineyards and gardens are these? He answered, They are the King's, and are planted here for his own delight, and also for the solace of pilgrims. So the gardener had them into the vineyards, and bid them refresh themselves with the dainties. He also showed them there the King's walks, and the arbours where he delighted to be; and here they tarried and slept.

Now I beheld in my dream that they talked more in their sleep at this time than ever they did in all their journey; and being in a muse thereabout, the gardener said even to me, Wherefore musest thou at the matter? It is the nature of the fruit of the grapes of these vineyards to go down so sweetly as to cause the lips of them that are asleep to speak.

So I saw that when they awoke, they addressed themselves to go up to the city. But, as I said, the reflection of the sun upon the city (for "the city was pure gold") was so extremely glorious, that they could not as yet with open face behold it, but through an instrument made for that purpose. So I saw, that as they went on, there met them two men in raiment that shone like gold; also their faces shone as the light.

These men asked the pilgrims whence they came; and they told them. They also asked them where they had lodged, what difficulties and dangers, what comforts and pleasures they had met in the way; and they told them. Then said the men that met them, You have but two dif-

If you see. . . . Quoted from Song of Solomon 2:5 and 5:8. There are times when the glories of heaven overwhelm the Christian. "Sick of love" = "faint from love."

refresh. The Law permitted pilgrims to eat from a neighbor's field or vineyard (Deuteronomy 23:24-25).

even to me. The gardener speaks to the author!

go down so sweetly. Quoted from Song of Solomon 7:9.

pure gold. Quoted from Revelation 21:18.

open face. "But we all, with open face beholding as in a glass [mirror] the glory of the Lord, are changed into the same image from glory to glory, even as by the Spirit of the Lord" (2 Corinthians 3:18). "Open face" means "hiding nothing." When Moses saw the Lord, he received some of God's glory on his face, and he had to wear a veil so that the people would not see the glory fade (Exodus 34:29-35).

faces shone. Not only did Moses have a shining face, but so did Jesus when He was transfigured (Matthew 17:1-8), and Stephen when he preached (Acts 6:15ff.).

asked. Another interrogation!

two difficulties. The two difficulties are: crossing the river (a picture of death), and gaining access at the gate of the city.

a river. Bunyan borrows this image from Israel crossing the Jordan and entering into the promised land (Joshua 3). However, nowhere in the Bible is "the crossing of Jordan" used as a symbol of death. The image of crossing a river is used in Christian hymns and poems (and in the writings of Dante and Virgil); but it is not a Bible image. Israel's experience at Jordan pictures the believer dying to self, leaving a life of wandering in unbelief, and entering into his inheritance in Christ *in this life.* After all, Canaan cannot be a picture of heaven because Israel fought battles there! However, we must confess that Bunyan's handling of this event is masterful.

Enoch and Elijah. Enoch was "translated" to heaven without dying (Genesis 5:21-24 and Hebrews 11:5). Elijah was taken to heaven in a chariot of fire (2 Kings 2:1-11).

trumpet. The last trumpet signals the return of Christ and the changing of the believer to be like Christ (1 Corinthians 15:51-54).

as you believe. "According to your faith be it unto you" (Matthew 9:29). Again, Bunyan teaches us that no two believers have the same experiences. Christian almost gives up and drowns, while Hopeful encourages him to continue crossing the river. The enemy attacks us at the time of death just as during life.

ficulties more to meet with, and then you are in the city.

Christian then, and his companion, asked the men to go along with them; so they told them they would. But, said they, you must obtain it by your own faith. So I saw in my dream that they went on together till they came in sight of the gate.

Now I further saw that betwixt them and the gate was a river, but there was no bridge to go over: the river was very deep. At the sight therefore of this river, the pilgrims were much stunned; but the men that went with them said, You must go through, or you cannot come at the gate.

The pilgrims then began to inquire if there was no other way to the gate; to which they answered, Yes; but there hath not any, save two, to wit, Enoch and Elijah, been permitted to tread that path, since the foundation of the world, nor shall, until the last trumpet shall sound. The pilgrims then, especially Christian, began to despond in their minds, and looked this way and that, but no way could be found by them, by which they might escape the river. Then they asked the men if the waters were all of a depth. They said, No; yet they could not help them in that case; for, said they, you shall find it deeper or shallower, as you believe in the King of the place.

They then addressed themselves to the water; and entering, Christian began to sink, and crying out to his good friend Hopeful, he said, I

174

sink in deep waters; the billows go over my head, all his waves go over me! Selah.

Then said the other, Be of good cheer, my brother, I feel the bottom, and it is good. Then said Christian, Ah! my friend, the sorrows of death have compassed me about; I shall not see the land that flows with milk and honey; and with that a great darkness and horror fell upon Christian, so that he could not see before him. Also here he in great measure lost his senses, so that he could neither remember, nor orderly talk of any of those sweet refreshments that he had met with in the way of his pilgrimage. But all the words that he spake still tended to discover that he had horror of mind and heart-fears that he should die in that river, and never obtain entrance in at the gate. Here also, as they that stood by perceived, he was much in the troublesome thoughts of the sins that he had committed, both since and before he began to be a pilgrim. It was also observed that he was troubled with apparitions of hobgoblins and evil spirits, for ever and anon he would intimate so much by words. Hopeful therefore here had much ado to keep his brother's head above water; yea, sometimes he would be quite gone down, and then ere a while he would rise up again half dead. Hopeful also would endeavour to comfort him, saying, Brother, I see the gate, and men standing by to receive us. But Christian would answer, 'Tis you, 'tis you they wait for; you have been hopeful ever since I knew you. And so have you, said he to Christian. Ah! brother! said he, surely if I was right he would now arise to help me; but for my sins he hath brought me into the snare and hath left me. Then said Hopeful, My brother, you have quite forgot the text where it is said of the wicked, "There is no band in their death, but their strength is firm. They are not troubled as other men, neither are they plagued like other men." These troubles and distresses that you go through in these wa-

I sink. Quoted from Psalm 69:2. "Selah" ends Christian's quotation. It is a Hebrew word that was probably a musical direction or notation for the Temple singers.

sorrows. Christian encourages himself by quoting from the book of Psalms, here Psalms 18:4-5 and 116:3. Jonah prayed in a similar way (Jonah 2).

darkness. Abraham experienced a "horror of great darkness" the night God made His covenant with him (Genesis 15:12).

my sins. The memory of past sins can burden and frighten the believer at the hour of death. Christian forgets all the blessings he had received from God along his pilgrimage. It is dangerous to trust our feelings.

There is. . . . Hopeful reminds Christian of the Word of God, which is the only source of assurance. Here he quotes Psalm 73:4-5.

Be of good. . . . Quoted from Acts 9:34. Christian finally gets his assurance from God's Word and quotes Isaiah 43:2.

spirits. "Are they not all ministering spirits, sent forth to minister for them who shall be heirs of salvation?" (Hebrews 1:14). The angels escort God's people to heaven at death (Luke 16:19-22).

mighty hill. "A city that is set on an hill cannot be hid" (Matthew 5:14). Christian climbs his last hill!

mortal garments. The body is like a garment, and at death it is shed so that we can receive the new, glorified body. See 1 Corinthians 15:53-57. 2 Corinthians 5:1-10 pictures the body as a soldier's tent, taken down to make room for a permanent and glorious building.

ters are no sign that God hath forsaken you, but are sent to try you, whether you will call to mind that which heretofore you have received of his goodness, and live upon him in your distresses.

Then I saw in my dream that Christian was as in a muse a while. To whom also Hopeful added this word, Be of good cheer, Jesus Christ maketh thee whole; and with that Christian brake out with a loud voice, Oh! I see him again, and he tells me, "When thou passest through the waters, I will be with thee; and through the rivers, they shall not overflow thee." Then they both took courage, and the enemy was after that as still as a stone, until they were gone over. Christian therefore presently found ground to stand upon, and so it followed that the rest of the river was but shallow. Thus they got over. Now upon the bank of the river on the other side, they saw the two Shining Men again, who there waited for them; wherefore, being come out of the river, they saluted them saying, We are ministering spirits, sent forth to minister for those shall be heirs of salvation. Thus they went along towards the gate. Now you must note that the city stood upon a mighty hill, but the pilgrims went up that hill with ease, because they had these two men to lead them up by the arms; also they had left their mortal garments behind them in the river, for though they went in with them, they came out without them. They therefore went up here with much agility and speed, though the foundation upon which the city was framed was higher than the clouds. They therefore went up through the regions of the air, sweetly talking as they went, being comforted, because they safely got over the river, and had such glorious companions to attend them.

Now, now look how the holy pilgrims ride,
Clouds are their chariots,
     angels are their guide:
Who would not here for him all hazards run,

That thus provides for his when this world's
done?

The talk they had with the Shining Ones was
about the glory of the place; who told them that
the beauty and glory of it was inexpressible.
There, said they, is the Mount Zion, the
heavenly Jerusalem, the innumerable company
of angels, and the spirits of just men made perfect. You are going now, said they, to the
paradise of God, wherein you shall see the tree
of life, and eat of the never-fading fruits thereof;
and when you come there, you shall have white
robes given you, and your walk and talk shall be
every day with the King, even all the days of
eternity. There you shall not see again such
things as you saw when you were in the lower
region upon the earth, to wit, sorrow, sickness,
affliction, and death, "for the former things are
passed away." You are now going to Abraham,
to Isaac, and Jacob, and to the prophets—men
that God hath taken away from the evil to come,
and that are now resting upon their beds, each
one walking in his righteousness. The men then
asked, What must we do in the holy place? To
whom it was answered, You must there receive
the comforts of all your toil, and have joy for all
your sorrow; you must reap what you have
sown, even the fruit of all your prayers, and
tears, and sufferings for the King by the way. In
that place you must wear crowns of gold, and
enjoy the perpetual sight and vision of the Holy
One, for "there you shall see him as he is."
There also you shall serve him continually with
praise, with shouting, and thanksgiving, whom
you desired to serve in the world, though with
much difficulty, because of the infirmity of your
flesh. There your eyes shall be delighted with
seeing, and your ears with hearing the pleasant
voice of the Mighty One. There you shall enjoy
your friends again that are gone thither before
you; and there you shall with joy receive even
every one that follows into the holy place after

Mount Zion. A reference to
Hebrews 12:22-24.

paradise. These descriptions
come from Revelation 2:7;
3:4-5; and 22:5.

former things. Quoted from
Isaiah 65:16-17 and Revelation
21:4.

taken away from. Quoted from
Isaiah 57:1-2.

reap. An allusion to Galatians
6:7-8.

crowns. Revelation 4:4.

see him. Quoted from 1 John
3:2.

serve him. "Therefore are they
before the throne of God, and
serve him day and night in his
temple" (Revelation 7:15). "Infirmity of your flesh" is an allusion to Romans 6:19 and Galatians 4:13.

eyes . . . ears. Allusions to
Isaiah 64:4 and 1 Corinthians
2:9.

you. There also shall you be clothed with glory and majesty, and put into an equipage fit to ride out with the King of Glory. When he shall come with sound of trumpet in the clouds, as upon the wings of the wind, you shall come with him; and when he shall sit upon the throne of judgment, you shall sit by him; yea, and when he shall pass sentence upon all the workers of iniquity, let them be angels or men, you also shall have a voice in that judgment, because they were his and your enemies. Also when he shall again return to the city, you shall go too, with sound of trumpet, and be ever with him.

Now while they were thus drawing towards the gate, behold a company of the heavenly host came out to meet them; to whom it was said, by the other two Shining Ones, These are the men that have loved our Lord when they were in the world, and that have left all for his holy name; and he hath sent us to fetch them, and we have brought them thus far on their desired journey, that they may go in and look their Redeemer in the face with joy. Then the heavenly host gave a great shout, saying, "Blessed are they that are called to the marriage supper of the Lamb."

There came out also at this time to meet them, several of the King's trumpeters, clothed in white and shining raiment, who with melodious noises and loud, made even the heavens to echo with their sound. These trumpeters saluted Christian and his fellow with ten thousand welcomes from the world; and this they did with shouting and sound of trumpet.

This done, they compassed them round on every side; some went before, some behind, and some on the right hand, some on the left (as 'twere to guard them through the upper regions), continually sounding as they went, with melodious noise, in notes on high: so that the very sight was, to them that could behold it, as if heaven itself was come down to meet them. Thus therefore they walked on together; and as

When he shall come. These statements about the return of Jesus Christ for His people come from 1 Thessalonians 4:13-18; Jude 14-15; Daniel 7:9-10; and 1 Corinthians 6:2-3.

Blessed are they . . . . Revelation 19:9.

guard. Satan is the prince of the power of the air (Ephesians 2:20). He seeks to prevent the saints from arriving at the heavenly city.

they walked, ever and anon these trumpeters, even with joyful sound, would, by mixing their music with looks and gestures, still signify to Christian and his brother how welcome they were into their company, and with what gladness they came to meet them; and now were these two men, as 'twere, in heaven before they came at it, being swallowed up with the sight of angels, and with hearing of their melodious notes. Here also they had the city itself in view, and they thought they heard all the bells therein to ring, to welcome them thereto. But above all, the warm and joyful thoughts that they had about their own dwelling there, with such company, and that for ever and ever. Oh, by what tongue or pen can their glorious joy be expressed! And thus they came up to the gate.

Now when they were come up to the gate, there was written over it in letters of gold, "Blessed are they that do his commandments, that they may have right to the tree of life, and may enter in through the gates into the city."

Then I saw in my dream that the Shining Men bid them call at the gate; the which when they did, some looked from above over the gate, to wit, Enoch, Moses, and Elijah, etc., to whom it was said, These pilgrims are come from the City of Destruction for the love that they bear to the King of this place; and then the pilgrims gave in unto them each man his certificate, which they had received in the beginning; those therefore were carried in to the King, who, when he had read them, said, Where are the men? To whom it was answered, They are standing without the gate. The King then commanded to open the gate, "That the righteous nation," said he, "which keepeth the truth, may enter in."

Now I saw in my dream that these two men went in at the gate: and lo, as they entered, they were transfigured, and they had raiment put on that shone like gold. There was also that met

bells. Bunyan had been a bell-ringer and had enjoyed the sport very much. During the time he was under conviction of sin, he felt that bell-ringing was a sinful practice; so he stopped. However, it was impossible for him to stay away when the bells were being rung. He carefully positioned himself lest one of the bells fall on him in judgment. How suitable that all the bells of heaven should welcome the pilgrims to their new home!

Blessed. . . . Revelation 22:14.

certificate. The roll that they carried proving they were believers.

That the. . . . Isaiah 26:2.

179

harps. Revelation 4:4 and 5:8.

Enter ye. . . . Matthew 25:23.

Blessing. . . . Revelation 5:13.

men. The description comes from Revelation 7:9.

Holy, holy. . . . Isaiah 6:3 and Revelation 4:8.

soon. Ignorance has an easy time getting over the river simply because he is ignorant. Vain-hope helped him get over. Ease in death is no assurance of entrance into the city. Note that Ignorance is not escorted by the angels.

I have eat. Quoted from Luke 13:26. Jesus warns in that passage that spiritual privileges are no guarantee of salvation. If anything, they make for greater judgment, unless they result in salvation.

certificate. Ignorance had no certificate; he was not a true believer. All his professions and arguments were vain.

answered. See 1 Kings 18:21, Matthew 22:12, and Romans 3:19.

bind him. "Bind him hand and foot, and take him away, and cast him into outer darkness;

them with harps and crowns, and gave them to them—the harps to praise withal, and the crowns in token of honour. Then I heard in my dream that all the bells in the city rang again for joy, and that it was said unto them, "Enter ye into the joy of your Lord." I also heard the men themselves, that they sang with a loud voice, saying, "Blessing, honour, glory, and power, be to him that sitteth upon the throne, and to the Lamb, for ever and ever."

Now just as the gates were opened to let in the men, I looked in after them, and behold, the city shone like the sun; the streets also were paved with gold, and in them walked many men, with crowns on their heads, palms in their hands, and golden harps to sing praises withal. There were also of them that had wings, and they answered one another without intermission, saying, "Holy, holy, holy, is the Lord." And after that, they shut up the gates; which when I had seen, I wished myself among them.

Now while I was gazing upon all these things, I turned my head to look back, and saw Ignorance come up to the river side; but he soon got over, and that without half that difficulty which the other two men met with. For it happened that there was then in that place one Vain-hope, a ferryman, that with his boat helped him over; so he, as the other I saw, did ascend the hill to come up to the gate, only he came alone; neither did any man meet him with the least encouragement. When he was come up to the gate, he looked up to the writing that was above, and then began to knock, supposing that entrance should have been quickly administered to him; but he was asked by the men that looked over the top of the gate, Whence came you? and what would you have? He answered, I have eat and drank in the presence of the King, and he has taught in our streets. Then they asked him for his certificate, that they might go in and show it to the King; so he fumbled in his bosom for

180

one, and found none. Then said they, Have you none? But the man <u>answered</u> never a word. So they told the King, but he would not come down to see him, but commanded the two Shining Ones that conducted Christian and Hopeful to the city, to go out and take Ignorance, and <u>bind him</u> hand and foot, and have him away. Then they took him up, and carried him through the air to the door that I saw in the side of the hill, and put him in there. <u>Then I saw</u> that there was a way to hell, even from the gates of heaven, as well as from the City of Destruction. So I awoke, and behold it was a dream.

there shall be weeping and gnashing of teeth" (Matthew 22:13). Jesus minced no words when it came to warnings about judgment.

Then I saw. From the City of Destruction to the gates of heaven: this is the scope of the book, and Christian has made the journey. Bunyan closes with this dramatic warning that a person may be near, and yet so far, from God's salvation. Ignorance was self-deluded. May this not be true of us.

The Conclusion

Now, READER, I have told my dream to thee;
See if thou canst interpret it to me,
Or to thyself; or neighbour; but take heed
Of misinterpreting; for that, instead
Of doing good, will but thyself abuse:
By misinterpreting, evil ensues.

Take heed, also, that thou be not extreme,
In playing with the outside of my dream:
Nor let my figure or similitude
Put thee into a laughter or a feud.
Leave this for boys and fools; but as for thee,
Do thou the substance of my matter see.

Put by the curtains, look within my veil,
Turn up my metaphors, and do not fail,
There, if thou seekest them, such things to find,
As will be helpful to an honest mind.

What of my dross thou findest there, be bold
To throw away, but yet preserve the gold;
What if my gold be wrapped up in ore?
None throws away the apple for the core.
But if thou shalt cast all away as vain,
I know not but 'twill make me dream again.

The Life And Times Of John Bunyan

"My descent was of a low, inconsiderable generation, my father's house being of that rank that is meanest and most despised of all the families in the land."

So wrote John Bunyan, Puritan preacher and author of *The Pilgrim's Progress*, the most popular Christian classic ever produced in the English-speaking world.

He was born in November 1628 in Harrowden, Bedfordshire, and was baptized at the parish church in Elstow on the thirtieth day of that month. Bunyan's father was a brazier, or tinker, who travelled from town to town mending pots and pans. The family settled in Elstow, a village one mile southwest of Bedford.

Bunyan's childhood was tempestuous. For some reason, he was plagued by frightening dreams and blasphemous thoughts. In later years he interpreted those experiences as the work of God to bring him to a saving knowledge of Jesus Christ. He attended a local school for poor children, but his education was interrupted so he could assist his father and help support the family.

Life was not easy, but it was not without its simple joys. Like many of the youths of his day, Bunyan enjoyed games on the village green, dancing, and music. If he read at all, it was in the Bible or Foxe's *Book of Martyrs*.

The year 1644 was a crisis year for Bunyan. In June, his mother died; then his beloved sister died a month later. In August, his father married again, an event that greatly hurt young John. In November, when he turned sixteen, Bunyan was taken into the army to help fight the civil war that had begun in August 1642. He was probably happy to leave home. It is not clear whether Bunyan fought with the Royalists or the parliamentary army, but it was probably with the latter. It is clear that many of the military images in his books were gathered during his three years in the army.

One interesting incident in his military career made a great impression on the youthful Bunyan. At the siege of Leicester a friend asked permission to take Bunyan's place; the man was shot in the head and killed. Bunyan had experienced several narrow escapes in childhood, and that additional one convinced him that God had a special purpose for him to fulfill, although at that time he was not a believer.

Back in Elstow, Bunyan worked as a tinker and enjoyed life as a sinner. "I had but few equals," he later wrote, "for cursing, swearing, lying and blaspheming the holy Name of God." There is no evidence that he was ever guilty of drunkenness or immorality, even though in his later writings he painted his picture very black.

Bunyan married in 1649. His wife was as poor as he, but she came from a godly home and brought with her two religious books: *The Plain Man's Pathway to Heaven* by Arthur Dent, and *The Practice of Piety* by Lewis Bayly. "In these two books I would sometimes read with her," Bunyan later wrote, "but all this while I met with no conviction." However, he did try to reform his life, and he began to attend the Bedford church where John Gifford was pastor.

The next three years saw Bunyan struggling against sin and with God. He wanted to escape hell, yet he enjoyed his sins and found them difficult to give up. One Sunday he was playing tip-cat on the village green, and he "heard" a voice in his soul that said, "Wilt thou leave thy sins, and go to heaven? or have thy sins, and go to hell?" He was momentarily stunned, but then he decided to go on with his game. After all, if he *was* going to hell, he might as well enjoy himself along the way!

While working in Bedford one day, he saw a group of poor women sitting in the sun and conversing. Wondering what their conversation was about, he drew near to listen. "I heard but understood not," he later confessed, "for they were far above, out of my reach. Their talk was about a new birth, the work of God in their hearts, and also how they were convinced of their miserable state by nature."

As a result of hearing that, he had a deeper conviction in his own heart and a desperate struggle to please God. He took a keen interest in the church and regarded the ministers, the vestments, and the services with almost a superstitious awe. "Their Name, their Garb, and Work, did so intoxicate me and bewitch me," he wrote. People noticed his radical self-reformation and wondered how long it would last. One day the pastor preached against Sabbath breaking, a bitter blow to Bunyan's new self-image. That was the end of his self-reformation. Bunyan returned to the village green and his favorite games. At the same time, he tried to quiet the voice within.

One day he was standing at a neighbor's shop window "cursing and swearing . . . after my wonted manner" when the woman of the house openly rebuked him. The fact that her own reputation was not too savory only made her words sting his conscience that much more. He resolved again to do better, and he succeeded for a time. "I was proud of my Godliness," he wrote. But still he had no peace or joy in his heart, and the more he tried to reform on the outside, the more he was miserable on the inside. Of course, many of those experiences found their way, in one form or another, into *The Pilgrim's Progress*.

It was the ministry and personal friendship of Pastor John Gifford that was used of God to bring John Bunyan to the place of assurance that he was a child of God. Bunyan was baptized by Gifford in 1653 and became a member of the Bedford church. "Conversion to God is not so easy and so smooth a thing as some would have men to believe it is," he later wrote. And all of *The Pilgrim's Progress* testifies to that fact.

In 1654 or 1655, the Bunyan family (by then he had two sons and two daughters) moved to Bedford, and Bunyan became more active in the church. But 1655 was another crisis year for him: his wife died and Pastor Gifford died. But that same year the church members encouraged Bunyan to start preaching, and before long it was recognized that God's hand was upon that simple tinker. In 1656 Bunyan published his first book, *Some Gospel Truths Opened*. It was the first of sixty titles he would publish, the greatest of which would be *The Pilgrim's Progress*.

In May 1660, the Commonwealth ended, and Charles II was recalled and put on the throne. At first, Charles gave evidence of wanting to cooperate with all the religious faiths in England, but it was not long before his policies changed. He began to move against the independents in favor of the established church. On November 12, 1660, Bunyan went to preach thirteen miles from Bedford. He had been warned that he was in danger of arrest, and the next day he was arrested and put into the town jail. In spite of pleas from his wife (he had married again) and friends, he was kept for twelve years.

One should not picture Bunyan as a prisoner languishing in a dungeon, for he did have a certain amount of freedom and was occasionally permitted to visit his family. While in jail he studied his Bible, wrote books, tried to minister to the other prisoners, and made lace, which he sold to help support his family. He wrote eleven books during that period, including the autobiographical *Grace Abounding to the Chief of Sinners*. In 1670 the Bedford church wanted to call Bunyan as its pastor, and when he was released in 1672, the call was made effective. On May 9, 1672, Bunyan was licensed to preach. On September 13 he was officially pardoned.

But in 1675 the Declaration of Indulgence was repealed, and Bunyan was returned to jail for six months. It is likely that he completed *The Pilgrim's Progress* during that time. The book was licensed for publication on February 18, 1678. Nathaniel Ponder of London was the publisher, and the book was an immediate success. Three editions were called for during the first year.

After his final release from jail, Bunyan continued his pastoral and preaching ministry, and God's blessing was upon him in a singular way. He drew huge crowds wherever he preached, and (as with his Lord) the common people heard him gladly. In August 1688, while riding to London, he was caught in a rainstorm and became ill. He preached his last sermon on August 19, and on August 31 he died. He is buried in Bunhill Fields, the Nonconformist cemetery located across from Wesley's Chapel on City Road in London.

The Puritans

It is unfortunate that today the word *Puritan* conjures up the picture of a stern man in a black hat: a humorless individual who goes about stopping people from having a good time. Quite the opposite ought to be true. The Puritans were a disciplined people, to be sure, but they knew that their discipline enabled them to enjoy the blessings of God. They delighted in the simple joys of life, especially their homes and children. They worked hard, "doing all to the glory of God." They believed in using their opportunities to provide for themselves and for others who were less fortunate.

The history of Puritanism is woven into the fabric of English political and religious history.

In 1534 Henry VIII separated the English church from the authority of the Pope. No major changes were made in doctrine except in those matters related to papal supremacy. Henry died in 1547. His heir Edward VI was only ten years old, so the government was controlled by a "protectorate council." Edward and his associates were strongly Protestant and brought about church reforms that strengthened the Protestant position.

When Edward died in 1553, his half sister Mary Tudor was crowned queen. A devout Roman Catholic, she sought to restore "the true faith" to her realm, even to the point of persecuting Protestants. It was under her authority that Latimer and Ridley were burned at the stake. Mary died in 1558, and Elizabeth I ascended to the throne.

In 1559 Parliament passed two laws that permanently settled the Protestant character of the English church. The Act of Supremacy made the reigning monarch the supreme governor of the church and The Act of Uniformity defined the worship and the doctrines of the church. In 1562 a church convocation accepted the Thirty-Nine Articles as the official doctrinal confession of the Church of England.

For the most part, Elizabeth was lenient with the Roman Catholics, but she had serious problems with the evangelical Protestants, most of whom had been influenced by the Reformers on the continent. Those men, many of whom were devout scholars, wanted to see the church purged of the Roman Catholic elements that were still evident, especially in the liturgy. The name "puritan" was attached to this school of thought as early as 1563, and it was definitely a term of reproach.

In 1566 Matthew Parker, Archbishop of Canterbury, published his "Advertisements" that required all clergy to follow a standard rule in wearing vestments. Of course, the Puritans opposed this ruling and asked again for a purifying of the church. Some of the Puritans became impatient and withdrew from the church; they became known as "separatists." Many of them fled to Holland or to the New World.

When Elizabeth died in 1603 the privy council named James VI of Scotland as the new monarch. We know him as James I of England, the man who authorized the King James translation of the Bible. During his reign in Scotland, James had experienced problems with the Presbyterians and their Calvinistic doctrines. He carried his prejudices against the Presbyterians with him to England and transferred the prejudices to the Puritans.

Soon after James I ascended to the throne, he was presented with a Puritan petition signed by one thousand clergymen. The petition asked again for reforms in the church. In response, James called a conference at Hampton Court, at which the Puritans and the Church of England bishops could confront one another. It is unfortunate that James confused the Puritans with the Presbyterians, for the Puritan divines had no desire to change church government. It was primarily the liturgy that they wanted the king to reform. The king's reply was, "No bishop, no king!" He was not about to make any changes.

One of the results of the conference was the formation of the Scrooby Manor congregation of Puritans, many of whom finally emigrated to America on the *Mayflower* in 1620. Another result was the authorization of a new translation of the Bible, the one we now know as the King James Version.

The Puritans were not a denomination, nor did they have any desire to divide or destroy the Church of England. The bonds that held them together were doctrinal, not political. The only spiritual authority they recognized was the Bible, the Word of God. They emphasized the preaching and reading of the Bible, not only in the churches but also in their families. They believed in an educated clergy, dedicated pastors who could expound the Scriptures, win the lost, discipline the church members, and be personal examples to the flock. Unfortunately, at that time there were many ministers in the established church who were unconverted, untrained, and unconcerned about the needs of the people.

The Puritans were basically Calvinistic in doctrine, following the teachings of the Geneva Reformer, John Calvin (1509-64). They believed in election by the Father and redemption through faith in Jesus Christ. They saw the work of the Holy Spirit as one of convicting sinners, giving sinners new life when they trusted Christ, sealing converts, and empowering them for life and service. The Puritans believed in a personal experience of conversion. It was not sufficient for a person to be baptized as an infant, enrolled as a member of the church, and asked to give assent as an adult to a certain set of doctrines.

The Puritans looked upon their beloved En-

191

gland as God's "covenant nation." If the people would only repent of their sins and trust Christ, God would do for England what He did for Israel: defeat her enemies, establish her kingdom, and bless her people. God was their King, and their supreme allegiance was to Him.

It was when Charles I came to the throne in 1625, three years before John Bunyan's birth, that matters moved to a crisis stage. The Puritans again requested reform of the liturgy and the clergy, but to no avail. Before long, Charles was in conflict with Parliament. He desperately needed money, and members of Parliament would not grant it. Charles attacked the Puritans, inflicting heavy fines, physical punishment (he cut off the ears of their leaders), and jail sentences. When William Laud became Archbishop of Canterbury in 1633, the pressures against the Puritans grew even worse as Laud sought to create a uniform church. The result was a polarized nation: persons were either for or against the king.

Such polarization inevitably led to civil war (1642-46), and Charles and his forces were defeated. Oliver Cromwell emerged as the leader of the anti-royalist forces. Charles I was beheaded January 30, 1649; Cromwell was named Lord Protector of the Commonwealth. It is worth noting that the Puritans did not present a united front against the king, because some of them fought on the Royalist side.

During the years of Cromwell's leadership, England's standing in Europe grew considerably. He was tolerant of the Jews and Quakers and truly sought to make England a place where the Word of God was faithfully preached by men of God. But this situation was not to last. Cromwell died on September 3, 1658, and his son Richard was named Lord Protector. However, Richard lacked the charisma and stature of his distinguished father, and Parliament asked him to resign. A military government took command, and forces were set in motion to bring the exiled Charles II back home. He was proclaimed king on May 8, 1660. The regency was restored, but the Puritans did not look to it for any spiritual encouragement.

In spite of his early promises to give liberty of conscience to his subjects, Charles II took steps to strengthen the state church. The Act of Uniformity (May 19, 1662) required all clergymen to accept the Book of Common Prayer and to take an oath of obedience to the king as leader of the church. It also required the reordination of those clergymen who had not been ordained by the established church. More than two thousand conscientious pastors refused to submit and were ejected from their churches. (From then on they would be called "nonconformists.") The Conventicle Acts (May 1664) prohibited Nonconformist meetings of more than five persons, unless the meetings were held in a private house. The Five-Mile Acts (October 1665) prohibited dissenting ministers from going within five miles of any town where they had served a church.

During that time of intense religious persecution, many Puritan pastors faithfully and sacrificially served their congregations; and some, like John Bunyan, were arrested and imprisoned. However, their churches grew both in purity and power.

Charles II died on February 6, 1685, and his Roman Catholic brother James II took the throne. James sought to do what Mary Tudor had failed to do, namely, restore the Roman Catholic faith to the realm. He authorized extensive arrests. It was at that time that the infamous Judge Jeffreys was in power and was arresting devout Christians, trying them illegally, and giving them terrible sentences. By June 1688 the people were ready for a change. An invitation to "bring over an army and secure the infringed liberties" was given to William of Orange of Holland, who was married to the daughter of James II. In 1689

William and Mary were crowned joint monarchs. That same year, the Toleration Act gave religious freedom to all groups with the exception of the Roman Catholics and the Unitarians. For the most part, the Nonconformists were now free to minister the Word of God without fear of persecution.

Puritan theology and the Puritan spirit of discipline and devotion are still with us to enrich the church. The United States in particular owes a great deal to the Puritan fathers who established the nation. The dignity of honest labor, the sanctity of the home, the living of all of life to the glory of God (there is no difference between "secular" and "sacred"), the honoring of the Bible as the Word of God, and the desire to see national leaders fear God and obey His law, are all principles that we have learned from the Puritans.

Important Dates Concerning Bunyan and the Puritans

English history	John Bunyan's life
1625 Charles I became king	
	1628 Born in Bedfordshire
1642-46 Civil war	1644 In the army; deaths of mother and sister
	1646 Returned to Elstow
1649 Charles I executed	1649 Married first time
1649-60 Commonwealth inaugurated; Oliver Cromwell made Lord Protector	1650 Blind daughter Mary born; John Gifford pastor in Bedford
	1653 Baptized, united with Bedford congregation
	1655 First wife died; John Gifford died; began to preach
	1656 First book, *Some Gospel Truths Opened*, published
1660 Charles II made king	1660 Arrested and put in jail
1665 The London plague	1666 Published *Grace Abounding to the Chief of Sinners*
1666 The great London fire	
1672 The Declaration of Indulgence	1672 Released from jail; licensed to preach; pardoned
1675 Declaration of Indulgence repealed	1675 Returned to jail for six months; completed *The Pilgrim's Progress*
	1678 *The Pilgrim's Progress* licensed for publication
1685-88 Reign of James II	
1688 "The Glorious Revolution"; William and Mary crowned	1688 Preached his last sermon (August 19); died (August 31)
1689 The Toleration Act	

Index of Scripture

OLD TESTAMENT

Genesis
3:1 — 119
4:1-15 — 68
5:21-24 — 174
6:5 — 163
8:21 — 163
9:27 — 62
12:1-3 — 62
13:10 — 127
13:13 — 127
15:12 — 175
18 — 39
19:14 — 67
19:17 — 24
19:23-28 — 21
19:24 — 25
19:26 — 24, 125
21:1-21 — 39
24:31 — 63
25:29-34 — 139
25:32 — 145
27 — 51
27:28 — 172
27:37 — 172
34 — 122
39:11-13 — 85

Exodus
1 — 113
4:2ff. — 70
19:16-25 — 35
20:13 — 133
24:17 — 123
25:10-22 — 159
25:17-22 — 28
28:4 — 65
32:8 — 36

33:15 — 149
34:29-35 — 173

Leviticus
11 — 97
16 — 159

Numbers
7:89 — 159
13 — 78
14 — 60
16 — 126
20:17-19 — 75
21:4 — 128
21:22 — 75
26:9-10 — 127
35:9ff. — 83

Deuteronomy
2:27 — 75
6:6-9 — 154
14 — 97
19:6ff. — 83
23:24-25 — 173
25:2 — 151
29:5 — 70

Joshua
3 — 174
20 — 165

Judges
3:31 — 70
4:18ff. — 70
6-7 — 70
15:15 — 70

1 Samuel
2:8 — 69
2:9 — 79
8:3 — 123
9:27 — 37
12:23 — 31
17 — 70
17:4 — 147
17:26-36 — 149
17:34-36 — 149
17:51 — 147
30:11-12 — 72

2 Samuel
12:7 — 37
22:43 — 80

1 Kings
10:1-10 — 74
18:21 — 181
18:28 — 114
19:9 — 36
21:27 — 151

2 Kings
1:2 — 41
2:1-11 — 174
2:11 — 114
4-5 — 125
4:29 — 44
9:1 — 44
23:10 — 24

1 Chronicles
11:4-9 — 41

2 Chronicles
6:27 — 151

Nehemiah		48:13	61	7	85
13:24	107	50:1-3	52	9:10	167
		50:22	52	10:19	91
Job		50:23	100	13:4	162
2:9-10	132	51:17	41	13:12	172
3:5	78	62:9	105	14:12	45, 58
6:6	95	65:9	127		129, 150
7:15	132	69:2	175	15:33	88
9:11	81	69:14	79	16:18	83, 88
10:21-22	23	71:16	80	18:12	88
10:22	78	73:4-5	175	19:27	153
11:2	91	76:10	115	21:16	139
12:4	106	86:5	75	22:13	61
12:22	81	88	149	22:14	85
22:24	119	88:18	131	23:23	107
28:28	167	95:6	158	23:34	54
29:3	82	107:10	78	24:10	62
31:1	86	107:30	71, 78	24:30-34	55
39:19-25	148	111:10	167	26:5	141
41:15	73	113:7	69	26:12	140
41:26-29	148, 149	116:3	175	26:13	61
		116:4	79	26:16	26
Psalms		116:6	30	26:25	115
1:1	37	118:8	129	28:20	124
2:6	41	119:34	99	28:22	124
2:11	41	119:37	107	28:26	162
2:12	40	119:105	24, 44	29:5	150, 170
3:6	149	125:5	163		
18:4-5	175	131:1	34	Ecclesiastes	
23:2	128			1:2	105
23:4	77, 80, 149	Proverbs		1:14	105
24:7-10	38	1:6	16	2:11	105
27:1-3	149	1:22	54	2:17	105
34:6	91	1:32	54	2:4-6	136
38:4	21	2:11	63	4:9	154
38:18	100	2:15	163	4:9-10	83
40:2	30	3:35	91	5:12	153
44:19	78	4:25-27	128	7:16	119
45	161	5:5	85	10:3	141
45:14	63	5:22	142	10:15	152
46:4	127	6:6	59	11:8	105
48:2	41, 61	6:24	85	12:11	53

Song of Solomon			64:4	177	7:10	52
1:3	63		64:6	22, 54, 156	7:13	70
2:5	173		65:16-17	177	7:22	70
2:10-12	172		65:17	27	8:18	37
5:8	173		66:2	22	10:8-19	37
7:9	173				10:13	77
			Jeremiah		10:21	77
Isaiah			2:6	77, 78	11:32	151
6:1-8	28, 37		2:13	40		
6:3	67, 180		2:24	146	Hosea	
8:8	71, 137		7:31	24	4:16-19	124
9:2	77		9:3	91	14:8	124
9:16	129		13:16	58	14:9	137
10:4	149		17:9	104		
10:6	80		17:15	152	Amos	
13:21	61, 78		20:10	24	5:8	81
14:30	128		29:12-13	158		
19:23	43		29:18-19	84	Jonah	
25:6	68		31:19	100	2	175
25:8	28, 67		31:21	130		
26:1	53				Micah	
26:2	179		Ezekiel		7:8	76
26:20-21	52		1:4-14	28	7:10	80
30:33	24		1:28	37	7:16-17	52
32:18	58		3:19	68		
33:17	71, 161		9	49	Habakkuk	
34:14	78		10:20	28	1:2-3	22
35:3-4	31		16:10-13	65	2:2	22
35:8	31, 43, 53, 75		20:43-44	100	2:3	159
36-38	148		22:14	23	2:4	37
38:15	151		33:1-9	102		
40:3	43		36:25	100	Zechariah	
40:17	105		36:25-27	45	3:1-5	75
40:31	58		47	127	3:4	54
43:2	176				4:11-14	48
49:10-11	58		Daniel		12:10	54
50:7	104		3	113		
55:1-8	29		6	113	Malachi	
57:1-2	177		6:10	158	2:4-7	44
62:4-12	172		7:5	73	3:2-3	52
62:5	172		7:9	70	3:16	64
62:11-12	172		7:9-10	178	4:2	52

Matthew		13:43	27	16:16	99
1:23	71, 137	13:44	128		
3:7	23, 41	14:31	142	Luke	
3:12	52	15:14	79	1:52	18
4:1-11	76	16:8	142	2:14	40
4:8-10	106	16:17	166	3:17	52
5:6	100	16:18	63	4:5-7	106
5:8	100	16:25	119	4:13	76
5:14	176	16:26	26	7:30	37
5:18	158	17:1-8	173	8:13	50
7:7-8	40	19:30	83	9:51	104
7:13-14	23, 38, 43	20:16	47, 137	9:62	26
7:13-20	45	22:12	36, 181	10:4	40
7:15	45	22:13	181	12:35	44
7:16	96	23:1-4	96	12:41-48	99
7:21	93	23:3	95	13:23-24	137
7:21-22	169	24:35	158	13:24	38
8:26	142	25:1-13	63	13:26	180
9:29	174	25:23	180	14:26	24
10:16	119	25:31	75	14:26-27	38
10:25	41	26:14-15	125	14:33	27
10:37-39	38	26:64	52	15:17	25
11:12	49	26:67	114	16:15	90
11:25-27	166	27:3-5	125	16:19-22	176
11:27	159, 166	27:18	110	16:19-31	47
11:28	158	27:26	114	16:25	47
12:24-27	41	27:50-53	52	17:10	156
12:31	37	28:18	104	17:32	125
12:43-45	84			18:9-14	141
12:45	142	Mark		18:13	159
13:1-9	27	2:5	54	19:14	50
13:18-23	27	3:21	26	20:46-47	122
13:20-21	29	4:40	62	22:19	68
13:22	123	5:9	105	22:54-62	148
13:23	96	8:34-38	38	24:32	48
13:24-30	52	8:38	89, 90		
13:30	96	10:21	137	John	
13:36-43	52	14:15	69	2:15	151

3:16	24	5:1-11	139	3:26	161
3:27	93	6:15ff.	173	4	158
4:36	103	8:1-24	123	4:5	158
4:42	99, 159	9:5	53	4:25	170
5:28-29	51	9:34	176	5:1	54
6:26	121	11:26	25	5:2	153
6:35	160	12:10	135	5:6-21	86
6:37	30, 41, 43, 160	13:10	124	5:20	46
6:70-71	123	14:8ff.	111	6	165
7:37	29	14:17	119	6:19	177
7:37-39	121	14:22	49, 104	6:21	155
7:48	89	15:9	46	6:23	73
10	56	15:26	119	7:7-11	46
10:1	56, 141	16:20-21	110	7:7-12	87
10:11	137	16:24	109	7:15-21	66
10:15	137	16:25	135	7:15-25	48
10:27-29	27	16:30	21	7:21	157
12:6	123	16:30-31	160	7:24	60, 62, 87, 99
12:25	28, 38	17:5	108	8:18	27
12:31	73	17:7	110	8:28	130
12:40	167	19:23	107	8:37-39	76
13:12-17	99	19:23-41	107	10:1-13	162
14:15	100	19:25	110	10:4	160
14:16-26	53	19:28ff.	113	10:9-10	100
14:21-23	46	20:23	104	11:25	140
14:30	73	20:26	102	12:16	140
15:3	46	21:8	22	14:23	129
16:8-9	99	22:1	112	15:2	99
16:11	73	22:22	112, 114	16:17-18	151
16:12	142	24:4	111	16:18	115
16:13	44	24:5	111	16:25-26	46
17:12	123	26:22	103		
18:23	112	26:24	26	**1 Corinthians**	
18:31	114	26:28	25	1:18-25	90
19:7	114			1:18-31	32
20:24-29	87	**Romans**		1:26	89
20:27	37	1:17	37	2:7-8	107
		2:14-15	52	2:9	177
Acts		2:24	95	2:14	26
2:37	21	3:10	163	3:2	142
4:12	100	3:17	163	3:9-17	63
4:33	147	3:19	123,181	3:18	89

4:9	108	10:18	100	6:13ff.	60, 72
4:9-10	106	11:1-3	39	6:16	41, 73, 149
4:10	90	11:3	75	6:17	76
4:15	45	11:13-14	15	6:18	79
5:10	106	11:26-27	33		
6:2-3	178	12:9	48, 160	**Philippians**	
6:19-20	50			1:6	48
7:29	32	**Galatians**		1:27	100
9:7	70	1:6	36	2:5-11	69
9:24	14	1:7	37	3:7-9	89
9:24-27	103	1:15-16	100, 166	3:14	18
10:12	83	1:16	100	3:17-20	100
10:25-27	120	2:11-21	129	3:20-21	107
11:24	68	2:16	39, 57,	4:6-7	69
12:3	166		156, 166		
12:28	30	2:21	39	**Colossians**	
13:1-3	97	3:1-18	62	1:14	158
13:2	98	3:10	39	3:5	124
14:7	97	3:11	37, 39	3:9	86
14:11	107	4:13	177		
15:1-4	23	4:19	45	**1 Thessalonians**	
15:3-4	53	4:21-31	39	1:10	41
15:45	86	6:1	83	2:1-6	118
15:51-54	174	6:7-8	177	2:7	45
15:51-58	51	6:9	103	4:13-18	52, 178
15:53-57	176	6:12	37	4:16	52
15:56	46			5:6	154
16:13	90	**Ephesians**		5:7-8	60
		1:3-14	54		
2 Corinthians		1:13	54	**2 Thessalonians**	
1:8	76, 131, 148	1:18-19	159, 166	1:7-10	51
1:24	117	2:1-3	73	2	71
3:1-9	38	2:2	178		
3:18	173	2:8-9	93	**1 Timothy**	
4:4	73, 153	2:19-22	63	1:15	160
4:17-19	27	4:11	22	1:20	139
4:18	25, 47, 104	4:14	16	2:3-4	41
4:20	95	4:22	86	2:5	160
5:1-10	176	4:30	50	3:3	123
5:2-4	28	5:6	155	3:8	116, 123
5:7	153	5:26	46	4:7	17
5:17	54	6:6	99	6:5	102

Reference	Page	Reference	Page	Reference	Page
6:9	124, 154	10:28-29	50	1:7	62
6:10	123	10:38	37	1:13	44
6:12	48	10:38-39	37	1:24	55
6:17	119	10:39	153	2:5	65
		11:5	174	2:5-10	63
2 Timothy		11:6	25	2:9	65
1:6	48	11:13-16	108	2:11	108
1:13	17	11:14-16	59	2:24	158
1:14	144	11:15	66	3:9	108
2:1-4	70	11:16	25	3:15	41, 137
2:14	92	11:25-26	38	3:15	137
2:17-18	138	11:27	104	4:7	50
3:4	113	11:33-34	28, 70	4:16	24
3:5	55	12:3	168	4:18	143
4:8	27	12:4	103	4:19	105
4:10	124	12:5	133	5:2	123
4:17	77	12:6	151	5:8	54, 59,
		12:16	139, 145		73, 147
Titus		12:16-17	51	5:10	27
1:2	27	12:21	35		
1:10	91	12:22ff.	41	**2 Peter**	
1:11	123	12:22-24	177	1:19	23, 158
1:16	91	12:25	37, 142	2:9	144
		12:29	123	2:22	85, 169
Philemon		13:2	137	3:9	41
24	124	13:8	164		
		13:17	62	**1 John**	
Hebrews		13:20-21	25	1:9	60
1:14	176			2:15-17	86, 107
2:1	37	**James**		2:21	153
2:14-15	69	1:3	62	3:2	177
4:12	76	1:22	96	3:12	68
4:16	159	1:26	96	3:15	133
5:7	158	1:27	96	3:18	100
6:4-6	50	2:19	162	4:5	37
6:5	27	2:26	96	4:5-6	108
6:15	133	4:7	76	4:14	99, 159
6:18	165	5:8	46	5:4	150
7:24-25	160	5:11	50		
9:17-22	25			**Jude**	
9:27	22	**1 Peter**		12	101
10:12-21	158	1:4-6	25	14-15	51, 178

Revelation		7:9	180	17:8	52
1:5	160	7:15	177	18:11-14	105
1:17	37	7:16-17	28	18:12	105
1:18	135	9:1-2	52, 147	18:16	105
2:4-5	60	9:11	52, 72,	19:9	178
2:7	177		73, 147	19:15	71
2:10	104, 135	9:17	73	20:1-3	52
3:2	62	11:7	52	20:11-15	51
3:4	27	12:3ff.	73	21-22	172
3:4-5	177	12:7-12	77	21:4	28, 67, 177
3:8	41	12:10-11	77	21:6	29, 100
3:11	103	13:1-10	71	21:8	25
3:17	166	13:2	73	21:18	173
3:19	151	13:3	76	21:23	172
4:4	28, 177, 180	13:11	76	22:1	127
4:8	67, 180	13:12	76	22:2	77, 128
5:8	180	13:14	76	22:4	54
5:13	180	14:1	54	22:5	27, 172, 177
6:12-17	52	14:1-5	28	22:14	179
7:1-8	28	17:3-4	105	22:17	29

Index to Persons and Places and What They Mean

The first number opposite the index entries is the page on which the subject is first mentioned and on which the explanatory note is given. This index does not give every page reference for Christian, Faithful, or other important persons because the references are too numerous.

Abiram, 126
Abraham, 119, 125, 177
Adam the First, 86, 87
Alexander, 139
All-prayer, 79
Ananias, 139
Any-thing, Mr., 116
Apollyon, 72ff., 91, 105. See also Devil
Apostasy, town of, 142
Arbor, the, 58, 87
Armour, 72, 149
Armoury, the, 70, 71
Arrogancy, 88
Atheist, 152

Beautiful (house), 61ff., 88
Beelzebub, 41, 77, 105, 106, 110
Bells, 179
Beulah, 172
Blind-Man, Mr., 113, 114
Broadway Gate, 142
Burdens, 21, 29, 32, 33, 34, 36, 43, 53, 54, 57, 65, 67
By-Ends, Mr., 115, 116, 124, 125
By-path Meadow, 128
Byway to hell, 139

Cain, 68
Carnal Delight, Lord, 112
Carnal Policy, town of, 32
Celestial City, 50, 59, 60. See also Mount Zion

Celestial Gate, 54, 57, 71, 114, 129, 140, 144, 174, 179
Charity, 63ff.
Christ, 16, 43, 50, 54, 65, 87, 99 106, 159, 160ff., 166
Christian, 25, 60, 62. See also Graceless
City of Destruction, 25, 30, 32, 36, 41, 44, 62, 63, 73, 83, 179, 181
Civility, 34
Clear (hill), 140
Coat, 54, 57, 59, 65, 66
Comforter, the, 53
Conceit, country of, 140
Coveting, county of, 118
Cross, 37, 53, 65, 67, 69, 158
Cruelty, Mr., 113, 114

Danger, road of, 58
Darius, 113
Dathan, 126
David (Hebrew king), 71, 79, 128, 147, 148, 149, 150
Dead Man's Lane, 142
Deceit, town of, 86
Delectable Mountains, 71, 136, 151, 153
Demas, 124, 125, 126, 127
Den (the jail), 21
Desire of Vain Glory, Lord, 112
Destruction, a way of, 58
Devil, 48, 50, 54, 64, 147. See also Apollyon, Beelzebub, and Satan

205

Difficulty, Hill, 57ff., 66, 86
Diffidence, 131
Discontent, 88
Discretion, 63
Dives, 47
Doubting Castle, 130ff., 139, 172

Elijah, 174, 179
Enchanted Ground, 140, 154, 172
Enmity, Mr., 113, 114
Enoch, 174, 179
Envy, 110, 112
Error, Hill, 138
Esau, 139, 145
Evangelist, 22, 30, 33, 35ff., 64, 103
Evil report, two men of, 78
Experience, 137. *See also* Shepherds

Facing-both-ways, Mr., 116
Faint-heart, 143, 147
Fair-speech, town of, 115, 116
Fair-speech, Lord, 116
Faithful, 72, 83ff., 155
Feigning, Lady, 116
Fire, 48, 52
Flatterer, 140, 150ff.
Formalist, 55ff., 65

Gardener, 173
Gehazi, 125
Giant Despair, 131ff., 139, 172
Gideon, 71
Goliath, 71, 147, 149
Good-confidence, city of, 143
Good-will, 41
Graceless. *See* Christian
Graceless, town of, 62, 169
Great-grace, 143, 147
Gripe-man, Mr., 118
Guilt, 143
Gulf of Despond. *See* Slough of Despond

Hamor, 122
Hate-good, Lord, 109ff.
Hate-light, Mr., 114
Having Greedy, Sir, 112
Heady, Mr., 113, 114
Hell, 23, 79
Help, 30
Heman, 148
Hezekiah, 148
High-mind, Mr., 113, 114
Hold-the-world, Mr., 118
Honesty, town of, 169
Hopeful, 115
House of the Interpreter, 44
Hymeneus, 138
Hypocrisy, 55ff., 65

Ignorance, 141ff., 161, 180
Immanuel's Land, 71, 137
Implacable, Mr., 114
Interpreter, 44, 45ff.
Isaac, 177
Israel, 60

Jacob, 122, 177
Jael, 70
Japheth, 62
Joseph, 85, 98
Judas, 122, 123, 125

King of Princes (Christ), 73
King's Highway, 75
Knowledge, 137. *See also* Shepherds
Korah, 126

Large Upper Chamber, 69
Law, 45-46. *See also* Mount Sinai
Lazarus, 47
Lechery, Lord, 112
Legality, 34, 35, 39, 42, 43
Legion, 105
Leviathan, 149

Liar, Mr., 113, 114
Light, 23
Lions, 59, 61, 62, 67, 88
Little-faith, 142ff.
Live-loose, Mr., 113, 114
Lot's wife, 126
Love-gain, town of, 118
Love-lust, Mr., 113, 114
Lucre, Hill, 123, 126
Lust of the Eyes, 86
Lust of the Flesh, 86
Luxurious, Lord, 112

Malice, Mr., 113, 114
Man clothed in rags, 21, 156
    in iron cage, 49, 64
    of Sin, 71
    of stout countenance, 49, 65
    rising out of bed, 51, 64
    with inkhorn, 49
    with seven devils, 142
Mark on forehead, 54, 57, 65
Michael, 77
Midian, 71
Mistrust, 59ff., 61, 143, 147
Money-love, Mr., 118
Morality, village of, 34, 37
Moses, 70, 87, 88, 96, 149, 179
Mount Caution, 138
Mount Sinai, 35, 39, 43
Mount Zion, 41, 44, 55, 62, 63, 67,
    69, 176, 177ff.

Narrow way, 43
Nebuchadnezzar, 113
No-good, Mr., 113, 114
Note of the way, 140

Obstinate, 24, 42
Oil, 48, 64
Old Man, Lord, 112

Pagan, 82
Palace Beautiful, 61
Passion, 46ff.
Patience, 46ff.
Peace, 69
Peter, 123, 148
Pharoah, 113
Pharisees, 122
Philetus, 138
Pickthank, 110, 111, 112
Piety, 63ff.
Pilgrim, 54
Pit, 129
Plain of Ease, 123
Pliable, 24, 31-32, 42, 84
Pope, 82
Prating Row, 94
Presumption, 54, 65
Pride, 88
Pride of Life, 86
Promise, key of, 135
Prudence, 63ff.

River
    of God, 127
    at Celestial City, 174
roll (certificate), 23, 54, 57, 58, 59,
    65, 66, 87, 144, 179, 180

Salvation, wall of, 53
Samson, 71
Sapphira, 139
Satan. See Devil
Save-all, Mr., 118
Save-self, 169
Say-well, 94
Self-Conceit, 88
Sepulchre, 53
Shame, 89ff.
Shamgar, 71
Shechem, 122
Shem, 62

Shepherds, 136ff., 150, 151. *See also* Knowledge, Experience, Watchful, and Sincere
Shining Ones, three (angels), 54, 65, 151, 172, 176, 178, 179, 180
Simon, 123
Simple, 54, 65
Sincere, 137, 142. *See also* Shepherds
Sisera, 70
Sloth, 54, 65
Slough of Despond, 29, 33, 36, 42, 75, 84, 85
Smooth-man, Mr., 116
Sodom, 126, 127
Solomon, 91, 119
Stately palace, 48, 61, 65
Steps (out of the slough), 30
Superstition, 110, 112

Talkative, 91ff.
Temporary, 169
Time-server, Lord, 116
Timorous, 59ff., 61
Tophet. *See also* Hell
Tree of life, 77
Trees of healing, 128
Turn-away, Mr., 142

Turn-about, Lord, 116
Turn-back, 169
Two-tongues, Mr., 116

Vain-confidence, 129
Vain-Glory, land of, 55
Vain-Hope, 180
Valley of Humiliation, 72, 88
Valley of Shadow of Death, 77ff., 91, 134, 172
Vanity, town of, 105, 111
Vanity Fair, 105, 134

Wanton, 85
Watchful (a porter), 62, 66, 72
Watchful (a shepherd), 137. *See also* Shepherds
Wicket-gate, 23, 30, 32, 36, 38, 40
Wilderness, 21
Worldly-glory, 88
Worldly Wiseman, 32, 35, 37, 38, 39, 42

Zion, City of, 59, 73, 104, 114, 115, 152, 153, 172, 173. *See also* Mount Zion